Helen Phifer is the bestselling writer of twenty-seven books, including the hugely popular Annie Graham, Lucy Harwin, Beth Adams, Maria Miller and Detective Constable Morgan Brooks series.

She lives in the busy town of Barrow-in-Furness surrounded by miles of coastline and a short drive from the glorious English Lake District.

Helen loves reading books that scare the heck out of her and is eternally grateful to Stephen King, Dean Koontz, James Herbert and Graham Masterton for scaring her senseless in her teenage years. Unable to find enough scary stories she decided to write her own and her debut novel *The Ghost House* released in October 2013 became a #1 Global Bestseller.

You can find her over on Instagram @helenphifer, or on her website at www.helenphifer.com

Secrets of the Shadows

HELEN PHIFER

ONE PLACE. MANY STORIES

HQ
An imprint of HarperCollins*Publishers* Ltd
1 London Bridge Street
London SE1 9GF

www.harpercollins.co.uk

HarperCollins*Publishers*
Macken House, 39/40 Mayor Street Upper,
Dublin 1, D01 C9W8, Ireland

2
First published in Great Britain by
Carina, an imprint of HarperCollins*Publishers* Ltd 2014
This edition published by HQ, an imprint of HarperCollins*Publishers* Ltd 2024

Copyright © Helen Phifer 2014

Helen Phifer asserts the moral right to be
identified as the author of this work.
A catalogue record for this book is
available from the British Library.

ISBN: 9780008737054

This book contains FSC™ certified paper and other controlled
sources to ensure responsible forest management.

For more information visit: www.harpercollins.co.uk/green

Printed and bound in the UK using 100%
Renewable Electricity at CPI Group (UK) Ltd

For Mum & Dad, thank you for everything

Prologue

June 30th 1984

Six-year-old Sean Wood didn't like this house; it smelled funny and all the furniture was dark and old. He didn't like the man who walked around wearing the long black dress either. He knew that the man was a priest because his mum had told him that he was. She'd also told him that they had to live in the presbytery next to the church, but he didn't know exactly what that meant. They had their own house two doors down from this one. It was much smaller, with three bedrooms and a tiny garden, but it was big enough to play in with his A-Team action figures. He wanted to go and dig out B.A. Baracus from underneath the rose bush in the front garden where he had buried him last week, before he got eaten by worms or went mouldy. His mum wouldn't let him; he had asked her this morning when he had finished his bowl of Snap Crackle and Pop. She'd gone mad with him when he said he wanted to go and get his toys and asked if she'd take him, so there wasn't much choice.

He was going to come up with a plan of his own – just like Hannibal always did – and go on a rescue mission. He would wait until his mum had a bath. She always spent hours in there and wouldn't notice that he had sneaked out of the door. He just hoped that the priest wasn't an enemy working for the other side and wouldn't drop him in it. His mum had been acting strange all week now and yesterday she hadn't let him go to his sister Sophie's funeral. Instead, she'd made him stay here, in this big smelly house with the woman the priest called his 'housekeeper'. He liked her because she baked nice cakes and would let him eat as many as he wanted when his mum wasn't looking.

Sean went upstairs to the room that had become his until he could go back to his own, with the Masters of the Universe and A-Team posters. This new room had a big wooden cross on the wall and the only thing to read was a thick black book, which had 'Bible' written in gold on the front. Sean had looked inside and then closed it again. The writing was so small it would take him forever to try and read it. He slumped onto the bed; it was boring here. At least when Sophie was alive he'd had her to play with – well, until she got poorly he did. It had started a couple of weeks ago, but a few days ago she'd got really poorly, saying words that he had never heard of and that were nothing like the French words they sometimes learnt in school. He didn't under-stand what was going on but he knew it was something bad.

Sophie had been screaming the day she'd died, really screaming, as if the priest and their mum were hurting her. It had been so loud that he'd crept from this bedroom to see if he could help her, but her bedroom door had been locked. He had looked through the keyhole to see his sister on her bed with the man in the dress standing over her with a book like the one next to his bed. The man had been throwing water onto Sophie. Sean had watched as the priest had bent down and placed a wooden cross onto her forehead. He'd stared in horror as the cross burnt into her skin; the sizzling sound had made him feel sick and he'd pushed himself away from the door. He'd thought he was going to puke all over the polished wooden floor.

2

Telling himself to be brave, Sean went back to look through the keyhole again, to see Sophie thrashing around. She looked angry and hurt, then her eyes rolled to the back of her head until he could only see the whites of them. It was then that she began to choke. The priest was trying to lift her head and his mum was watching. Sean didn't understand why she didn't rush to help Sophie. He watched as his sister's face turned blue and, just like that, the noise stopped. It was over and Sophie was dead.

The scream that came from his mum was far worse than seeing Sophie lying perfectly still, frozen in time. Sean scrambled to his feet and ran towards his room. Clutching a plastic toy to his chest, he fell to the floor and crawled under the bed, where he curled up in a ball and cried himself to sleep. He stayed there, hidden from sight, until the priest came looking for him hours later. Father John tried to talk him out but Sean didn't want to leave his hiding place. The priest reached under to pull him out and Sean sank his teeth into his hand. There was a loud shout and a few bad words but then the priest lay flat on the floor so he could see Sean's face. 'Come on, son; you can't stay there all day. Let's go and get you something to eat.'

Sean shook his head, curling himself up even tighter. 'I want to see my mum . . . Where is she?'

'She's fast asleep at the moment; the doctor has been to visit Sophie and your mum. He had to give your mum some medicine.'

'What about Sophie? Did he give her some medicine?'

'No, there is no medicine that will make your sister better, I'm very sorry to say.'

'I want to go and see Sophie then!'

'Are you sure? Sophie's soul has left this earth and gone to a much better place. All that's left is her body.'

Sean nodded; he needed to see if Sophie's face was still blue and if she had the mark of the cross burnt into her forehead. He crawled out and stood up. Father John reached out and took hold of his hand. As brave as Sean felt, he still grasped it and held tight. They walked to Sophie's room and Father John pulled a key from his pocket. Unlocking the door, he turned to Sean. 'You're sure?'

Sean nodded and stepped forward, pushing the door open as he did so. His legs were shaking and he knew he had to be brave, just like B.A., so he held his head up and stepped into the room, which was much colder than the rest of the house. He walked across to the bed. Sophie looked as if she was asleep, her long platinum-blonde hair spread out on her pillow. Her blue eyes were closed and her face was a funny white colour but it definitely wasn't blue. Her forehead didn't have a big mark on it and she looked like one of the dolls she played with all the time. Her lips were still pink and in her hand she had a cross and a Bible. Sean pulled his spare Hannibal action figure from his trouser pocket and reached out to tuck it behind her fingers. He touched them and snatched his hand back – they were so cold. Reaching out, he tried again and this time he managed to tuck it behind her hands, shuddering as he did so. Then he ran away from Sophie, the priest and the end of his childhood to the empty room, where he scrambled back under the bed.

*

Now Sean wandered along the dark passage until he reached the bathroom, then pressed his ear against the door. He could hear his mum splashing in the water. Good, she would be in there for ages; she had the same long blonde hair as Sophie and it took her forever to wash it. He crept along to the huge oak staircase with the world's smallest carpet and ran down. So light on his feet the treads didn't creak once, he looked around the hallway. There was no sign of the housekeeper or the priest. He strode across to the front door as if he was allowed to be going outside and turned the handle. The door opened and he screwed up his

4

eyes against the harsh sunlight. He grinned. Playing outside was his favourite thing; he hated being cooped up inside – especially in this house.

Sean wanted to go home more than anything. He looked across the huge lawn over to the church. The door was shut, so if the priest was in there he wouldn't notice Sean sneaking out. The street was empty. He stepped out of the doorway and ran down the steps and across the lawn to the low wall that surrounded the front garden. He was on a mission now; it was important. He had to save B.A.'s life – the A-Team couldn't survive with just the three of them; it had to be all four.

He stopped outside his house and reached out to touch the gate; the metal was cold even though it was bathed in sunlight. He opened the gate, took three steps forward and then fell to his knees in front of the rose bush, where he began to dig in the soil with his fingers. Soon he felt the hard plastic of the figure he'd buried last week and smiled – he'd done it and saved the day. He stood up and went back out of the gate, closing it behind him. A shadow passed over the upstairs window, catching his eye. Lifting his head, he put his small hand to his forehead to shield his eyes from the burning sun, then looked up and squealed to see Sophie standing at the window staring down at him. He frantically waved his hand and grinned at her but, before she could wave back, a darker, much taller figure stepped behind her and pulled her away from the window.

Sean ran back to tell his mum that Sophie was in their house, he'd seen her and they could go home now. He ran into the presbytery and up the stairs to the bathroom, where he hammered on the door. 'Mum, Mum. You don't have to be sad now – Sophie's OK. I saw her looking out of your bedroom window. We can go home now.'

There was no sound of splashing water like there had been earlier; there was no sound, apart from the steady drip of a tap that hadn't been turned off. Sean took hold of the doorknob, twisting it until it turned and the door opened wide. That was when all the normal thoughts that a six-year-old boy should be thinking left him. He walked closer to the bath, which contained his mother's lifeless body in a pool of bright red water. His stomach clenched and the voice in his head told him to run but he carried on until he was close enough to reach out and touch her. As he pushed her shoulder, her head lolled to the side and her glassy, open, dead eyes stared through him.

Sean looked down into the bath and saw her arms and it was then that he opened his mouth and began to scream.

Chapter 1

2014

Annie Graham downed the tequila then shuddered. She hated the stuff but it got you drunk fast. Jake – fellow police officer and best friend – whose house they were in, laughed at the grimace on her face. 'You are such a girl – you know that, don't you?'

She squeezed her eyes shut. 'Yes, I'm a total girl and I'm not ashamed of it either; this stuff is bloody awful. I don't understand how you could even begin to actually enjoy it.'

Jake spluttered, managing to spit his tequila all over the black marble of the breakfast bar. 'Because I quite like the taste now I've got used to it and it does the job in half the time of six cans of lager. One more and then we'll be brave enough to go ghost-hunting.'

Annie giggled. 'I've had enough of that to last me a lifetime, thank you. After discovering I could see ghosts in a haunted house and being stalked by a serial killer six months ago, I'm quite happy *not* to go ghost-hunting. I can't believe you want to drag me to a cemetery when we're drunk. You'll be screaming at every shadow you see and then what happens if we actually do see something?'

'You're a wimp. I'm not going to be the one screaming and anyway don't you want to see if you can still see dead people or if it was all just a figment of your twisted imagination?' He managed to dodge the piece of chewed-up lime that she threw at his head. 'Sorry.'

Annie began to laugh so hard that she slid off the stool. 'I'm drunk and I don't think going to the cemetery in this state is going to be too productive. What if someone reports us and we end up getting arrested? There have been loads of metal thefts up there this month. Can you imagine the gossip that would spread around the station if we got caught in there?' Tears were rolling down her cheeks, smudging her mascara and leaving black trails.

Jake bent down; putting both of his hands under her armpits, he dragged her up from the floor. 'Nah, bollocks, we'll just tell them the truth. That we're ghost-hunting.'

'Your call, but if you insist – who am I to argue?'

He shrugged his huge shoulders and took hold of her hand. 'What the hell. Come on, if we get caught we'll say we were looking for vampires. I want to go now, before I chicken out. I've always wanted to do this but never had anyone drunk or stupid enough to go with.'

They looked each other in the eye and nodded. Jake helped her into her coat and wrapped her scarf around her neck. His fingers brushed her thick black curls, which had grown back and now covered the scar that had once been on show. She looked so much happier and healthier now she didn't have Mike in her life. He bent down and planted a big wet kiss on her forehead and held her close. Annie wrapped her arms around him and whispered, 'Don't you go getting all soft on me, Jake. I'm OK now and I've never been happier. Everything that happened six months ago is done; life is getting better.'

Jake squeezed his friend even tighter. 'I'm not; I just hate what happened to you.' They pulled apart. Jake took hold of her hand

8

and dragged her to the front door. 'Come on, there's no time like the present and, besides, your dream man Will might turn up soon and you know what a spoilsport he is. He'd never let you loose in a cemetery with your track record.'

They left the house holding hands and began the short walk to the cemetery gates.

'How are we going to get in if they're locked?' Annie asked.

'Sometimes you amaze me. You can climb walls, can't you? I'll give you a bunk-up if you can't get those short legs up high enough.'

She slapped his hand in a half-hearted gesture; Jake squeezed hers back, a silent apology. Annie couldn't walk straight; her legs were wobbling as they approached the tall black cast-iron gates, which loomed in the distance. Behind them was a blanket of pitch-black, which made her heart beat faster.

*

Will shivered. He hated cemeteries when the sun was shining and he could see everything around him, but to be here in the dark with no moonlight gave him the creeps. It didn't help that he was sitting in a car with Twit and Twat, the two specials who were very nice blokes but far too keen to get a piece of the action. They couldn't sit still and were talking utter crap. Every time a shout came over the radio the one sitting next to him would sit up, his body taut and his fists clenched, raring to get going. Will smiled to himself – at least he was getting a bit of fun out of it by torturing the pair of them; they needed to learn that police work wasn't all rescuing damsels in distress and blue-light jobs. As bored as he was, he really hoped that nothing would happen tonight with these two in tow because it was all bound to go tits up in a big way.

Two of his best detectives, Stu and Laura, were hiding behind some mausoleum near to the crematorium. He would rather

9

have been with one of those two, but after the head injury and broken kneecap he'd got whilst trying to save Annie six months ago and the fact that it was freezing, he'd decided to pull rank for once and sit in the car.

He switched off from the two chattering voices and began to think about Annie. He was parked not too far away from her husband Mike's grave. He looked out of the side window and squinted; he could just make out the hilly mound of soil. Will would have loved to have given him what he deserved, but the town's first serial killer had beaten him to it. He had to admit that Annie was by far the best thing that had happened to him and he loved her more than he'd loved anyone, but he was still afraid of committing and, to be honest, she was still a mess.

He hated the nightmares she had almost every night. She would brush them off as if nothing was wrong but he had seen her pale face and eyes wide in horror as she crept out of the bed and into the bathroom. The first time he'd heard her stifling her sobs it had broken his heart and he had lain there dithering about whether to go and comfort her or give her some space. He'd opted to stay where he was, feeling useless. When she had finally come back to bed he'd turned and wrapped his arms around her, holding her tight and stroking her hair until her breathing slowed and she fell back asleep.

Tonight he'd left her at Jake and Alex's house; if his grave-robbers didn't turn up he might go round for a coffee and see what they were up to.

*

Jake threaded his arm through Annie's and the pair of them weaved along the tree-lined road towards the cemetery. The blackness behind the gates looked ominous; she didn't want to do this. Why did she let Jake talk her into these things? She hadn't been here since Mike's funeral.

'We can't get in – it's all locked up.'

Jake looked at her in disbelief. 'Are you serious? You're a copper; you should know how to scale a fence.'

'Of course I know how to scale a fence, just not when I'm drunk. I don't want to land head first in someone's grave. I have a bit more respect than you do.'

'Wimp. Come on, I'll give you a bunk-up.'

Annie ignored his offer of help and wobbled on ahead of him, scaling the gates before Jake could offer her his hand. She jumped off the other side and slipped. Jake bent over laughing.

'Come on then, big man, let's see if you can do any better.'

Jake took a run at the gate. For his size, he was surprisingly nimble and he managed to climb over it and land on his feet next to her. Annie tutted and began to walk away in the opposite direction to Mike's grave and Jake followed. She let out a loud scream at a statue in the distance and he started to laugh again. Her elbow landed sharply in his side and he stopped. She decided to walk up towards the old chapel, which was now boarded up and fenced off. Annie had been drawn towards it last year when she had come looking for Alice's grave – she had seen Alice's ghost in that area of the cemetery so it was the logical place to go. Jake, who had finally stopped laughing, whispered in her ear, 'Come on, you're right; this is stupid. Let's go and order a Chinese.'

Stubborn as ever, she carried on walking. 'Now who's the wimp? You were the one who wanted to come here in the first place. I'm not leaving until we see a ghost. I'll prove to you I'm not full of crap.'

'I never said you were, but it is kind of hard to believe.'

Annie shook her head; it felt muzzy – too much tequila. She would pay for it in the morning but maybe tonight when she finally made it to bed she wouldn't have any of those terrible nightmares about a secret room in a cellar with dead bodies inside.

*

Stu and Laura huddled together to try to keep warm. They couldn't really see the chapel from their position but this was the only place where they could keep out of sight yet still be near enough to get there in a hurry. Will's voice echoed through their earpieces. 'Two people just climbed over the gate and are heading your way up towards the chapel. It looks like a man and a woman but hard to tell from here.' Stu crept to the side of the wall. Straining his eyes, he could make out a tall man and a much shorter woman who were stumbling hand in hand. Laura popped her head around to take a look and rolled her eyes at Stu. 'I can't see those two getting up to anything other than a quickie. That's if he can get it up. Those two are hammered and I'm freezing in a bloody cemetery of all places. How do we get roped into these crappy jobs? Join CID, become a detective, solve serious crime. Yes, right, what a load of rubbish.'

They watched as the dark figures finally reached the chapel and then the taller one bent down to give the shorter one a bunk-up the fence. Will's voice echoed in their ears. 'Go, go, go.'

*

Jake's hand pushed Annie and she grabbed hold of the top of the fence just as two figures came hurtling up the path, followed by a car with headlights on full beam, blinding them. Jake landed on the ground with a loud thud as someone rugby-tackled him. He landed on his back with some bloke on top of him. Annie, blinded by the light, began to shout, lost her grip on the fence and then slipped to the ground. She landed next to Jake and whispered, 'We are so fucked.'

The car stopped in front of them and a familiar figure climbed out, shouting, 'Police, don't move.' Laura slapped a pair of handcuffs on Annie whilst Stu cuffed Jake. Annie took one look at Jake's shocked expression and began laughing. Will stepped closer to take a look, pushing Twit and Twat out of the way, who were

12

standing with batons and CS gas drawn, ready for battle. 'Jesus.'

Jake grinned at him. 'All right, Will; fancy meeting you here.'

'Would you like to tell me exactly what you two are doing in here at this time of night?'

Annie was speechless, her laughter getting more hysterical by the second. Composing herself as best as she could, she screeched, 'Sorry, officers, whatever it was, it was me.'

Will clenched his fists in anger. Annie hiccupped so loud it echoed around the graves. 'Sorry, Will. Jake and I decided to do a spot of ghost-hunting.'

Will's voice shook as he barked at Stu and Laura to uncuff them. His cheeks were flushed red and he leant down to grab Annie's arm. 'Jesus Christ, I can't leave you two alone for five minutes; you are a bloody liability.'

Jake had sobered up remarkably well compared to Annie, who was trying to stifle her laughter and not doing it very well. Jake looked at Will. 'Sorry, it's my fault. I begged her to come with me.'

Will shook his head and grabbed Annie's arm much more roughly than he'd intended, instantly regretting it as her face became a mask of fear. She pulled away from his grip. 'I can manage on my own.' Annie sobered instantly; she knew that Will would never mean to harm her, not like Mike used to, but still, her feelings were hurt.

'Sorry to interrupt your little party, sir.' She spat the words out. 'Come on, Jake, let's go back to your house and finish that tequila. Oh, and Will, don't bother coming round after you finish whatever it is you're doing in here. I'll be far too busy holding a séance.' She stormed off, making Jake jog to catch up with her. Neither of them spoke until they reached the gates, where they looked at each other and started laughing once more. The wind carried the sound up to the chapel, where Will was standing shaking his head and trying to figure out what had just happened.

Stu and Laura waited for Will to tell them what to do. 'Right, since those two have almost certainly messed up any chance of catching our grave-robbers tonight, I think we should leave. I can't see anyone coming in here now after all that racket.'

The two specials looked relieved to be able to escape the boredom; they wanted to be out where the action was, although, judging by what jobs had been passed over the radio in the last hour – a group of kids throwing stones at a taxi and a pensioner who had fallen out of bed – they wouldn't get much excitement working 'response' either. Will was just glad to get rid of them; he'd had enough for tonight. He waited for them to get in the car and then muttered, 'Come on, first round's on me. If I get drunk I may just find all of this slightly amusing.'

Stu smirked. 'It was kind of funny, Will. What are the odds on those two deciding to give *Most Haunted* a run for their money while we were on observations in here?'

Laura laughed; she agreed with Stu. They got into the car and Will drove down to the gates, where Jake was trying to give Annie a bunk-up. Jake turned and saluted them. Will passed the keys to the gate to Stu. 'Open the gates and let the stupid buggers out and don't say a word. I'm really not in the mood.'

Stu got out and opened the gates. Will watched as Jake and Annie giggled at something Stu had said to them. It would be all around the station tomorrow but it wouldn't be his fault; they only had themselves to blame. He waited for Annie to turn and look at him so he could smile but she didn't. Instead, she clutched hold of Jake and stumbled off in the direction of his house.

Laura had been watching Will; she had seen the look in his eyes when Annie had marched off. He wouldn't admit it but he was upset. Laura had never met a woman with so much baggage and even more bad luck. Fingers crossed Stu would be his normal wimpy self and leave them after half a pint of lager to get home to his wife. For all his bravado, he was nothing more than a henpecked husband; it would be nice to be alone with Will in the pub. She'd had a thing for him for the past twelve months yet he'd not once looked at her in anything other than a professional capacity. She grinned to herself at the thought of what she could do for him if she was given the chance. Stu looked at her and whispered, 'Never in a thousand years; he's in love.'

Laura shook her head. 'Twenty quid says I at least get a kiss off him.'

Stu growled, 'For twenty quid I'd want a blow job, not a kiss. Tenner and you're on.' Laura smiled sweetly and nodded in agreement.

June 25th 1984

Sophie and Sean were playing hide-and-seek upstairs. Sean wasn't very good at it because he was too small to climb up into any of the cupboards, which meant that Sophie always found him. She had laughed at him last time she found him behind their mum's bedroom door, hiding underneath her long fluffy dressing gown. This was his favourite hiding place and he felt safe there because it smelled of coconut shampoo and his mum's perfume. He buried his head into the soft robe to stifle a giggle when he heard Sophie shouting, 'Fee- fi-fo-fum, I smell the blood of an Englishman.'

He could hear her footsteps as she ran along the landing, the creak of the bathroom door as she looked inside and the bang as she slammed it shut again and ran to the next bedroom. He was too young to understand that she was making a fuss so as not to make him feel bad about being too little to find a good hiding place – she was kind like that. She could be horrible to him, especially if he had taken one of her Sindy dolls for his A-Team men to rescue, but most of the time she was nice.

He heard her footsteps as she ran closer to his hiding place. He was staring down at his feet, so he didn't see the dark shadow that walked past the door, but he shivered and felt his teeth begin to chatter. It was so cold; he hugged the robe tighter to him to keep warm. He sniffed and then gagged; there was an awful smell in the room – a bit like when his mum made veg for dinner and they didn't eat it all because it was horrible. She would forget and leave the pan on the cooker for days. He wondered if his mum was cooking veg for tea and he pulled a face. He didn't like any of it except for the green peas and he only liked them because they made good ammunition for the A-Team to flick at the bad guys.

The light left the room and Sean felt the hairs on the back of his neck begin to prickle. It was sunny outside so he didn't understand why the room had gone so dark. He wanted to peek out from his hiding place but his Hannibal voice was telling him 'No'. He had to stay hidden, then he would be safe. Sophie had stopped running about and he heard her make a funny high-pitched noise. It wasn't very loud at first but then she let out a really loud screech, which made him jump with fright. There was a loud thud, followed by more screaming. Sean was scared but he had to go and see what was wrong with his sister so he ignored Hannibal and ran from the room onto the landing, where Sophie was curled into a ball screaming. He didn't know what to do but then his mum came running up the stairs and bent down to see what was wrong with her. He had never seen anyone with a face as white as Sophie's and he was afraid for her.

'What's wrong, Sophie? Tell me what happened!'

Sophie stared at their mum and shook her head. 'There was a man . . . he was all black and he smelled really bad.' She let out a sob and began crying.

'What man – where did he go? Did he hurt you?'

Sean began to feel scared; he had smelled that bad smell but hadn't seen any man. He turned his head to look around and make sure that the man wasn't behind them. Sophie nodded and Sean watched his mum's face turn the same colour as Sophie's. 'He pushed me over and told me to get out.'

Sean felt his knees begin to shake; he was so scared and he needed to pee really badly.

'Sophie, where did he go – is he still in here?'

His mum pulled Sophie up from the floor and then she grabbed him by the shoulder and pushed both of them behind her. She picked up a vase of flowers off the small table, discarding the flowers and dropping them to the floor.

'Sophie, I need you to tell me where he is – which room did he go in?'

'I don't know, Mummy. I think he's gone. He walked into the wall.'

She lifted a shaking finger and pointed at the wall opposite them and whispered, 'He went through there but I think he will be coming back . . . He doesn't like me.'

Sean watched his mum put the vase back on the table and then she turned to face both of them. 'Sophie, if you are telling me lies you will be in trouble, young lady. No one can walk through walls. Now, do you want to tell me what really happened or are you going to continue telling fibs?'

Sean wanted to tell her that there was a man who had smelled bad but he didn't want to make his mum even angrier so he kept quiet and didn't look at Sophie. He felt sorry for her and she would be angry with him if he knew and didn't speak up. But then his mum picked up the vase again and walked into each bedroom to look under the beds and in the wardrobes. Sophie and Sean followed her. She even checked the cupboard in the bathroom where the hot water tank was but the only things in there were piles of towels. The only place his mum didn't check was the attic, but since there was no ladder he reasoned that the man couldn't be hiding up there, not unless he had super powers and could fly like Superman.

He felt Sophie's hot breath as she let out a sigh of relief; she was standing so close to him, clutching his arm so hard he couldn't move it. Their mum turned to them both. 'Now, I don't know what game you were playing or why you are telling lies, Sophie, but you mustn't do that ever again. You nearly gave me a heart attack; I thought someone had attacked you.'

Sophie bent her head as big teardrops fell from her eyes onto the floor. Sean reached out his hand and curled his chubby fingers around Sophie's cold, much more slender ones then squeezed hard. He believed her. Their mum went downstairs and they followed her, neither of them wanting to be upstairs without her in case the bad-smelling man came back through the wall.

Chapter 2

2014

He perched on the arm of the sofa, admiring his handiwork. The woman lay there and didn't move once, which was exactly how he liked it. He didn't want to fight with her and he was glad there was no blood. He didn't like it – no, that wasn't a strong enough word; he hated blood. The smell of it made his stomach churn and his knees go weak. A couple of times he had passed out because of it and he was getting better but he avoided it at all costs. When he had first put the plastic bag over her head she had tried to claw her way out of it but he had tie-wrapped it and the plastic was too thick and her nails too short to make a difference.

Satisfied that she was dead, he walked towards her, pulling the Stanley knife from his back pocket. He slid the button up so the blade was pointing out and slowly sliced the plastic in half, making sure the blade didn't touch her skin and spoil everything. He didn't have time to pass out or feel faint. He sliced through the thick plastic tie and loosened the bag, pulling it away from her face and her soft pink lips. He stroked her long blonde hair. He tucked back the fringe, which had come loose when she had been struggling, and stared. She looked as if she was asleep – a sleeping angel. He had expected to feel deep regret at what he had done but he didn't; what he felt was satisfied. For the first time in his life he felt as if some basic primal need had been filled and he was intoxicated with a feeling of well-being, which his normally troubled mind rarely experienced.

It was still early yet; he would have a couple of hours with his perfect angel before taking her to her final resting place. He hoped the priest would be the one to find her and not a little old lady, but it didn't really matter who found her because people would soon come running to see what the fuss was about and the news would soon spread about his gift to God's messenger.

He sat in the armchair and closed his eyes, memories from a long time ago filling his mind. His mother was to blame for everything that had gone wrong in his life. He wished that she was here to understand how messed up she had made him, but she wasn't. He was on his own, always had been and always would be. He must have dozed off because when he opened his eyes he didn't know where he was and his tongue was stuck to the roof of his mouth. Blinking a few times, he looked over to see if the woman had come back to life and walked out. But she was still there and very dead. He stretched out his hand, letting his fingers brush her cheek; it was much cooler. Her lips had a blue tinge to them now; they didn't look as kissable as they had done earlier. Standing, he picked up his iPhone and took a few pictures of her, sending them to the wireless printer he had in his small office upstairs. Best not to get these pictures printed out at the shop in town; they would raise some eyebrows!

He went upstairs and unlocked the door to the office, which was actually his spare bedroom. All the walls were painted white and on one wall were four large cork noticeboards. Three of them were blank. He picked the two photos up off the printer and pinned them to the board he'd named Operation Gabriel. On this board were pictures of his victim's house, views of the street from both ends. There was a small map of the surrounding area and her house was marked with a big red cross. Post-it notes were pinned to it as well, with her name and phone number. There was a picture of the coffee shop she used two or three times a week to get her skinny latte with a dusting of chocolate sprinkles on top. Once she'd bought a slice of lemon cake, but even this had been to go. He'd never seen her sit down and relax, take five minutes. He'd stand in the queue behind her and twice when she'd turned he'd grinned at her. Flustered, she'd smiled then turned back to face the barista and wouldn't look around again.

She had no family or friends who visited her and she never went with anyone to get her coffee. He'd been watching her for four weeks now and the only visitor she had was the electricity man to read the meter. It looked as if Tracy Hale was as lonely as he was. He had no idea who would be the one to report her missing. It was quite sad, really. He stepped back to admire his work. Op Gabriel was almost over. He just needed to secure her in the church grounds without getting caught and then it would be time to start the next operation. He enjoyed the information-gathering part of it almost as much as the killing and he wondered if he wasn't wasting his talents in his current job.

He went back downstairs to watch out of his living room window, pulling the curtain to one side to see if anyone was around. The small cul-de-sac was quiet; he had a small black book with a record of all his neighbours' comings and goings. He knew that Bob at number eight went to the pub every Thursday, Friday and Saturday, leaving the house at seven and not coming back until midnight at the earliest. Mrs Wallace from number twelve never went out of the house after five p.m.; the latest he had ever seen her come home had been ten to five one night when a taxi pulled up outside her house and she had scurried inside, shutting and bolting her door. She would then go into each room and close the curtains. She never had any visitors and she never opened the door – ever.

The problem was number fifteen. He didn't know what the young couple who lived there were called but they came in at all hours and were very unpredictable. They both worked shifts at McDonald's; he knew this because of the distinctive olive-green polo shirts and khaki trousers the staff at the drive-through wore. When they weren't working they were out drinking and sometimes brought friends back to play extremely loud music and party. He was glad that he lived a short distance away from them, otherwise he might have gone in there and smashed their music system or whatever it was they used to play the damn music on. However, it was a pretty safe bet that they didn't come home between the hours of eight and nine p.m.

They were the only ones left in the street; the other houses had been bought by the council and boarded up. There had been talk about regeneration and knocking the houses down to build an urban park but that was over two years ago now. The council had run out of money and now the last few residents were making the best of what they had until a better opportunity came along.

He looked at his watch; it was almost eight – time to put his plan into action. His truck was on the small drive directly in front of the house. He had made a point of taking things on and off the back of the truck to avoid arousing suspicion when he actually had more than some planks of wood or bits of old furniture. He slipped on his thick black leather gloves and opened his front door. It was a dry night, which was all part of the planning; he wouldn't be able to do this in the rain. He unlatched the tailgate of the truck and let it drop down. He moved some of the old bits of wood around and took the folded-up plastic sheeting he had in the cab into the house.

He began to wrap the plastic around his sleeping angel, tucking it around her and rolling her from side to side to make sure she was completely covered, then he took the roll of duct tape he had left on the table and began to secure the plastic, being careful not to use too much – he didn't want to make it harder than it was already going to be when he got her to the church. He bent down to pick her up; it was quite a struggle and much harder than he'd imagined. The plastic sheeting made it difficult to grip and even though she was a tiny little thing she was a dead weight – he smiled to himself at the pun. With everything he had, he threw her over his shoulder and made his move.

He walked out of the house and placed her in the back of his truck. He didn't look around to see if anyone was watching because he never did; he relied on his senses to alert him. After slamming the tailgate shut, he went back inside his house and shut his front door. Give the neighbours time to come over and investigate if they thought he had put anything untoward on the back of the truck. He left the hall light on and the front door unlocked. He was breathing heavily from the exertion but he was buzzing with excitement. He went into the darkened living room to sit down and wait in the chair, giving the police a chance to arrive in case anyone had called them. He couldn't go around suffocating girls in public places; it had to be done in private. He couldn't abide mess and it would have been too risky killing her at her house so it had to be here.

Ten minutes passed with no police cars flying into the street with blue lights and sirens wailing. Perfect – he just hoped he could manage to get her out of the truck at the church without anyone noticing. He had been a busy boy this last month because he had a red book with every activity and service that was held in the church. Thursday nights were quiet – no tap-dancing teenagers in the church hall or flower-arranging pensioners in the church. Thursday was an unpopular night in St Mary's Church social calendar, which suited his needs just fine. He left the driveway and drove the short distance to the church. Recently he had done a few odd jobs in the area so his truck was a regular sight parked near to the church. If he said so himself, he was a very organised person.

There were no houses which overlooked the church, just the

presbytery a short distance away. He noted that the blinds were closed. The front of the church was illuminated but the rear was in darkness. He parked at the side, as close to the gate as possible. There wasn't anyone in the area but he got out and had a stroll around to make sure. Reassured, he unlatched the back of the truck and dragged her out, throwing her over one shoulder. He had to duck as he went through the gate to make sure he didn't catch her on the low branches that hung over the entrance, not wanting to get her caught in them, dangling like a life-size puppet. His hands began to sweat inside his gloves, making it harder to grip her, but a few more paces and he would be at the grave he had chosen. It was in the perfect position; it couldn't be seen from the street because of its close proximity to the wall and it was sheltered by a huge oak tree.

Panting now, he bent and tried to put her down without dropping her but she slid from his grasp and he grunted as her body hit the gravel. Pulling the knife from his pocket, he sliced open the plastic. Working fast, he pulled it off and screwed it up – tossing it to one side. He undressed her, taking every item of clothing off, then he laid her on her side, taking the time to position one hand under her face, palm upwards, her other arm across her chest, so they were as close together as he could make them without fastening them together. He then set about picking up leaves, branches and twigs to cover some of her nudity, wanting her to look tasteful. Posed in death as if she were a sculpture, this had taken him a lot longer than he had anticipated but when he finally finished and stepped back to admire his work he felt like applauding. She looked truly beautiful in death. He pulled his gloves off and took his phone out of his pocket, snapping a couple of photos. He didn't think he would see her again but he wanted to remember everything about his first angel.

Dragging himself away, he turned and began picking up her clothes and the plastic sheeting; they smelled of her and he would keep them hanging up in his office in the wardrobe he had bought specially. He lifted the blouse to his nose and inhaled her perfume, unsure what it was but knowing it was something expensive. He knew every time he smelled it on a woman he would be reminded of these precious memories. His heart pounding with excitement and exertion, he forced himself to walk away from her. As he reached the gate he turned to steal one last glance and blew her a kiss. Then he climbed into his truck and drove away. He was pumped full of adrenalin – nothing could destroy how he felt at that moment. Gloating but not stupid, he drove around the empty streets aimlessly for the next twenty minutes – he didn't pass one police car, which didn't surprise him.

When he was ready, he began to drive home and back to his mundane life.

Chapter 3

The Black Dog was quiet. Will went to the bar and bought himself a double vodka and drank it neat. Then he ordered two pints of lager, a large glass of wine and three bags of salt and vinegar crisps. There were two men playing pool in the corner and Will, Stu and Laura – that was it. At least it saved time at the bar – he wanted to get drunk and forget that tonight had ever happened. In a couple of weeks he might see the funny side of it but he doubted it; he might even throw a sickie tomorrow so he wouldn't have to face the eight hours of piss-taking. He carried the drinks over and went back for the crisps. Laura was telling Stu about some festival she was going to in a couple of weeks with a minibus full of mates. Stu asked who was headlining and Will downed his pint before they had had a chance to sip their drinks.

He got up and went to the bar for another shot of double vodka and a pint. He swallowed the vodka at the bar and knew that they would be whispering about him; he never usually drank more than a couple of pints on shift nights out, preferring to stay sober and not be the cause of any gossip. He took out his phone and called Annie; even though he was mad with her, he'd still rather be with her than stewing in the pub getting pissed. This was the first time they'd really fallen out and he didn't like it. If she answered he'd get a taxi home and leave Laura and Stu to it.

He let her phone ring and ring until it went to voicemail. He didn't leave a message because he wasn't sure what to say: 'Stop being stubborn and come home'? He tried again – still no answer – so he rang Jake, who didn't answer either. Now Will felt even more angry than before and ordered another shot of vodka. After downing it, he turned and stumbled back towards the table to join the others. He caught the look that Laura gave to Stu but ignored it and began talking about any old crap that came into his head.

After twenty minutes Stu looked at his watch. 'I really should get going. Debs will kill me if I'm really late.'

Will nodded. 'You're a lightweight, Stu. What's that on your forehead? Hang on, it's beak marks – henpecked is what you are.'

Laura stifled a giggle and held her empty glass towards Will. 'Well, I'm not in a rush – same again.'

Stu frowned, shaking his head at her, but Will stood up to go back to the bar and she rubbed her finger and thumb together and whispered, 'You're going to owe me a lot more than a tenner.'

Stu shrugged. 'I seriously doubt it. He's going to get so tanked up you'd need a flagpole to strap to his dick.'

She let out a loud screech, which made everyone, including Will, turn to look at them. Stu lifted his hand and walked out of the door, leaving them to it.

*

Annie was sitting in Jake's kitchen drinking the frothy cappuccino that Alex had just made. Now that she had got over the initial shock of what had happened in the cemetery it didn't seem quite so funny. She knew she'd upset Will and embarrassed him in front of his colleagues and she felt like crap.

Alex grabbed her hand. 'Penny for them?'

'Why do I let Jake talk me into doing such stupid stuff? I'm

27

such an idiot and now Will's mad with me and going into work tomorrow is going to be an absolute nightmare.'

'Annie, I've lived with Jake for the last two years and he still talks me into doing stupid stuff and I really should know better. Last month it was having our cards read by an old dear who nearly passed out when she realised we were a couple. She'd told Jake he was going to settle down with the woman of his dreams in the next three years and would have lots of children.'

She grinned at him. 'Poor woman. I know what he's like and that's why I should know better. I'm fed up with feeding the station gossips with my life.'

Jake walked in and patted her on the head, then he went and stood close to Alex, slipping his arm around his waist. 'Have we sobered up yet, Ms Graham? That was pretty hilarious, though.'

'It was funny at the time but I'm not so sure now. I think I should go and find Will and apologise.'

'I wouldn't if I were you. I'd let him calm down. He was pretty mad at you. Why don't you sleep in the spare room? Give you both a chance to breathe and then you can go and see him in the morning. He's not at work till twelve.'

Annie thought about it. She'd have to get a taxi to Will's house and then get one back here to come for her car tomorrow, and it wasn't payday for another week. It would be easier to stay the night and drive home first thing; she didn't have to be in work until nine. She opened her mouth and let out a huge yawn. 'Ooh, excuse me; if you don't mind, I'll stay here. It's easier than messing around with taxis and stuff.'

Alex nodded then left the kitchen. Jake lowered his voice. 'He's gone to turn down your bed and make sure the bogeyman isn't hiding in the wardrobe.'

Annie pushed Jake's arm. 'Don't be so mean; he's adorable and sometimes far too good for you and your sarcasm.' She sipped the rest of her coffee and this time managed to get down from the stool in an elegant manner. 'See, I can be a lady when I try.'

Jake laughed and bent down to kiss her on the cheek. 'Goodnight, my crazy ghost-seeing friend. Sleep tight.'

She turned to go upstairs; Alex had turned the heating on and pulled the bed covers down, placing one of Jake's T-shirts on the bed for her. 'Sleep tight, Annie; everything will be OK. You and Will are destined to be with each other and I bet he's tried phoning – have you checked?'

She felt in her pocket for her phone but it wasn't there. 'Damn, I think I might have dropped it when I fell in the cemetery.'

'I'll send Jake to go and look for it in the morning. I'm not as brave or foolish as you two. There is no way I would go in there at this time of night. Do you want to borrow mine to ring him?'

She shook her head. 'No, it's late. Let him stew for a while; it may make him realise that he can't live without me.'

Alex hugged her. 'I'm pretty sure he can't.' He left and she undressed and pulled Jake's huge T-shirt over her head then climbed into bed. Within five minutes she was fast asleep.

*

When Will couldn't see straight he decided it was time to call it a day. He stood up and felt his legs wobble. Falling into the table, he knocked the rest of Laura's wine into her lap. She jumped up and grabbed Will's arm. 'Come on, Will, I think it's time to leave.'

He felt her arm slide under his and she gripped his elbow, directing him towards the door. 'Sorry, Laura, I got you all wet.'

He slurred his words and Laura giggled. 'It's OK. I'll dry out but I think I should make sure you get home OK.'

Will turned and aimed his lips at her cheek to plant a kiss on it but she moved fast and he felt his lips connect with hers. She kissed him hard, pulling him closer, and for a second he forgot about Annie and kissed her back, then his senses returned and he pulled away from her. 'Whoa, steady on. I'm not supposed to be doing this.' A taxi pulled up and he stepped away from her towards it and knocked on the window. 'Who is this taxi for?'

'Corkill.'

Will nodded and opened the door. 'That would be me then.' He shook his head at Laura, who was stifling a laugh, and she climbed in after him. He gave his address and wound the window down; he'd had nothing to eat since dinner except for a packet of crisps and he felt sick. Laura had snaked her arm through his again and was now leaning her head on his chest. It was wrong but he was so drunk he couldn't think straight and was putting all his concentration into not puking all over the taxi floor.

When they got out of the taxi, Will struggled to get the money from his pocket to pay the driver. It was a huge effort to keep standing upright. He felt Laura's slender fingers slip into his side pocket and begin to root around for his money. He watched her pay the man and then she took hold of his hand and dragged him up the gravel path to his front door. She had his door key in her hand and put it in the lock. She opened it and stepped inside. Will stumbled in behind her and tripped on the hall mat, trying his best to keep upright, but gravity won and he lost his balance and fell to the floor. He lay there and began to laugh. Laura tried to drag him up but he was too heavy and instead she ended up falling on top of him. She kissed him again but this time he didn't kiss back. 'I'm sorry, Laura; I can't do this – I love Annie.'

He watched her begin to blink back tears and he did feel bad, even though he was drunk. He managed to pull himself to his knees, knocking the framed picture of himself and Annie face down onto the small table in the hall. He then wobbled his way into the living room and collapsed onto the sofa. Within sixty seconds he was snoring.

Laura wanted Will so badly that it hurt inside her chest. She couldn't afford a taxi home and Annie must not be home or she would have come down to see what all the commotion was. She looked at Will then bent down and tugged off his shoes, then she undid his trousers, pulled them down and dropped them on the floor next to his shoes. He had a pair of tight black boxer shorts on and for a man much older than her he looked well decent. It was warm in the house and she didn't want to crease her best suit so she stripped down to her underwear and climbed on the sofa next to him. She hoped that when he woke up he would be like most men and not be able to resist her charms and the offer of some hot sex. Then the wine began to take effect and she found herself falling asleep.

June 26th 1984

Sophie couldn't bring herself to watch this stupid TV programme that Sean was obsessed with – as if those men could make tanks out of some metal sheets and a hairdryer. It was total rubbish but he loved it. He really wanted to be B.A. – the one with the crazy haircut. Sophie hadn't really spoken much since she'd seen the man yesterday – he had been real in one way but not in another and he'd smelled so bad. She didn't know why he didn't like her or where he had come from but she knew he would be back. He had told her to get out and she hadn't. Where could she go? She was only nine years old. She couldn't just leave because some horrible, stinky shadow of a man had told her to. What made everything worse was her mum thinking she had made it all up. Why had she not been able to smell him? Sophie would never lie about anything unless it was one of those white lies so she didn't upset someone.

She looked down at the picture she had been drawing to show her mum exactly what he looked like so she could be careful if she saw him too, but she couldn't get him right. He had looked both grey and black but at the same time transparent, and she knew that if she had been brave enough to reach out her hand and touch him, it would have gone straight through him. He must be a ghost and Crayola didn't make a crayon called 'ghost', although she knew it would be a pretty popular one because she would bet ten Black Jacks she wasn't the only kid to have seen him. She shivered; she didn't want him to come back.

When she was finally happy her picture was good enough, she took it to show her mum, who was busy talking to Father John, who was always around lately. She hovered at the kitchen door until the priest took his eyes off her mum and smiled at her.

'Hello, Sophie, what have you got there? Let me see.'

Sophie walked reluctantly towards him and handed him the piece of paper. He took it from her and smiled. 'I didn't know you were a budding artist.' He looked at the picture and his face froze. Sophie knew then that the priest had seen the shadow man before.

'Why have you drawn this? Have you seen this man, Sophie?'

She nodded but didn't speak; she didn't want to make her mum angry again.

'When did you see him?'

She looked across at her mum, who had turned from stirring whatever it was she was cooking on the stove to watch them. Sophie walked up to Father John and, standing on tiptoe, she whispered in his ear, 'Yesterday, upstairs, and he doesn't like me.' Sophie's mum, Beth, looked at her daughter, whose face was pale, and then at Father John. His face was whiter than Sophie's.

'What's going on . . . what are you talking about, Sophie? What did I tell you about making things up?'

Father John stood and passed the picture to her; she took it from him and blanched. 'Sophie, that's horrible. Why would you want to draw someone who looks like that? No wonder you're scaring yourself. What have you been watching on the television?'

Father John turned to Sophie. 'If you see him again I want you to tell me. Was he mean to you?'

Sophie nodded.

'He doesn't like me either, but I can make him go away. He

may just have been passing through on his way somewhere else.'

The thought of this made Sophie feel better and for the first time since yesterday she didn't have that sick feeling in her stomach. 'I will. Do you really think so? Because I don't like him. He's like a shadow man and he smells really bad!'

Father John grinned at her. 'I'm sure and, yes, he does smell really bad, like an old dustbin.'

They both started giggling and Beth shrugged her shoulders; she had no idea what they were talking about but let them get on with it.

Father John stood up to leave. 'I'm going now but I'll be back later. I'll bring some holy water and bless Sophie's room.'

Beth nodded. 'You two are crazy but if it makes you feel better then knock yourself out.'

Father John winked at Sophie. 'He doesn't like holy water either; it smells too clean for him so he won't come into your room.'

Sophie watched as he put his coat on, not wanting him to go. She felt safe with him here, especially if he knew about the shadow man. Father John walked to the front door and she followed him. He paused then fished around in his pocket. He pulled out a small bronze St Michael medal and handed it to her. 'Wear this or keep it with you; it will help.'

Beth looked at him. 'Come on, Father John, what are you trying to do: brainwash my daughter? Sophie, go and get Sean and take him up to clean his teeth; I'll be upstairs in a minute.'

Sophie turned and ran back to the living room to drag her brother away from the television. The priest waited until she was out of earshot. 'I don't think you understand, Beth, but there is a very real threat from this shadow man, as Sophie calls him. I saw him myself when I was a bit older than Sophie is now and he isn't very nice.'

'Are you expecting me to believe that my daughter has seen a ghost? Because I don't believe in any of that nonsense. You're

33

supposed to be a man of God; next you'll be telling me that he'll be popping around to speak to the children as well. I don't want to hear any more about it and please don't encourage her. I have enough to worry about.'

'I'm sorry. You're right, Beth, but you need to know, whatever or whoever this shadow man is, he is real. I was terrified of him when I was a boy. It was such a shock to see that drawing.'

'Bye, Father.'

She shut the door and Father John walked to the gate. He turned to look up and saw Sophie at the window with her face pressed against the glass, waving at him. He waved back and said a prayer to keep her safe. No one knew what they were dealing with except him and he had blocked it out for twenty-three years.

Father John walked the short distance to his church. The house that Beth and her children were living in belonged to the church. It was used as a house for poor families or anyone in desperate need. Beth had been in a dire situation when Father John had met her for the first time, with a black eye and broken nose. He had found her huddled at the corner of the church with her two children and a suitcase. He had only just joined the parish but he couldn't ignore them. He had led them around to the presbytery, cradling a sleeping Sean in his arms. Beth had followed with Sophie and the battered suitcase.

That had been nine months ago and he had watched Beth grow in confidence and they had become good friends. In fact, truth be told, he was in crisis at the moment because he very much wanted to be more than good friends and he knew that this could never be. He knew that he should be trying to distance himself from her but he couldn't. He found himself drawn to her, to them, more than ever. He hadn't felt this way before and wondered if it was only because he wanted to protect them, protect her.

Now this – how could the shadow man be here after all these years? Father John needed to speak with Father Robert, who was much older and wiser than him. He twisted the black iron ring on the church door and walked inside. He needed to pray. The silence inside the church reassured him and he felt as if he had come home, that God was waiting for him and it was a good feeling. Despite the internal conflict he was suffering, he knew that this was where he truly belonged and that somehow God would help him.

Chapter 4

2014

Annie woke to the smell of frying bacon and her stomach groaned; she was starving. Throwing the duvet back, she swung her legs out of the bed, sitting on the edge for a minute in case she was mega hung-over. She stood up and felt fine, no pounding head or churning stomach – Annie 1, alcohol 0. She got dressed and went into the bathroom to freshen up. Her hair was much better; it was now a short shoulder-length bob and suited her much better than the half a skinhead she had been sporting last year. Wetting her fingers, she ran them through her hair and scrunched it up and then she squirted some toothpaste onto her finger and rubbed it all over her teeth. At least she wouldn't smell and she was excited to see Will and make it up to him. Last night was the first night they had spent apart since she had moved in with him.

Going downstairs into the kitchen, she was greeted by a bright and breezy Alex, who was making bacon and egg butties. Jake was nowhere to be seen.

'The big guy's in bed; he can't move his head and has been up all night throwing up. Tequila obviously doesn't agree with him as much as he thinks it does, but you, my dear, look fabulous so you can gloat over him all day if you want.'

'I'd love to but I'll save it until he's back at work. I'd love a quick sandwich if it's OK and then I'm off to go and see Will. I think I have a bit of grovelling to do.'

Alex grinned. 'Well, just don't grovel too much and remember he was at fault as well.' He handed her a sandwich made from two thick slices of freshly baked bread. Annie took a bite and groaned. 'Thanks, Alex, you know how to look after a girl.'

He began to laugh. 'I do indeed.' He looked in the direction of the stairs. Annie stood on tiptoe and kissed his cheek. As she turned to leave he shouted her back – he had her phone in his hand.

'Where did you find that?'

'Under one of the bar stools; it must have fallen out of your pocket.'

She thanked him then went out the front to get in her car to go and see the man of her dreams.

Annie reached Will's house and parked up outside. She loved where they lived; it was so pretty. She had always liked the idea of living in a country cottage with a porch covered in sweetly smelling roses and honeysuckle around the door and his house had it all. She hoped he was still in bed so she could climb in next to him and show him exactly how sorry she was. She jogged along the gravel path and pulled the key from her pocket. The door wasn't locked, which wasn't like Will. He was the king of telling people to 'Lock it or lose it', the force's burglary motto.

She opened the door and stepped inside. It reeked of stale beer, and her eyes fell on the table and the photo of them both, which was face down. Her stomach began to churn; she hadn't felt this way since she'd left Mike and she knew something was wrong. Call it a woman's intuition or a copper's instinct. A loud snore came from the direction of the living room and she forced herself to move towards it.

She wasn't too sure what she had expected to see but it definitely wasn't Will lying next to a practically naked Laura, who had her arm thrown over his chest and her legs wrapped around his. The pain that shot through Annie's heart made her gasp out loud. Deep down, her worst fear had been that it would end like this. She had managed to forget about Will's reputation as a womaniser because he had changed since he'd fallen in love with her. Tears welled in her eyes and as much as she wanted to grab skinny blonde Laura's hair and drag her off the sofa and throw her naked into the street – she couldn't do it. Will murmured something into Laura's ear and that was it. Annie turned to run out of the house and out of Will's life forever, but she tripped over his shoes and clattered into the wall. Will's eyes flew open and he looked in her direction, confused. Annie stared back at him, composing herself as she turned and walked out, slamming the door shut behind her.

Will felt the warmth from the body next to him and was shocked to see Laura. 'Fuck me, Laura, what are you doing?'

He shoved her and she rolled off the sofa onto the soft rug below. He fumbled to get up, his head swimming. His stomach lurched and his mouth filled with bile. Still he ran for the front door, noticing the picture frame he'd knocked over last night and had been too drunk to bother picking up. A loud screech as Annie's car sped off was enough to make him puke all over the hall floor. When he finished retching he threw open the door to make sure that it had been her car and that she wasn't still sitting outside. She was long gone and he stood on his front porch mentally begging her to come back. He turned to go inside and noticed his elderly neighbour watching him. He realised that he was almost naked. 'Sorry, Mrs Jones.'

He went back in and shut the door. Laura was standing there, with her clothes on now. 'I should get going. Can you ring me a taxi? My phone's dead.'

He pointed at the phone next to the overturned picture. 'Ring one yourself. What were you thinking . . . what was I thinking . . . did we . . .?' He couldn't bring himself to say the words.

She shook her head. 'I don't know; I can't remember.'

'Phone your taxi then wait outside; you can shut the door behind you.' He walked to the kitchen to get a pint of water and four paracetamol; he felt like shit. Hangovers at his age weren't so much fun anymore and he had just royally fucked up his life. He wanted to cry but instead he took a roll of paper towels to mop up his vomit and then went upstairs to bed. He dialled Annie's number but it went straight to voicemail. Not able to do much else, he shut his eyes and fell into a deep sleep, one in which he hadn't just broken the heart of the woman he loved and ruined his whole life.

Chapter 5

Father John had a busy day ahead of him; he had two funerals and a christening to arrange. He also had a sick parishioner to visit who needed to speak to him about something they wouldn't discuss with anyone else. But, first things first, he wandered into the kitchen in his SpongeBob pyjamas and fluffy slippers. He needed coffee. Not just a spoonful from a jar – proper coffee. He rarely spent money on himself but the one thing he had finally succumbed to was a coffee machine, one that could match the industrial-size one in the local Costa without breaking a sweat. In fact Father John's cappuccinos were the stuff of legend; if they were to make him a saint it would be Father John – Patron Saint of Coffee Drinkers. The Women's Union would congregate around the large kitchen table once a week with a plate of homemade biscuits and twelve of his coffees, then he would bow out gracefully and leave them to it. For the first time in history there was actually a waiting list to join them and he knew it was because he was running a parish coffee shop.

He ground the beans and set about making his coffee, popping two slices of wholemeal bread into the toaster. Once he'd eaten his breakfast and read the daily paper he would shower and put on his sin-busting suit, as he fondly called it, and get to work.

He was on his second cup of coffee and halfway through reading the paper when he heard an ear-splitting scream outside. He jumped up, throwing his paper to the side, and ran to the window to see what the hell it was. He peered out and could see the bent figure of Mrs Higgins come hurtling through the churchyard and into the front garden. For an old woman she could move fast! He rushed to the front door and opened it for the woman, who was now standing there breathing heavily and pointing towards the churchyard. She couldn't speak, so John slipped on his boots and began jogging in the direction she was pointing. He couldn't see anything and looked around, expecting to see some young couple having sex or some drunken homeless guy, but there wasn't anything.

He looked back at her and shrugged. She lifted a shaking hand and pointed towards the wall. He turned around slowly this time, looking at the graves, and then he saw her; he had to blink to make sure his eyes weren't playing tricks on him. She was lying on one of the much older graves and she looked as if she was asleep, only John knew she was in a much worse state than that. He nodded to Mrs Higgins and made his way towards the grave, not wanting to go any further but knowing he had a duty of care towards this poor woman.

He stood in front of her and crossed himself, saying a quick prayer, then he bent down and placed two fingers to her neck to check for a pulse. He knew there wouldn't be one but he had to make sure. He stood up and walked back to the house to phone the police. Dear God, what was the world coming to?

*

Will dragged himself out of bed and into the shower. He couldn't spend all day wallowing in self-pity and hiding away from the world; he needed to sort this mess out now. The combination of alcohol and the thought of how much he had hurt Annie was

41

giving him butterflies. He was positive he hadn't actually had sex with Laura – he'd been pissed as a fart – but he remembered telling her that he loved Annie so how had she ended up naked next to him? He knew from past experience that when he got that drunk he wouldn't be able to get it up for Jennifer Aniston so there was no way he would have been able to do it with Laura.

The hot water cleansed his skin but he still felt like a dirty, rotten cheat on the inside. He rubbed the lemon shower gel that Annie had bought all over himself. He hoped to God he would be able to sort it out with her because the last six months had been the best of his life. He had even been thinking about asking her to marry him and up until he'd met her he'd never really believed that he'd ever feel that way about a woman – ever. His phone was ringing but it was only when he turned the shower off and began to dry himself that he heard it; his heart skipped a beat and he crossed his fingers it was her. Dashing naked through to the bedroom to reach his phone, he picked it up and saw it was a blocked number and knew it was work.

'Will speaking.'

He listened as the control room operator informed him that a body had been found in St Mary's churchyard, it looked suspicious and would he attend. 'Yes, I'll be there in ten minutes.' He ended the call. *Bollocks,* now it was going to be hours before he would get to speak to Annie. He didn't want to do it over the phone but he had no choice so he dialled her number. She didn't pick up and he hadn't really expected her to, so he left her a message. 'Annie, it's not what you think. I swear to God I don't know how she ended up there. I was so drunk I wouldn't be able to . . . well, you know what I mean. I love you so much. I've got to go; there's a suspicious death at St Mary's and it might be hours before I can come and see you. Please, Annie, I love you with all my heart – let me explain.'

He ended the call and slumped on the bed. Today was going to be a long day.

*

Annie had driven around aimlessly for a couple of hours. At one point she ended up on Walney Island and parked the car on the seafront, watching the waves crashing onto the shore with tears rolling down her cheeks. She finally decided it was time to go home and parked the car outside her semi-detached house. Her phone was vibrating on the seat next to her but there was no way she would answer it. She couldn't bear to hear Will's voice right now. He had hurt her so much, yet she wasn't surprised. She knew she had got too involved so soon after Mike.

She looked at her house. It had been over a month since she'd been inside. The For Sale sign that was swaying in the wind would be coming down; there wasn't another option. It looked as if she would be moving back after all. She couldn't stay with Jake; he'd smother her with love, and the last time she'd stayed at her brother's it had caused no end of heartache for everyone. She'd run there to escape from Mike after he'd smashed her over the head with a bottle and almost killed her, which had led her to discover the haunted house in the woods, where she had also discovered her new-found ability to see ghosts. Oh, and she'd managed to attract the attention of a man called Henry who was a serial killer.

Her phone beeped, shaking her from the memories that were filling her mind with horror; the only good thing that had come out of it all had been her falling in love with Will. He had turned into her knight in shining armour, and now this morning he'd put an end to all of it. Her phone beeping told her she had a voicemail so she opened the glove compartment and threw the phone in there, slamming it shut. She needed some time on her own, time to think, and this was as good a place as any.

She got out of the car and walked up the three steps to reach her front door. Once she opened it and stood inside, she waited for a couple of minutes to see what would happen. To see if the memories of the beatings Mike used to give her would come flying back, but they didn't. In fact, she didn't feel anything. She went into her living room, which had once been full of mismatched, antique painted furniture. Now it was an empty shell; everything had been packed away and stored in one of her brother's barns at his farmhouse in Abbey Wood. The only thing of any comfort was the carpet that she'd had fitted just before Mike had tried to kill her; it still smelled new.

She went through into the kitchen and checked the cupboards; there were a couple of mugs, a plate and two forks and a spoon – at least she had something to eat and drink with. She filled the sink with soapy water and plonked the lot of it into the bowl to soak. She needed to go and buy some groceries. In fact she needed to buy quite a bit, unless she waited until Will was at work and went back for all her stuff – she would have to because she didn't have much spare cash. Turning to look at the kitchen door where Mike had decided to try and cave the back of her head in, she expected to feel upset, but the only thing she felt was relief that she was still alive, even if her life was one fucked-up mess.

She ran up the stairs to check the bedrooms and turn the heating on to air the house through. It didn't feel much like summer today. She didn't even look into the master bedroom; instead she went into the much smaller spare bedroom, which looked out onto the tree-lined front street. This house was by no means as pretty as Will's but it was her house and it was time to reclaim it.

Tears filled her eyes but she blinked them back. She had wanted to spend the rest of her life with Will, but she wouldn't let him treat her like a fool. She stripped the single bed, shook all the covers and pillowcases and then put them back on. They had never been used before so there was no point washing them; she was just checking for spiders and dust.

Annie turned to peer out of the window and caught a glimpse of a little girl standing on her front doorstep. She was wearing a long white cotton dress and had platinum-blonde hair, which had been parted down the middle and braided into two plaits. She didn't recognise the girl as one of the neighbours' kids; the poor thing must be frozen because there was a bitter wind today. And then she noticed that the litter on the street was whipping around on the pavements in a frenzy, but the girl's hair and dress weren't moving at all. Annie looked up and down the street to see if there were other people around; the only one was the elderly man across the road and he was hanging on to his battered old trilby to stop it from blowing away.

Her heart raced and the palms of her hands were damp. The girl didn't move; she carried on staring up at her. Annie pressed her face to the glass and opened her mouth to speak but the girl lifted a finger to her lips to shush her. Then she turned and walked down the first two steps . . . By the time she should have touched the third one she had disappeared.

Annie ran down her stairs and opened the door. There was no sign of the girl. She stepped out of the house and down the steps to check the front street. As she trod on the bottom step something crunched underneath her shoe. She stopped and bent down, picking up a broken toy figure; it was a head and body with no legs or arms. It was a pretty creepy toy because, whoever he was, he looked far too old to be an action figure – his hair was grey. She looked up and down the deserted street then turned and went back inside her house.

She went into the kitchen and opened one of the empty drawers, throwing the figure into it. She didn't like it but, for some reason, she knew it was important to someone – maybe the girl had played with it when she had been alive. As much as she didn't want to admit it, she knew that the girl was dead; normal kids didn't disappear into thin air. If only Jake had been here – he would have had a shit fit.

*

45

A car horn beeped outside and Will pulled himself up from the bed. He went downstairs, picking up the overturned picture. He kissed his finger and pressed it to Annie's lips – *sorry, babe.* The hall still stank of stale vomit and his stomach lurched once more. He opened the front door and inhaled the fresh air, lifting his hand to wave at the officer waiting for him in the patrol car. After slamming his door shut, he went down the steps and opened the car door. 'How's it going, Sean?'

'Oh, you know how it is, Will – same shit, different day and all that.'

Will nodded; he knew exactly what he meant. 'So what's happened?'

'I haven't been to the scene. I heard the shout come over the radio that an old dear had found a dead woman in the church grounds. They've been in a flap ever since.'

'Christ. As if we need any more murders. I take it that it doesn't look like natural causes?'

'Not from what I've heard on the radio. They were shouting about getting a tent there from CSI to cover her up. I spoke to Smithy who's on scene guard; he said she was totally naked.'

'Not good, Sean, not good at all.'

The church steeple loomed in the distance and Will thought he would give anything to be anywhere other than there. But he would push his problems to the back of his mind and do his best for whoever it was that needed his help. They hadn't asked for what had happened to them – unlike him.

June 27th 1984

Father John wanted to speak to Sophie without Beth present but it was impossible. Beth knew that something was going on but she didn't want to admit it.

He'd woken in the night after a terrible dream where he was taking part in a tug of war. He was on one side and the shadow man on the other – Sophie had been the rope. When he had opened his eyes his hair was plastered to his head with sweat. The room smelled terrible, like rotting vegetables. He'd sat up and reached out to turn on the bedside lamp, smelled that stench then jumped out of bed and turned the main light on because the lamp cast too many shadows. It had been years since he'd encountered that particular smell and he felt unsettled; the shadow man had been here – in his room. John knew that whatever it was wouldn't be able to touch him in a house that belonged to God but it scared him that it still believed it could go wherever it wanted. The sooner Father Robert came back from Manchester the better because at this very moment in time John felt violated in God's house.

He knelt down at the side of his bed and began to recite a prayer that he hadn't really used since he was a child. He paused, sure that he heard a deep voice repeating each word, and every hair on the back of his neck stood on end. He whipped his head around, looking for a shadow lurking in a corner, but he was alone. He finished his prayer then stood up. 'I'm not afraid of you anymore. I don't know why you are here but I think it's time you moved on, because if you don't I will send you back to whatever hellhole you've come from and you will never see the light of day again.'

With that, John left the bedroom and went straight downstairs and out of the front door to check on Beth and her children. Beth's house was in darkness, which was a good sign; they must all be sleeping. Unsettled, he went back to the presbytery and took the key for the church from the large pewter dish on the sideboard in the hall. He needed to be close to God, so he made his way over to the church, which was shrouded in darkness. The spotlights that illuminated it every evening had turned off. They ran on a timer to save money but he wasn't scared; this place was his life and he believed in God and the power of good. This also meant that he believed in evil and, somehow, in the hours of darkness, it was far easier to believe that evil was lurking in the shadows.

As he strode across the damp grass he sensed someone walking behind him but he brushed it off as his imagination. It wasn't until he reached the small cemetery where the grass ended and the gravel began that he heard definite footsteps behind him. He didn't turn to look but continued in the direction of the church. When he reached the huge oak door he inserted the key in the lock and opened it. His heart was hammering inside his chest but he would not show his fear because he knew that it would be a sign of his weakness. Stepping inside, he felt along the wall to the left of him for the light switch. When his fingers located it and pressed it down, the relief that washed over him was over-whelming as the entrance was bathed in glorious light. He stood there, leaning against the closed door until his breathing slowed and was back to normal.

The door felt as if it was vibrating the tiniest bit. He had never noticed that before, but then he had never had cause to come in here in the middle of the night after a bad dream, being followed by a man who wasn't from this world. The inner sanctum of the church was still in darkness and for the first time in his life as a priest he felt scared of that darkness and what could be waiting in there. *Get a grip, John; you are in the Lord's house. There is no way that God is going to let such evil enter his house; this is a place of safety and love.*

He marched across to the glass door and threw it open; if that repugnant smell had entered his nostrils he would have screamed, but it didn't. The church smelled like it always did: a little bit damp with the lingering aroma of candle wax and the smell of the fresh flowers that the Mothers' Union brought in and arranged each week. This week it was lavender, roses and lilies and they smelled fabulous. He crossed himself. *Thank you, God. I'm glad you kept to your side of the bargain; I need all the help I can get.*

I'm still a beginner at all this stuff, you know. Please don't leave me to deal with it on my own because I don't know whether I can.

He turned on the lights and the shadows were banished. John felt his nerves begin to steady and his heart slowed to a more regular pace. He busied himself lighting candles and arranging hymn books into neat piles. When he'd done this he walked to the altar and knelt down to pray harder than he'd ever prayed in his life.

Chapter 6

2014

Annie loved Sunday morning shifts; usually there wasn't too much happening. Sometimes there was the odd drunken prisoner to deal with from last night's shenanigans on Cornwallis Street, which was famed for the number of drunken brawls at the weekend. It always amused her seeing their faces as they were released from custody to do the 'walk of shame' home. Nine times out of ten a look of bewilderment was etched across their faces as they had no recollection of what arseholes they'd been to get locked up in the first place. Kav, her sergeant, had looked at her when she had come into the parade room at the start of her shift and nodded. Annie guessed that he knew or had heard something; he seemed to have a sixth sense when it came to her. When Mike had attacked her, Kav had been the one to find her unconscious and he had dealt with it himself after she had confided the whole sordid story to him. He had stopped it from becoming public knowledge and she was eternally grateful to him.

At the briefing he had put her double crewed in the van with Jake and it was over a greasy breakfast in the hospital canteen that she blurted to him about finding Will with Laura yesterday morning. She hadn't meant to but Jake had asked if they wanted to come round for supper tonight and she didn't have the energy to make up a plausible excuse; besides, he would hear it soon enough so it was better he heard it from her. His face had turned redder than the sea of tinned tomatoes that were swimming around on his plate; he'd dropped his knife and fork and clenched his huge fists so hard his knuckles were white.

'Please tell me that this is some kind of joke, because I will kill him. I warned him, if he didn't keep his dick in his pants I would rip his head off.'

'Calm down, Jake, please. It's OK. I sort of expected it to happen; in fact I'm surprised he lasted this long, given his reputation.'

'What planet are you on? It is not bloody OK. I don't give a flying fuck; he promised me he wouldn't mess you around. That's it – I'm going to kill him.'

'No, you are not. Keep out of it. This is between me and Will. I've moved out and gone back home now anyway. He left a voicemail yesterday, trying to apologise, and said he had to work the murder at the church that came in so I went and packed up most of my stuff after tea. He isn't worth you getting in trouble and losing your job over and I can't be bothered anymore. I've cried it out of my system and from now on I'm staying single. No more men. Now, promise me you won't do anything stupid?'

'I can't, Annie. You can't expect me to let him do this to you and not say anything – it's not right. He's my friend but you're like my sister and I wouldn't let anyone treat my sister like that.'

'Thanks, Jake, but you don't have a sister so how do you know? Look, I'll deal with Will – just leave it.'

'Why do you have to be such a goody two-shoes? OK, I promise to try not to do anything stupid. That's the best I can do.'

As they were walking back to the police van, a call came in for a domestic on Marsh Street. They ran and jumped into the van and Annie held on to the side of the van door as Jake blue-lighted it through to the other side of town. She loved working with him but he was a crap driver; it was like watching her life flash before her eyes whenever he drove them to an emergency call. As they turned into the street one of their regular customers was kicking his ex-girlfriend's front door. Jake screeched the van to a halt and they both jumped out.

'Now then, Peter, what have we got here? From where I'm standing, it looks like you're causing a shit-load of criminal damage.'

'Fuck off – she's a total bitch. Won't let me see the kids and she has another bloke in there.'

Peter turned and began kicking the door again. Jake took three steps and grabbed his arm, dragging him away from the door.

'Peter Low, I'm arresting you on suspicion of criminal damage, section four, and for being a prick. You do not have to say anything but it may harm your defence if you do not mention now something which you later rely on in court. Anything you do say may be given in evidence. Do you understand, Peter?'

'Fuck off.'

Annie turned away to hide the grin on her face and opened the van doors as Jake snapped his cuffs over Peter's wrists.

'Is that any way to talk in front of a lady? Get in the cage – I'm taking you to the town's worst bed and breakfast so you can sleep off your six bottles of cider and until you understand the error of your ways.'

Peter tried to resist being put in the van and began to scuffle with Jake, who was almost twice his size. Jake grabbed him and threw him in.

'Don't be a dick all your life; I can add police assault and resisting arrest to that nice little list of charges.'

Jake slammed the cage door shut and then the van doors. Annie started laughing. 'Sorry.' She walked towards the house and knocked on the door, which was opened by a woman in her early twenties who was clearly pregnant, with a two-year-old clinging to her legs.

'Are you OK, Julie? We've arrested him so he'll be in until at least tomorrow because we can't interview him until he's sober.'

'Thank you – why can't he just leave me alone? He's a pain in the arse.'

'Typical man, if you ask me, Julie. Look, I'll let you get sorted out and then I'll come back in an hour for a statement – is that OK?'

The woman nodded. 'Thanks, Annie. I'll have the kettle on.'

Annie grinned at her. 'You're on.' She got back inside the van. Peter was now hammering on the cage and shouting about police brutality.

Jake looked at her. 'Is she OK? For Christ's sake, Peter, pack it in or I'll come around there and show you the meaning of police brutality.'

'Fuck off.'

Annie smothered her laughter with her hand. Peter stopped banging and shouting, having realised that he didn't really want to go face to face with a pissed-off copper the size of Jake.

They drove to the station and parked in the rear yard; there was already a shoplifter in the traps waiting to be processed so it would be at least fifteen minutes before they could take Peter in. After five minutes an unmarked CID car drove into the yard, with Will at the steering wheel and Laura in the front passenger seat. Annie felt her heart break a little more at the sight of them together. Before she could say anything, Jake was out of the van and marching towards the car. *Oh, shit.* Jake began to shout at Will, which roused the now sleepy Peter from his drunken snooze.

Annie could only watch in horror as Jake wagged his finger in Will's face; Laura put her head down and darted across the yard and into the station. Jake shoved Will and he stumbled backwards against the bonnet of the car. He caught his balance then shoved Jake back just as hard. A loud cheer came from the cage, followed by a lot of whooping. Annie jumped out of the van, running over to separate them, but before she reached them they began to grapple with each other. She could hear the drunk in the van hammering on the cage and shouting. Kav came running out of the back door. He was the same size and build as Jake, if not slightly bigger, and he grabbed him, pulling him away.

'Get in the station now and calm down, you bloody idiot. It's a good job there's nobody important on duty or you two would both be out on your arses.'

Will regained his composure and walked away, his face red and blotchy. He didn't even look across at Annie. Kav had Jake pinned to the wall. 'Calm down, you stupid moron. Do you want to lose your job? Honestly, sometimes I wonder where your brain is because it's not in your bloody head. My office now and don't move out of there until I come and see you.'

Jake muttered, 'Sorry, boss.' He walked across the yard and into the station. Kav turned to Annie. 'I can hazard a guess at what this is about. Annie, are you OK sorting out your prisoner? Is there anything I should know before my officers start killing each other again?'

'I'm fine, Sarge. I told Jake to keep out of it but you know what he's like. He thinks with his fists, not his head and, yes, I'll sort the prisoner out.'

She walked back to the van and got inside, slamming the door. She looked in the rear-view mirror at Peter, who was grinning. 'Those two wankers better get locked up for section four . . . bloody brilliant . . . you couldn't make it up. There's more action here than outside the pub last night.'

'Shut up and go back to sleep. I'll wake you up when it's your turn.'

She sat there with her face on fire and a pounding headache, wishing the last few days had never happened.

Chapter 7

Will threw the office door open and it slammed into the wall. Everyone looked up from their computers at him. He didn't speak, just went and sat down at his desk and slouched behind the computer monitor so they couldn't see his face. Laura was nowhere to be seen, which suited him just fine; he didn't care if he never set eyes on her again. Jake was well pissed off with him but he could cope with that. What he couldn't cope with was seeing the look of betrayal on Annie's face. He began reading his emails – anything to take his mind off the last twenty-four hours. He wanted to make it up to her but he didn't know if he could. She hadn't returned any of his calls. He had an email from Grace Marshall, who was a profiler from Manchester they had drafted in to help search for the last killer. She was telling him all about the wonders of geographical profiling and how she had just helped to solve a series of rapes in the Blackburn area because of it. She also told him she was off to Corfu for two weeks and planning on coming down to Barrow to pay him and Annie a visit.

He considered asking for her advice on the woman found in the churchyard yesterday, but she would probably cancel her holiday and he didn't want to make her do that. They should be able to figure this one out without any outside help. He hoped to

55

God no more turned up but if another body did appear then he wouldn't wait around; he would ask for her help. There was no way he would wait while bodies stacked up; one serial killer in this town was enough and they didn't want another. The sound of movement made him glance up to see Stu and Laura whispering to each other. She must have sneaked back in because he hadn't noticed her. He nodded at them. They were both holding clipboards.

'Sarge, is it OK if me and Laura revisit some of the houses near to the church? See if we can catch anyone who wasn't in earlier.'

Will nodded once more; he couldn't bring himself to speak. As far as he was concerned, they could drive to bloody Blackpool for some candyfloss and a stroll on the beach – as long as he didn't have to look at them. He leant back, putting his feet up on the desk, then he put his hands behind his head and shut his eyes.

*

Annie finally got to book her prisoner in twenty minutes after the fiasco. He was now snoring loudly in the back of the van and she had to shake him to wake him up. He fluttered his eyelids at her. 'What . . . where am I?'

'You're about to be booked into the cells, Peter – again.' She emphasised the *again* bit, seeing as how she had arrested him twice this month already.

'What for?'

'What do you mean, what for? What did you get arrested for the last two times I met you?'

'Oh, yep, I forgot about that.'

She shook her head in disgust. 'You can't just forget about making someone's life a misery.'

She helped him get out of the cage and led him to the door, which clicked open. The internal door to the custody suite buzzed and they walked into the small room, where they went through the process of getting him booked in until court tomorrow. Once this was done and he was tucked up safely in his cell, Annie went to find Jake. She stuck her head through the community office door; it was empty. So was the parade room. Surely Kav wasn't still bollocking him. Not really wanting to go and face Kav but not knowing what else to do, she walked into his office, where he was sitting on his own reading the paper.

'Erm . . . Sarge . . . where's Jake – is everything OK?' She could feel the cooked breakfast she'd eaten earlier rolling around in her guts.

'He's gone to get me a McDonald's to make up for his bad behaviour.'

She let out a sigh of relief and he pointed to the empty chair opposite his desk. 'Take a seat and don't look so worried. What did you think I was going to do – send him to the inspector? I have the feeling that, whatever it is, Jake had a pretty good reason for it, but do not tell him I said that.'

'Thanks. I suppose he did and he is very good at protecting my honour, but sometimes I'd rather live without all the drama. It's knackering.'

Kav nodded. 'I should imagine it is. Anyway, enough of that. How are you?'

'I've been a lot worse.' Images of her lying in casualty last year filled her mind. 'I just wish I could lead a simple life, away from all the hassle. Maybe I should take up flower arranging.'

'I actually think that's a good idea – how much trouble could you get in making pretty bouquets?'

She laughed. 'Knowing me, probably a lot. I think I need a change of scenery or a lottery win; either one would be nice.'

'Then this might just interest you. There is a vacancy about to come up in Windermere, which is top secret because you know how many people would like to escape and work up in the heart of the glorious English Lake District, dealing with lots of tourists and sheep.'

'Really? Do you think I would be able to apply for it?'

'Well, I can't make any promises but if I have a quiet word with the inspector up there and tell her you need to get out of here for the sake of your sanity, but more for the sake of mine, it might just be possible. Plus she owes me for not arresting her teenage daughter a couple of weeks ago for being drunk and disorderly and trying to fight every copper outside that new nightclub where you can drink yourself into oblivion for a quid.'

'That would be amazing. I need to put everything behind me and have a fresh start.'

'Yes, Annie, I think you do. Although I will be gutted to lose you from my team because nobody provides me with the excitement or entertainment that you do, but it might mean I can hang on to what's left of my hair. Leave it with me and if you go and really hate dealing with all those Japanese tourists who've lost their cameras then you know I'll have you back tomorrow.'

She stood up to leave. 'Thank you; I really appreciate it, Kav.' She walked out of the door and back to the office to wait for Jake to turn up so he could give her a lift back down to Marsh Street for that statement. It wasn't long before Jake walked in carrying a greasy brown paper bag and slurping on a giant-size drink. 'I have no idea where you put the amount of food you eat or why you're not fifty stone. What did Kav say to you then?'

'Just told me I was a prick and basically I need to wind my neck in, but he also said that Will was an even bigger prick and I told him I didn't know about that because I'd never had the pleasure. Soon stopped him in his tracks – he didn't know where to look so he sent me out for food.'

'Well, at least you're not in any real trouble. I appreciate you sticking up for me but, like I told you before, I can handle it.'

She felt her eyes fill with tears and Jake began rooting around in his bag. He pulled out a cheeseburger and held it out. Annie shook her head.

'You know you could always try batting for the other side;

58

you might have a bit more luck with a bird. We could go to Manchester to the Gay Pride parade as a foursome.'

He dodged the desk stapler that came flying across the room. 'Just a thought.'

'Hurry up – I need to get out of here and go get that statement.'

Jake shoved the last of his burger into his mouth. He was still slurping from the paper cup. 'Do you want some? It's chocolate milkshake, your favourite.'

'No, thank you.'

'Suit yourself, but I bet it would make you feel better.'

She walked out of the office with Jake behind her, head bent and straight down the corridor just in case anyone was looking. She couldn't be bothered with polite conversation. There was no way she'd be coming back in here until it was finishing time.

Chapter 8

Sean parked the Ford Focus in the car park opposite the police station just in time to have a front-row seat for the fight that had just kicked off. In reality he should have run over to break it up but he was enjoying the show far too much. He did feel sorry for Annie; the poor woman didn't have much luck with her men. A bit like him and his women, he chuckled to himself. He placed his bet on Jake; he definitely wouldn't want to get on the wrong side of him and he got scary when he was angry. Sean had worked with him enough times to see him in action. Just as he thought about getting out of the car Kav intervened, saving him the trouble.

He knew that stuck-up bitch Laura was the cause of all this because he'd heard a couple of officers gossiping before the briefing this morning in the parade room. Sean had never liked her – well, he had until the last Christmas night out, when he had bought her a couple of drinks and thought he'd been doing all right until Will had walked in. She'd then spent the rest of the night hovering around Will and completely blanking him. He hated women like that and an idea began to form in his head.

He stayed in the car until it had all calmed down across the road then, just as he was about to get out, his radio crackled to

60

life as the control room asked him to attend a job. He started the engine and reversed out of the parking space to go all the way to the other side of town because a group of ten-year-olds were playing football in the street.

*

It had been four days since Kav had told Annie about Windermere and yesterday he had taken her to one side and told her the job was hers if she wanted it. The only downside was that if she did she had to start there in two days' time, they were so understaffed. She had gone home and dithered. Was she doing the right thing? Should she not let her pride get the better of her? For a couple of hours she had gone over and over it. Then she'd taken a note-book and a pen, writing down a list of reasons she should go and reasons she shouldn't. It took her ten minutes to realise the list for the move was much more impressive than the list not to. She'd phoned Kav and told him yes, thank you.

She spent the last hour of her shift boxing up her stuff and her various pieces of uniform. Jake, who had hovered around her all day, helped her carry them to her car. 'I can't believe this is it, that I'm never going to work with you again.'

Once more she asked herself if she was doing the right thing, but all that was keeping her here was Jake. She would miss the banter in the office and Sally and Claire, the PCSOs, but apart from them that was it . . . oh, and Kav – she couldn't forget him; he'd been more like a dad to her than her boss. She wouldn't tell him that, though. She had left a huge box of cream cakes in the fridge to help ease the pain a little; she had never really understood the tradition that if it was your birthday or you were leaving, you had to buy the cakes.

'Don't be soft; I'll still see you out of work. It's not as if I'm moving to London or somewhere far away.'

Jake pouted. 'Well, I feel as if you are. I want a phone call every

61

day and plenty of emails and if there's any eye candy up there of the male kind then that's super-important because I might have to get a transfer up there myself.'

Annie laughed. 'I promise I will.' She loaded the last box into the back of her now full car and slammed the door shut. 'Anyway, it's time to book off duty now. Come on, let's go to the pub for a drink.'

Jake brightened up at the thought of alcohol. 'Excellent idea. Should I see if Sally and Claire are coming?' He went back inside and again she wondered if she was doing the right thing but then a car pulled into the yard and she caught a glimpse of Laura with her bleached blonde hair and felt the familiar pain shoot through her chest. Yes, she was doing the right thing. She had spoken to Will briefly yesterday as she had been leaving the station and he had begged her to come home with him so they could speak but she couldn't. She didn't want to go back to his house – it was easier to blot things out this way.

'Please, Annie; we need to talk about this. One minute we were fine, then, within the space of twenty-four hours, you moved out and I know it's my fault entirely. But I need to explain it to you.'

'Just give me some space. Every time I see you with her it's like a bloody great knife gets twisted in my heart. I might be soft but I'm not an idiot, Will. I won't have anyone laughing at me behind my back.'

A van had pulled into the yard and she'd walked away before the officers got out and took an interest in their conversation. She'd turned to look at him. 'I think you should know I am transferring to Windermere. Kav told me they're even more understaffed than we are and need someone pretty quick.'

She had walked away before he even had time to digest what she'd said.

Now, she got into her car and drove it home, parking it on the drive and hoping that no one would break into it with all her stuff inside or else she'd be in trouble. After locking it and double-checking the doors, she pulled out her phone and began dialling the number for a taxi just as Jake pulled up in a police van. 'I thought that you might need a lift back to the station.'

She grinned at him and climbed in. 'So who's coming to the pub?'

'Kav, me, Sally, Claire and of course you.'

'Perfect, my favourite people.'

He drove them back to the station, where he parked the van and then handed her the keys. 'Go stick them on the whiteboard while I nip and get changed.'

She took them from him and did as she was told. A wave of sadness washed over her as she walked into the sergeant's office for the last time. The whole station was a complete shit-hole but she loved it and would miss it. Kav walked in behind her. 'I believe the first drinks are on you, Miss Graham.'

She nodded. 'They are – after everything you've done for me this last year I owe you far more than a drink.'

'Steady on, Annie, it's only five o'clock. You'll make me blush.'

But he winked at her and she laughed. 'Sergeant, you know exactly what I meant.'

He pulled his jacket off the back of the chair and put it on, then, opening the door for her, he waved her through and whispered in her ear, 'You're doing the right thing, Annie, trust me. Everything will work out just fine.'

They walked down the street to the Railway, which played no music but the beer was cheap and it was always busy. True to her word, Annie bought the first round and they all squeezed around a corner table in the window, where they could watch the world go by and get drunk. At the table opposite them was a group of men, one of them an old friend of Mike's who waved at Annie and shouted hello. She waved back. Mike's so-called friends had no idea that he was a wife-beating thug. Or, if they did, they never let on. She hadn't liked any of them because he always went for the loud, cocky ones who would laugh and joke at everyone's expense.

After half an hour she went to the bar for another bottle of wine. It was packed and she had to squeeze in. She felt a hand squeeze her behind and turned around, about to give whoever it was a mouthful, and was shocked to see Mike's friend grinning at her.

'All right, darling; fancy seeing you in here. You know, word has it you were already sleeping with one of the coppers before Mike's coffin hit the ground. You didn't do much mourning for him then?'

She wanted to tell him to fuck off but was too polite. 'No, I didn't, not after he almost killed me. His death didn't have quite the same effect.'

She paid for the bottle of wine and turned around. There were people pushing in all over the place and he took advantage and pushed himself as close to her body as he could. She shoved him away with one hand, a bit too hard, and he stumbled back into a tall man who was behind him, making him spill his pint. 'Watch it, mate.'

Annie muttered an apology and squeezed through the throng of people to get back to her friends. She put the wine on the table and turned her back to the group of men, who were laughing.

After five glasses of wine she knew that she'd had enough. Claire and Sally had left a while ago and Jake and Kav were discussing the football. She wanted to go home, put her pyjamas on and then crawl into bed. If she told them she was leaving they would make a fuss; instead, she told them she was going to the ladies'. Neither of them looked up as she made her way through the crowds to the door and some fresh air.

It was dark outside and slightly drizzling. She thought about phoning a taxi but she rarely used them; she would rather walk around to the bus stop outside the police station and get a bus for a quid. She didn't notice Mike's friend follow her outside. Putting her head down, she began to walk briskly around to the back of

64

the pub to take the short cut across the car park, which was in a quiet back street. Most of the streetlights weren't working and it was dark but she wasn't bothered; there was no one around. She had walked these streets at four in the morning on her own when she was working. The alcohol making her brain foggy, she forgot that she wasn't at work and didn't have the benefit of CS gas or handcuffs should she need them.

She crossed the road and was almost at the other side when she fell forward as someone shoved her hard from behind. Unsteady on her feet because of the wine, she fell to her knees and cried out. Before she could do anything, a weight pressed on her and she felt herself being dragged across to the open rear yard of an empty shop. She opened her mouth to scream and a fist hit her in the face, missing her nose but hitting her square in the eye. Annie lost it then and began to fight with everything she had, but her attacker was strong. She could smell the beer on his breath and knew it was Mike's friend from the pub, whose name she didn't even remember. She was managing OK but as she lunged forward she tripped and fell, landing on her back. He straddled her and memories from last year filled her mind. She opened her mouth to scream but he clamped his hand over her mouth so she bit him as hard as she could.

Another punch hit her on the side of the head this time and then his weight lifted off her chest and she watched in slow motion as he flew through the air like a balloon. Kav bent down and helped her up and Jake had the prick shoved against the bonnet of a car in an armlock. The guy was struggling so Kav walked over and sucker-punched him in the guts, knocking the wind out of him. The blackness was illuminated by flashing blue lights and Annie groaned as she looked across at Kav. 'Really?'

'Yes, Annie, really. Do you want to let that piece of scum go on his way after he just assaulted you and tried to do God knows what else?'

Annie shook her head. 'No, but I don't want any more hassle

either. Christ, I just want an easy life. Please, Kav – I can't do this.'

He put his arm around her shoulders. 'Come on, kid; it's like a parting gift for your colleagues. You're going to leave them all bored shitless so at least they'll get a little entertainment whilst you're away.'

She shook her head and pulled away from him. Jake had passed the drunken bastard over to Sean, who had him cuffed and was shoving him into the back of the van.

'Are you going to come back to the station and do a quick statement so I don't have to piss around trying to catch up with you, Annie?'

Before she could answer, Jake spoke up. 'Yes, Alex is on his way and will bring us round in a minute; she'll type up your statement and be on her way home in less than thirty minutes.'

They watched the van drive away and Jake turned to face her.

'Don't even say it, Jake. In fact, don't even speak. I really can't be bothered.'

He looked at Kav, who shrugged. 'Women.'

Alex's Mercedes turned into the street. He stopped the car in front of them and they climbed inside. 'Where to, my friends?'

Annie saw Alex look at Jake, who shook his head and rolled his eyes at her. Her eye was smarting now and beginning to swell shut. Alex looked in the mirror again and gasped. 'Annie, are you OK? What happened?'

'Another stupid prick, that's what, and this town is full of them.'

No one spoke as he drove them to the station. As he stopped outside, Jake turned to him. 'Wait here; we won't be too long. We just have to type up a quick statement each and then you can take us all home.'

Alex had parked in the bus lane, put his hazard lights on and just hoped this wasn't going to turn into a two-hour wait. They got out of the car and Annie began to laugh. Jake looked at her. 'What exactly is so funny?'

'And here was me thinking I'd seen the last of this place. I just can't keep away.' As all three of them stumbled through the side door, laughing, Will walked past, a sheaf of papers in one hand and a mug of coffee in the other. He took one look at Annie and his eyes opened wide as the shock registered in his brain. Before he could speak, Jake ushered her past and down to the community office, where he shut the door and all three of them sat down and logged onto their computers.

Chapter 9

Annie finally walked through her front door as the clock in her hall chimed ten; she had sobered up remarkably well. All she wanted now was a hot shower and her bed. She kicked off her shoes, locked the front door and ran upstairs to the bathroom. She stripped off and looked at her eye in the mirror. Jake had wanted her to go to the hospital but she'd soon put him right. It wasn't the first black eye she'd had and it probably wouldn't be the last. It was swollen and puffy; the dark blue bruising had begun to form a semicircle underneath her lower lashes. She poked it with her finger and winced.

Turning on the shower, she stepped underneath the hot spray and stayed there until her skin was red and she couldn't stand the heat any longer. But she felt clean. She got out and towel-dried herself then rubbed Chanel No. 5 body lotion all over her arms and legs, missing out the graze on her right knee, which was stinging. She loved the smell of the lotion; Will had bought it for her birthday. Her heart felt heavy, thinking about him. She hated how it was between them, and the look on his face earlier had been one of shock and concern. Annie had never been very good at holding grudges; she'd put up with Mike's violent outbursts for long enough, but she didn't know what to say to Will. She slipped her fluffy bathrobe on, another present from him, and went into her temporary bedroom.

She walked across to shut the curtains and paused, staring down into the street. There was a very familiar BMW parked outside her house and her breath caught in the back of her throat. She could make out Will's solitary figure sitting in the dark, his head in his hands. Closing the curtains, she didn't know what else to do. She would give anything to turn back the clock and change it all but she also knew she was too stubborn to give in, so she slipped off the dressing gown and got into bed. Her exhaustion long gone, she lay there, looking up at the ceiling.

The clock in the hall ticked loudly, every tick amplified. She tossed and turned but couldn't get to sleep. She threw back the duvet, got up and looked out of the window. Will was still outside in his car. Muttering under her breath, she went downstairs, slipped her battered pink Converses on and opened the front door. She walked down her steps, onto the street and knocked on the passenger window. Will jumped, swearing, but realised it was Annie and put the window down.

'Just what, exactly, are you doing sitting outside my house like some stalker?'

'I'm waiting . . . well, watching. I just wanted to make sure that you were OK.'

'Well, that's very kind of you but I'm fine, so you can go back to work or wherever it is you're supposed to be.' She felt like a total bitch.

'Good, I'm glad you're OK. I was worried about you when I saw you earlier. I couldn't believe it. I'm sorry, Annie, so sorry that I messed up. I promised myself that I would look after you and all I've done is hurt you and then stand back while other people hurt you.'

Sighing, she opened the car door and got into the passenger seat. It was warm in the car and it smelled of leather and Will's aftershave. Leaning back, she closed her eyes.

'I heard from Jake, of all people, that you were so inebriated that you wouldn't have been able to shag a porn star the other night. If Jake was sticking up for you then there must be some element of truth to it, so why did it happen? Why did that skinny blonde bimbo end up sleeping next to you almost naked?'

Will shook his head. 'I honestly don't know – I was really drunk. I was so shocked when I woke up and she was there; it was like a bad dream – a really bad dream. I don't even like her, apart from as a colleague. I heard the bang as you fell over and it woke me up. I thought I was lying next to you and when I turned and saw her it made me physically sick. I threw her out and then I threw up all over the hall floor. The rest you know. That day, when I got home late after working the crime scene at the church and you had packed your things and left was the worst day of my life.'

She knew exactly how he felt. 'Look at me – another disaster and another black eye. I think I must be destined to live the most messed-up life possible. I'm sorry too, Will – you were the best thing that ever happened to me.' She stretched out her hand, reaching for his, finding it in the dark and squeezing it tight. 'How long were you planning on sitting out here, anyway?'

'I don't know – until I was sure you were safe. Probably the rest of my life.'

'Well, you can rest easy; I think I'm OK for the time being. What time are you working till?'

'Eight. I was about to finish when I saw you come into the station. I was so shocked I had to go back and check the logs to see what had happened to you. Are you OK?'

'Yes, I'm OK and I'm sorry. I always seem to mess up your social life.'

He laughed. 'I don't have a social life – you are my social life. I was just so angry with you and Jake that I ended up sinking vodka shots as well as pints of lager. I won't ever be doing that again.'

'I do believe you, Will, but it still really hurts and I'm in a bit of a mess at the moment. I really need to clear my head. Maybe it was all too soon after Mike.'

Will felt his stomach drop to the bottom of his shoes. The last thing he wanted was for her to regret the last six months they'd spent together. He knew he needed to let her have some space; he wouldn't put pressure on her, but he also realised more than ever just how much she meant to him. In fact he wanted to spend the rest of his life with her. He released his tight grip on her hand. 'So what are you going to do about that wanker? If Kav and Jake hadn't gone looking for you . . .' The word *rape* hung in the air but he couldn't say it. Just the thought of another man putting his hands on her without her consent made his blood boil.

'I can't face going to court, Will. I've given a statement but I don't really want to. If he had gone any further then it might be different, but Jake and Kav managed to give him a few good punches, so that will do for me. He was drunk and it's surprising how many people act stupid when they're drunk.'

Will didn't argue with that – hadn't he been stupid? She yawned. 'I think I'd better go and get some beauty sleep; that wine is doing the business better than two Temazepam any day.'

'If you need me, Annie, you know where I am, where I'll always be for the rest of your life. I love you so much, Annie Graham, and I'm a total idiot.'

'Yes, you are.' She got out of the car and went back inside her house, tears rolling down her cheeks.

June 28th 1984

Beth yawned then stood up to go and turn the television off; she was tired but had started watching a film and then, before she knew it, the clock had chimed midnight. She checked the front door then made her way upstairs. Since Sophie had begun to talk about that shadow man she hadn't slept very well. It freaked her out but she didn't believe any of it and knew they would be OK. She had got away from her last boyfriend who was a bully; she wasn't about to let some imaginary man who smelled of rotten cabbage ruin her life.

She could hear gentle snores coming from Sean's room and she pushed his door open. He was splayed on the bed. His sheet was dangling on the floor and his hand was wrapped around one of the plastic action figures that never left his side. She bent down and kissed his soft cheek; he smelled so good. Then she pulled his cover up and crept back out of the room and into Sophie's bedroom across the landing. She still had her My Little Pony night-light switched on. The orange glow illuminated her daughter's face; it was so pale and underneath her eyes were dark circles – she looked so old. The innocence she'd last week had been replaced with the harried look she wore now.

Beth made up her mind to talk to Sophie tomorrow and this time listen to what she was telling her. Maybe she could ask Father John to come round and they could all sit down and try to put Sophie's shadow man to bed. Beth shivered; it was much colder in here than in Sean's room. Sophie was restless. She began murmuring and her left foot kept jumping as if someone was tickling it. Beth bent down and kissed Sophie's forehead; an awful smell wafted across her nostrils and she grimaced but then it was gone. She pulled Sophie's covers up and walked back out of the room. As she pulled the door closed she didn't notice the blanket that she had just tucked around her daughter being slowly tugged off the bed.

She made her way to the bathroom, brushed her teeth and then crept into her own bed. She was thinking of Father John, too scared to think about anyone or anything else. He made her feel safe; he treated her better than any man she had ever met, yet she would never be able to have a relationship with him because he was already married – to God. For now she could live with that; she was grateful that he was her friend. Her eyes began to close and she was almost asleep when an ear-piercing scream made her sit bolt upright. 'Sophie.'

She ran out of her room and straight into Sophie's to see her daughter huddled at the top of her bed, her knees drawn up to her chest and her arms wrapped around them. Sophie lifted her hand and pointed a finger to the corner of the room. Beth felt her knees tremble and threaten to give way as she turned to see Sophie's blanket was suspended in mid-air. There was a man standing underneath it. Beth screamed and picked up the heavy silver cross from the chest of drawers. She threw it at the blanket, which fell to the floor in a heap. A hand tugged hers and she screamed again, turning to see Sean rubbing his eyes behind her. She kept tight hold of his hand and ran across to the bed. Sophie was shivering so much that Beth could hear her daughter's teeth clashing together. She grabbed Sophie's arm and dragged her from the bed.

After running with both of her children down the stairs, she unlocked the front door and ran outside. She kicked it shut and the sound echoed around the deserted street. She ran down the path and along the road to the presbytery, where she hammered on the door until a light turned on upstairs.

*

Father John woke at the sound of the banging on the front door. He ran downstairs and opened the heavy wooden door. He was shocked to see Beth and her children, dressed in only their night-wear and with bare feet. They were huddled together; Sophie was staring into space and Beth was crying. John ushered them inside and shut the front door behind them.

He led them into the kitchen, which was bathed in a warm glow. All of them were shivering. He turned the oven on to give off some heat. He then set about pouring milk into a pan to

73

make them all mugs of steaming hot chocolate. He didn't know what to say. He looked at them one by one. Sean seemed the least bothered; he was sitting looking down at the toy figure in his hands. Beth looked as if she had seen a ghost and poor Sophie looked traumatised. Once the milk began to boil he took the tin of chocolate powder from the cupboard and added several heaped spoonfuls into it. Stirring the whole time so as not to scald the milk, then taking a tea towel from the drawer and four mugs, he poured the chocolate milk into each of them, making Sean's the smallest and adding some cold milk to it so it wouldn't burn him. Then he carried the tray to the table and set it down.

Beth nodded at him and he smiled. The look of terror on her face said it all and his stomach felt as if someone had forced him to swallow a rock, it felt so heavy. They blew the steam from their drinks and slowly sipped; not one of them spoke of what had just happened and John was far too afraid to ask.

Chapter 10

2014

Annie woke to the sound of a young girl singing. It was hard to hear the words but she could make out the tune and it sounded like 'Ring a Ring o' Roses'. She blinked and turned onto her side, thinking it must be kids playing on the front street but then she reached out for her phone, which was on the chair next to the bed. It was only seven and not very light outside. After last year's events Annie slept with a night-light on, afraid of the dark. The voice was still singing. She climbed out of bed to peer through the window; pulling the curtain back, she looked onto the street. It was deserted. She shivered; the heating must have turned off because it was freezing.

As she turned to climb back in the bed she caught a glimpse of something white in the mirror. She turned slowly to see the girl from the other day staring at her and her insides turned to slush. The girl stepped nearer to the glass and slapped the palms of her hands against it; Annie heard the sound as clear as if she had done it herself. The girl smiled then whispered, 'You have to help me. I don't want him to do it but he won't stop. He doesn't understand that John tried to help.'

And then she was gone, leaving behind two small white handprints on the inside of the mirror. Annie looked around the room to make sure the girl wasn't standing behind her with an axe. The room was empty – cold and empty. She stepped forward and lifted her hand and, with a shaking finger, touched the glass, afraid she might get pulled through into the other side and stuck in a different world. The handprints were starting to fade. Annie reached for her phone and snapped a couple of photos, but when she looked back at them the prints had completely disappeared and the picture showed only the mirror and her reflection. No sign of the girl from inside it who had been singing to her. She wasn't sure whether she was afraid or curious; her insides were churning regardless. Who was that kid and why did she think that she could help her? If she had been staying at Will's, would the girl still have come looking for her?

Today was her first day stationed up at Windermere and she wondered at how much her life had changed in the space of a week. She knew that the change of job could have happened in the blink of an eye; a few of her colleagues had been shipped off to Kendal or The Lakes with little or no notice. At least this was her choice. She just wished that she was still coming home to Will every night. He had swept her off her feet at a time in her life when she'd never expected it would get better. Tears filled her eyes – why had that bloody Laura spoilt everything? She felt like a heartbroken, lovesick teenager. At least her appetite had disappeared; for the first time she wasn't looking to find comfort in food.

She decided that now she was wide awake she might as well get showered and ready for work. Better to be early and make a good impression on her new boss than be late and get off on the wrong foot. Downstairs, she made some wholemeal toast and jam and a large mug of coffee. Sitting down on the kitchen chair, she couldn't help thinking about Will. They both needed a clean break, or so the voice in her head kept telling her; the one in her heart disagreed and kept telling her to ring him. It was tough trying to ignore it. With a bit of luck, by the time she'd made the forty-minute trip, worked a ten-hour shift and then driven home, she would hopefully be too knackered to even say his name.

Finally ready, she set off on the very pleasant drive to Windermere. The sun was rising and it felt much warmer than it had all year. When she got there she parked her car right outside the station and smiled. There would be no worrying about getting a parking ticket or driving round and round looking for a parking space; she loved it already. The building itself was tiny compared to the mausoleum in Barrow; it was quaint, built from local slate, and blended in seamlessly with its surroundings. She felt a little bit nervous but not as much as she'd expected. She checked her phone for the text that Kav had sent her earlier, with the door code to get into the building along with a good luck message that ended, 'and try not to cause a major disaster on your first day'. Annie grinned to herself; she was going to miss him.

She walked into the station, lugging her heavy black bag, which was full of her police kit, and began to look for the locker room to dump it in. She was glad to be away from Will, Laura and the station gossips. Work affairs were a part of the job; it was one of the pitfalls of working for the police. It was well known that coppers were in and out of each other's beds and the usual excuse was to blame it on the stresses of the job, when in actual fact the truth was plain and simple – they just couldn't stop shagging anything that walked and talked. As unhappily married as she was to Mike, she had always frowned on her colleagues who did just that, yet here she was, transferred to a different part of the county because of exactly the same thing. The only advantage was the transfer had been at her request and she hadn't been shafted out of the station for sleeping with a senior officer, which happened all too often.

She found the locker room and let the heavy bag drop to the

floor. Across the hall was an office, which was empty. She went to look for the duty sergeant to introduce herself and couldn't find whoever that was either. She could hear a raised voice coming from an office further up the corridor so she walked in that direction to see the sign that said 'Inspector' on the door. Annie paused outside, not wanting to intrude.

'Yes, I know, Georgia, darling; we did discuss you going to Chloe's party tonight and what time did I tell you to be in for?' There was a slight pause. 'Yes, I did say midnight but that was before you went out last night and got pissed out of your head and had to be brought home by one of my response officers. This alone tells me that you don't give a shit about embarrassing me and secondly it proves that you can't be trusted. Put it this way: I'm grounding you for the good of your liver. Fifteen is far too young to have cirrhosis of the liver and I refuse to be the gossip of the station because you think you can drink every piss-head under the table.'

Annie winced at the scream of 'I hate you,' which echoed around the tiny office. The line went dead and the woman holding the phone growled.

Annie coughed, knocked on the door and walked in. She didn't know Inspector Hayes. However, she did know of her reputation as a hard woman to please and, by all accounts, a bit of a bitch. The woman looked up at Annie and grinned. 'Bloody teenagers – they should come with a health warning. They're bad for your mental health and bank balance.'

'Sorry, I wasn't eavesdropping. I'm Annie Graham.' She held out her hand and shook the inspector's.

'Don't worry; if you work here for more than a week you will know all about everyone's home life, their horrible brats, miserable spouses and what we all drink down The Angel. One of the perils of working in a small station. On the plus side, you won't get hassled about your monthly submissions, moaned at about your arrest rate or told to do more traffic because at the glorious

Lakes we're all about the tourists and keeping everyone happy, so they keep coming back and spending more money.'

'It sounds perfect to me; I've had enough of the other side of policing for a while. I need a change.' Annie wondered how much Kav had filled the woman in on her eventful life over the last year. If he had, she didn't let on. She stood up and showed Annie to the small kitchen, where the woman actually switched the kettle on and started to make two mugs of coffee. Regardless of her reputation, Annie liked her; in fact she really liked her. The inspector poured the boiling water into the cups, added the milk, and then opened the cupboard and pulled out a packet of chocolate biscuits.

'I'm Cathy; you only need to bother with the inspector shit if the superintendent or higher puts in an appearance or if you're really crawling because you've messed up, but I doubt that. I've heard a lot of good things about you, Annie, and – in case you're wondering – I also know that you've had an even crappier past six months than I have. But that's your business and you only have to talk about it if you feel you need to. I have an open-door policy. If something is bothering you don't bottle it up; get it off your chest, because I'm telling you there will be days when the diva I brought into this world will do my tits in so much that if I don't sound off at someone I might just go home and strangle the bitch.'

She winked and it all sounded wonderful to Annie. Taking their mugs of coffee and the packet of biscuits, Cathy gave her a quick tour of the building, explaining all the various bits and pieces, then they sat down in her office and had a good old catch-up about what was happening down in Barrow.

Chapter 11

He walked into his office and stared at the board for Operation Ariel. It was beginning to fill up nicely. Although this one was a bit more rushed than the last one, he'd decided there was no point hanging around; he'd made his mind up who his next angel was going to be. He didn't want to rush it too much but he'd read on Facebook she was going out with some work colleagues for one of their birthdays and he realised it was the perfect opportunity. He'd spent two full days this week watching, following and stalking his victim. She was blonde and pretty and reminded him so much of his mother. The more he'd watched her, he'd come to realise that she was quite a selfish person, which made her even more like his mother.

He pinned the photos of the street she lived in and the flat above the hairdressers to the corkboard. He had printed out a small map of the streets surrounding and added that. He couldn't gain access to her flat; he had no reason to go inside and she would recognise him if he tried. He didn't think she would be very approachable, unless she was drunk, because she was a naturally suspicious person. If he couldn't get to her when she left the pub he would have to follow her back to her flat; he had checked there was no CCTV in the street. The shop on the corner had a camera but he knew for a fact that it didn't work and when it did it only covered the shop's entrance. He felt confident that even if she put up a fight and screamed he'd still be able to drag her into her own flat or his truck before any of the residents bothered to get out of their warm beds to see what was going on. He just hoped that if she did put up a fight she wouldn't draw blood – he shuddered.

He closed his computer. He'd been following the thread she had started about what to wear for tonight. He wasn't actually friends with her but he was a friend of a friend, which was almost as good. He could read any of the conversations the two of them had; the joys of the internet – it was a stalker's paradise.

He set about checking his bag. Everything he needed was in there: gloves, duct tape, plastic bags, tie wraps, sheet of polythene. He took the small brown medicine bottle out of the fridge; inside were two finely crushed Flunitrazepam, more commonly known as Rohypnol tablets. They were his emergency backup. If all else failed he would drug her, slip them into a glass of the white wine she seemed to like so much. He could feel his nerve endings tingling at the thought of what he was going to do; it was the biggest rush ever. He'd chosen St Martha's Church; they were all covered by the same priest. It looked as if the church was having the same funding crisis as almost everyone else.

He'd been and chosen the grave two days ago. He'd had a walk around the church and grounds with a baseball cap and some dark sunglasses on, his camera around his neck. He'd looked like a typical tourist and he hadn't seen anyone else while he'd been looking around, which suited him just fine. He wanted to be there to see the priest's face. He wasn't sure if he would be the one to find her but, one way or another, two bodies in two church grounds would certainly make the priest a person of interest for the police to talk to. He would love to be around when that happened.

June 29th 1984
02.00

After they finished their hot chocolates and both the children started to yawn, Father John showed Beth, Sophie and Sean up to one of the guest rooms, which had a huge double bed, big enough for all three of them to snuggle up together. If they needed to stay longer they could each have the rooms they had stayed in when he'd first found them. He left them to it and went to his own room. Beth hadn't said as much, but he knew it was the shadow man who had brought them to his door, terrified and shaking. He knelt at the foot of his bed and began to pray to God for all the help he could give him.

07.00

Father John opened his eyes and stared at the crucifix on the wall opposite his bed. Today was the day that he was going to go into that house and bless it from top to bottom. He looked at the alarm clock next to his bed – seven o'clock, but he couldn't sleep even though he felt exhausted. All night he had tossed and turned, so many thoughts running through his brain, and he had kept listening out in case his unexpected visitors needed his help. He got up and pulled on his faded jeans and a black T-shirt. When he went to do the house blessing it would be in full priest ensemble; whilst he planned exactly what he was going to do and made everyone breakfast he could be plain old John.

After a quick wash he ran his fingers through his thick, wavy black hair to calm it down a little. He needed a haircut but that wasn't going to happen today. As he threw his head back to gargle some mouthwash he caught movement in the mirror and whipped around to see Sophie standing at the bathroom door. 'Phew, Sophie, you scared me. How are you this morning?'

'He won't leave me alone.'

John knew exactly who she meant but he had to hear her say it. 'Who won't leave you alone?'

'The shadow man; even when I'm asleep he's there – in my dreams.'

John walked over to her and crouched down to her level. 'I know you're scared but you are also incredibly brave, Sophie, and you have to tell him to go away. I'm going to go to your house later and bless it with holy water from top to bottom.'

'Will that make him go away?'

John looked at the pale face staring back at him. He didn't want to lie to her and give her false hope but he couldn't tell a nine-year-old girl that he might not be able to get rid of the scary shadow without help. 'I hope so; I'm going to try my best but until I do I want you all to stay here with me. What do you think about that? My housekeeper, Mrs Brown, makes the best cakes; she will let you help her bake some when she comes at dinner time. Make sure you tell her which ones are your favourite. Come on, let's go and get some breakfast; I'm starving.'

He took hold of her hand and led her to the stairs. Her fingers gripped his. They were so cold; the poor little thing was frozen, even though it was summer.

In the kitchen John began to grill bacon and fry eggs; there was something therapeutic about cooking. He didn't do fancy but he was good at the basics. He asked Sophie to get him the mushrooms from the fridge. She put them next to him and he passed her a knife which wasn't very sharp and a dish. 'Do you think you could help me and chop those up?'

She nodded and began concentrating on the task he'd just given her. John was trying to take her mind off the living nightmare she was constantly thinking about. Even though his stomach was a bag of nerves, he was starving and needed a full belly to help him decide what to do. Between them they made enough to feed a small army and he plated some up for Beth and Sean, placing it in the oven on a low light to keep it warm until they woke up. He didn't think Sophie was going to eat any of hers but, after tipping half a bottle of tomato sauce over her food, she began to tuck in. She made a sandwich from the two slices of toast he'd put on her plate and she giggled as the warm butter dribbled down her chin. 'Oops, I'm such a messy eater – Mum always tells me that.'

John laughed. 'Me too – I had no idea you could eat so much.'

'That's because I like it here; this house smells clean. I didn't want to eat much in ours; it smells dirty. Only Mum doesn't really smell it, but I can and it makes me feel sick. I think Sean can as well but he doesn't understand.'

John smiled; she was old way beyond her years and that was sad. He cast his mind back to when he was a teenager, a few years older than Sophie was now, and he'd felt exactly the same. At the time he'd thought his house smelled as if someone had died in it, as if there was something rotting that only he could smell because his mother never could.

'I know exactly what you mean, Sophie. I was the same, only I had no one who believed me and my mother didn't understand. Every day I used to feel more and more tired, as if every little bit of energy was being sucked from my very soul. Just getting dressed for school used to be a real battle. I couldn't concentrate in school and my teachers thought I'd been taking drugs.'

He stopped talking. Sophie was nine years old and here he was, giving her a full and frank confession about his encounter with the shadow man when he was thirteen.

'What did you tell them?'

'Nothing – I was too scared. I thought that I was going a little bit mad. I did try and tell my mother but she didn't believe me and told me to stop telling fibs.'

'My mum said that but I think she changed her mind last

night when she saw him. He was standing in the corner of my bedroom. Grown-ups should realise that when children say they see people nobody else can it's because we really can.'

'What happened last night? I don't think your mum will tell me everything. Can you?'

Both John and Sophie pushed their breakfast plates to the side and were leaning with their arms on the table, heads bending towards each other.

'What are you two up to?'

Beth's voice made the pair of them jump and John had trouble trying to speak without his voice cracking. He felt overwhelmed. For the first time in twelve years he had faced his childhood monster. Beth wandered towards the table and picked up both of their plates, scraping what was left into the small stainless steel bin.

Sophie looked across at her mum. 'Tell Father John what you saw last night in my room.'

Beth, who was filling the sink with water, froze.

'Please, Mum, tell him you saw it; tell him you believe us.'

Beth turned around. A big tear glistened in the corner of her eye. 'I don't want to talk about it; we must have been dreaming.'

Sophie burst into tears and John didn't know who to comfort first but then Beth rushed over to Sophie and wrapped her arms around her, hugging her tight. She took a deep breath and then told John why they'd ended up banging on the presbytery door at one o'clock in the morning.

After breakfast John left the kitchen and went into the library to sit at his paper-strewn desk. He began looking through his papers. He could bless the house without the Vatican's permission but if he needed it to be exorcised then he would have to request permission and it could take weeks, even months, for it to be granted. He also knew they would need a whole lot more evidence than what he could give them at the moment.

He opened a drawer and pulled out the scrapbook he'd been keeping since he was a teenager. In it he had newspaper cuttings from every article he'd ever found about a haunted house or demonic possession. He knew that the shadow man was in between the two of them because he didn't want to *be* Sophie – what he wanted was Sophie's soul – and this was where it was going to get complicated. He laughed to himself. *Are you mad, John? You are worrying about fighting a shadow man that you have no idea how to deal with. How did you escape him years ago?* For the life of him, he couldn't remember exactly what it was he did to get rid of him; it was as if the memories were being blocked from his mind.

He shivered; the room was much colder than it usually was and he wouldn't be surprised if the entity was skulking around, listening. Maybe it was blocking his memories so he wouldn't be able to fight it again. He knew he didn't have much choice because Sophie looked exhausted, her skin was so pale and those black circles under her eyes made her look like an old woman and not a child. He needed to take action and quickly. Picking up the telephone, he began dialling the number for the local bishop – Father Robert. John prayed he was back from visiting his sister because he needed to ask for his help.

Chapter 12

2014

Laura raised the glass to her lips, draining the remaining drops of wine; she was more than merry, quite possibly drunk. Until she stood up and tried to walk in a straight line she couldn't say for definite. One thing she did know was that she was starving; two cans of slimming shake and a banana didn't really do much to fill you up. The man on the bar stool next to her smiled; he'd been chatting to her for the last thirty minutes. Don't ask what about because she didn't care. He was nice-looking – he was broad-shouldered and looked as if he worked out at the gym every day; at the moment he was the best-looking shag in the pub. Will, Stu and the others were sitting behind her in a semicircle and she hoped Will was watching. She wanted him to intervene, drag her back to the stool next to him and tell her how sorry he was; he did like her. In reality, he was completely ignoring her. He hadn't spoken more than ten words to her since last week.

She would have to go to plan B, which was to make him jealous, prove to him she could have anyone she wanted and it was him who was missing out. She turned her head slightly to see if he was watching her but he was nodding his head at something Stu was whispering in his ear – *losers, the pair of them.* Muscle man offered her another drink and she didn't refuse. This was Will's last chance and then she was leaving with muscle man and either taking him back to his place or hers. It didn't matter as long as she left the pub with him and Will watched her leave. She bent and whispered in his ear, 'Do you fancy going somewhere quiet for a coffee?'

The man nodded with a big grin on his face and she stood up from the bar stool, stumbling slightly. Muscle man, who had just told her he was called Ryan, caught her elbow, helping her to steady herself. She smiled at him then linked her arm through his, squeezing it tightly. Will nodded at her and then looked away. *Did his cheeks just flush?* She hoped so. It would serve him right; he'd had his chance. Laura did actually feel bad for Annie; she hadn't meant for her to catch them like she had, but in Laura's world all was fair in love and war. Ryan kept tight hold of her arm. They got outside the pub and walked down the street to the taxi rank. He gave his address and Laura wasn't about to argue; it was easier for her to sneak away after what she hoped would be some hot sex with no strings attached. He was a real gentleman and helped her into the car. Once it drove off he leant over and kissed her and she hungrily kissed him back. The taxi stopped outside a large detached house. The only buildings nearby were a church and small primary school and she realised it was the presbytery.

'Forgive me, Father, for I have sinned.' She giggled and reached out to touch his groin.

Ryan made the sign of the cross on her forehead and whispered, 'No, my child, you are about to sin – you haven't yet.'

She got a fit of the giggles as they got out of the taxi. Ryan slipped the driver a ten-pound note, then he took hold of her hand and led her towards the house, which was all in darkness.

'Are you really a priest?'

He shook his head. 'No, but my uncle is. I live with him while I'm working down here, but we have the place to ourselves. He's been asked to cover for a priest up in the Lakes so he's staying there for a bit. We'll be all on our own and you should see the size of my bed.'

He opened the front door and then turned and swept Laura off her feet, kicking the door shut behind him. Too drunk to even think about locking it, he carried her upstairs. Laura knew this was going to be fun and, for the first time in over a year, she forgot all about how much she fancied Will Ashworth.

*

Laura groaned, blinking one eye open. She wasn't in her own bed; her head felt as if it belonged to someone else and it was too heavy to lift. She turned to see the naked body of the man she had come home with and for once she thought: *not bad, not bad at all*. This made a change from the shock, horror, gasp and quick escapes after most nights out. She gazed around the room: it was pretty basic – king-size bed, wardrobe, chest of drawers and a huge crucifix on the wall. She'd forgotten he was the priest's nephew and hoped his uncle hadn't come home early. It would be a bit awkward if he'd heard them having sex in his house.

She sat up on the side of the bed; her head was banging and her stomach lurched as the bitter taste of stale wine lingered at the back of her throat. There was a bottle of water on the bedside table and she picked it up and took large gulping mouthfuls, glad to relieve the dry feeling at the back of her throat. After sitting with her head in her hands for ten minutes she forced herself to stand up. She wobbled across to the chair where she'd thrown her clothes last night and got dressed, but she didn't want to just leave. She actually liked Ryan and would love to see him again. Searching the pocket of her trousers, she found a crumpled business card with her phone number. Not wanting to wake him up because she didn't want him to see her looking so rough, she tiptoed around to his side of the bed and placed it on the bedside table next to him.

She bent down to kiss his forehead and her legs began to tremble. It was a struggle to hold her own body weight. Her stomach lurched once more and the room went black as she crashed down onto the floor. Semiconscious, she wanted to move but couldn't; her body was refusing to do what her mind was telling it to. From the corner of her eye she became vaguely aware of movement – someone was walking around the room. She looked at Ryan's glazed eyes. He was dead. What was happening? Her brain felt as if it had turned into treacle and she couldn't think. The footsteps stopped and she blinked, trying to focus, but the room was fuzzy and she was unable to see clearly. She knew it was a man – she could tell by the heavy footsteps that he was wearing boots. He approached her and she tried to speak but a mumbling noise came out. Her mind was screaming at her to move and her heart was racing – she knew the man wasn't here to help her – and then she heard his voice as he spoke into her ear.

'Say your prayers – it's time to go to sleep.'

*

He pulled the thick plastic bag over her head and watched as she took her last gasps, trying to suck in precious gulps of air – her pretty, thin face the same colour red as the old-fashioned carpet she was lying on. Her unfocused pale blue eyes bulged from the sockets, taking away some of the prettiness.

He had been parked across the road from the pub and followed the taxi as it drove away. When it had driven towards St Mary's Church he had almost given himself a heart attack – surely not; this was too good to be true! He hadn't wanted to use the same church twice, but why not? This was a gift from God himself. It would be foolish not to make use of it. When Laura and the man who was not his vicar stumbled drunkenly into the house they hadn't bothered to lock the door behind them, too absorbed in kissing each other. He had left them to it. He couldn't take them on now; they would be much easier once they'd had sex and tired themselves out.

He'd walked around the church grounds to see if there was a suitable grave he could use; he couldn't use the same one as she deserved her own. This time he chose one that wasn't overlooked by the school or the house. At least this would throw them; they would waste time and effort staking out the church, waiting for him to strike again, and next time it would be one on the other side of town, far away from St Mary's. After taking his bag from his truck, he'd finally crept in through the front door, locking it behind him. He'd overheard the man tell Laura about his uncle so it was all perfect. This house might belong to God but they said that the devil looked after his own. He'd sat down on the stairs and listened whilst they had very noisy sex – at one point he'd found himself getting a bit too excited and had to walk around the house to concentrate on what he was doing.

Eventually the bed stopped creaking and it went quiet. He wondered what would be the best way to do this without too much mess and blood. The man upstairs was much bigger than him. As much as he hated the sight of blood, he didn't really have much choice in how to kill him. It needed to be quick and the only thing he could think of was to stick a knife straight through his heart. At least he would be able to pull the duvet over him and if he did it fast enough maybe he wouldn't see any blood at all.

He'd gone into the kitchen and looked in the fridge. There were plenty of bottles of mineral water inside. He took one out and unscrewed the cap; then, tipping the contents of his medicine bottle in, he put the cap back on and gave it a good shake. There should be enough in there to render a bull defenceless. He would put it by her side of the bed for when she woke up. There was a butcher's block with an assortment of knives on the worktop and he'd pulled out the one with the biggest handle and the sharpest point. Just holding it made him feel queasy but he knew there was no way he could overpower the big man and a struggle would wake Laura up. He didn't want her to wake up until he was ready for her.

Worried that this could all go wrong in a very big way, he'd cautiously made his way up the stairs and in the direction of the room that all the noise had emanated from. He'd crept inside and placed the bottle of water next to Laura and then he'd crept around to the other side, where the man was lying naked and snoring gently. His legs began to tremble before he'd even lifted the knife but he took a deep breath and pulled his arm back, aiming straight for his chest. As the knife had plunged straight through the man's heart his eyes had opened and he'd made a gurgling sound. It must have been a lucky shot because the man's eyes had begun to glaze over. He'd left the knife where it was – he had his thick black gloves on so there would be no prints – and then he'd pulled the duvet over him so he didn't get distracted by the blood.

Laura had stirred and he'd looked across at her. Why did people feel the need to drink themselves into oblivion?

When he looked back down at Laura now she had stopped jerking and was still. It was a shame, but she wasn't a very nice person and she looked so much like his mother it was never going to end any other way. The moon had appeared from behind the dense black clouds and illuminated the church enough that he wouldn't have to struggle with her body and a torch. He bent down and removed the plastic bag from her head, scrunching it up and pushing it deep into his trouser pocket. He undressed her and then he bent down and heaved her up into his arms, which was a lot trickier than it sounded. She was very slim but still heavy enough to make beads of sweat form on his brow as he manoeuvred down the stairs with her. Using the tip of his Magnum boot to open the door he'd left ajar earlier, he stepped outside and paused, double-checking there was no one around.

He crunched his way along the short gravel path that led into the churchyard towards his chosen grave. He gently laid her down. It was easier this time with no plastic sheeting to contend with. After putting her in the recovery position, it took him a while to get her arms just right; they needed to be raised slightly, almost caressing each other. Then he set about looking for something to cover her with. When he was satisfied he'd done the best he could, he stood up and stretched – his back was aching. This wasn't as easy as he'd imagined but it was well worth the effort. Stepping back to admire his work, he smiled. Laura made a very beautiful sleeping angel and he wanted to sit down on the stone bench opposite and watch her, but he couldn't risk anyone seeing him. He snapped a couple of pictures on his phone and then pressed his right boot into the ground; give the detectives who would be working the case something to get excited about.

He left the way he'd come through the presbytery garden and out of the open gate. He stopped and remembered he hadn't shut the house door so he jogged back and slammed it shut. There was no point in making it too easy for the police. He wanted to give them a real challenge and see if they were up to the mark.

Chapter 13

The smell of new rubber plimsolls and the *flip, flack* of the too-big soles hitting the tarmac of the playground made Ella feel safe. It reminded her of her days playing hopscotch, when the only thing worth worrying about was if she would get put into the red or green team for sports day. Nobody wanted to be in yellow or blue.

'Miss, Miss – Billy has taken my bouncy ball.'

Ella sighed, turning around to sort out the first drama of the day. She smiled at the six-year-old girl with strawberry-blonde hair and a smattering of freckles across the bridge of her nose. Rosie Garnett would tell tales on her own mother; in fact, she often did. Ella looked at Billy, whose surly expression made her struggle to hide the smile on her face. 'Come on, Billy, give it back. Rosie, I'm sure he just wanted to play with you; isn't that right, Billy?'

Billy held out his small pudgy hand. Concealed inside his tight fist was the tiny bright green ball. Uncurling his fingers, he passed it to Rosie, who smiled so sweetly at him that it made Ella grimace. Rosie ran off after the bouncing ball she had just launched towards the other side of the playground and Billy stood, waiting to be told off. Ella patted him on the head. Then a piercing scream froze her to the core – something bad had happened and she was almost too afraid to turn around and see what it was, but her instinct took over and she turned and ran in the direction of the scream. It was one long, shrill noise and it sounded almost like the high-pitched peal of the fire alarms. It was emanating from the churchyard that adjoined the school.

Ella, closely followed by Miss Smith, reached the gate that led into the church grounds to see Rosie standing on the other side, her mouth open and that awful noise coming from it. Ella rushed towards her to see what was the matter; the girl didn't look as if she'd hurt herself. Ella grabbed hold of Rosie and gently shook her to make her stop. Rosie stared at Ella and lifted a small finger and pointed at something.

Ella turned to look and felt her heart skip a beat. The naked body of a woman lay across one of the graves. Her lifeless eyes told Ella everything she needed to know and she pulled Rosie against her, hugging her and gently turning her away from the dreadful sight. Picking her up, she carried her over to Miss Smith, who was standing with one hand clapped over her mouth; she hadn't ventured past the gate. 'Get the children back inside and phone the police now.' Miss Smith nodded and, taking the girl from her, she began blowing the whistle to signal that playtime was over and told the children to go back in. Ella stood blocking the gate so nobody could see through until all the children had been rounded up and ushered back inside.

As the last one walked through the hall doors she turned and approached the woman. She needed to check that she didn't have a pulse and, although Ella had never seen a dead body except for on the television, she was pretty sure that this was one. She cautiously walked over to the grave, careful not to trample anything that could be evidence – she had read enough crime thrillers and they had taught her well. Bending down, she pressed two fingers against the woman's neck to check for a pulse. Her skin was icy-cold and Ella knew that it had been a while since she had last taken a breath – there was nothing she could do for her.

The luminous green of Rosie's bouncy ball made a stark contrast to the marbled blue and white of the woman's skin; it had come to rest in the crook of her bent arm. Ella doubted that Rosie would ever be able to look at a bouncy ball again. Feeling sad for whoever this woman was, she made her way back to the small black cast-iron gate to wait for the police, and judging by the wail of the sirens they would be there very soon.

Mr Michaels, the head teacher, came barging through the narrow door that led into the hall where the children were milling and got tangled up in a web of arms and skipping ropes. The view through the large glass patio doors made Ella turn around so he wouldn't see the grin on her face. It was totally inappropriate but the man irritated her beyond belief. He strode across to her. 'Are you quite sure the woman is dead and not just some drugged-up homeless tramp who has dossed down in the church for the night?'

Ella tried not to roll her eyes at him and instead shook her head. 'Well, I'm no expert, Mr Michaels, but if you take a look yourself you will clearly see that she has been dead for some time. Although I don't know if you should go in there.'

He ignored her and pushed past. Ella watched and wondered if he was about to trample through the crime scene like he trampled through life but she didn't need to worry. He took one look at the grave and the colour drained from his face. 'Dear God, how did this happen, and in a church of all places?'

Ella shrugged; she had no answers. Just a feeling of desperate sadness for whoever the woman was, placed on show for everyone to see. She breathed a sigh of relief as two policemen came rushing through the hall doors and over to where she was standing. Ella pointed to the grave and was pleased to see Mr Michaels squirm his way back through into the playground, his face burning. He looked like a kid caught peeking into the girls' locker room. The first policeman made a strangled noise in the back of his throat and she thought he said 'Laura'; the second one stepped through the gate and his hand flew to his mouth. He muttered, 'Oh, my God.' Ella realised that the woman was someone they both knew.

Her legs began to quiver and her head felt fuzzy; she blinked a few times to try and clear her mind but she needed to sit down before she passed out. Leaning back against the rough red-brick wall, she felt herself begin to slide down it, her brand-new Per Una cardigan snagging on all the rough bits of brick all the way down until she reached the ground. How embarrassing – she felt like an idiot – but then she looked across at the two policemen and they didn't look much better. There was a lot of shouting into the radios that were clipped to the bright yellow body armour they were wearing. Her eyes shut. Through the daze she heard the words *ambulance, CID, foxtrot* but the last words the bigger of the two men spoke would forever haunt her dreams.

'It's our Laura . . . I mean it's Detective Constable Laura Collins.'

Chapter 14

Will opened his eyes. He'd only drunk two halves of lager and an orange juice but he felt as if he'd drunk ten pints. He would never drink like he had last week ever again; it had ruined his life. He thought about Annie – if he was honest, she was all he thought about. He wanted to do something to make it right but he had no idea how to prove to her that he wasn't a total screw-up and that she should give him another chance. Bloody Laura – he could kill her; what had she been playing at? She hadn't really spoken to him since he'd thrown her out of his house and he'd been relieved when she left the pub last night with the big bloke who'd bought her drinks all night. Let her make some other poor sod's life a misery.

His phone began to ring. He glanced at the screen – unknown number – work could bugger off. He wasn't on duty until twelve. He still had two hours to feel sorry for himself, play a bit of Adele; that was music to slit your wrists to – if only he had the energy. He reached across the bed to the iPod docking station on his bedside table and pressed play. 'Rolling in the Deep' filled the air and he buried his head underneath a pillow, feeling like shit. Half an hour of self-torture then he'd get up, have a shower and go face the world of fuckwits that waited for him at work.

Pounding on the front door awoke him from his dream; he had managed to go back to sleep. Adele was still reminding him that he could have had it all. The knocking didn't cease. He was going to get whoever it was by the scruff of their neck and ram their bloody head right through his letterbox. Pulling his trousers and a sweatshirt on, he ran down the stairs to the front door, throwing it open, about to shout at whoever it was. He was greeted by a white-faced Stu.

'This'd better be bloody good, Stu. I'm not due in until twelve.' Will turned away, expecting Stu to follow him inside but he didn't. 'Stu, what are you doing? Has Debs finally thrown you out?'

He watched Stu gulp, struggling to find the right words to say. 'It's Laura. She's dead.'

Will continued moaning at him, not really taking in what he'd just said, and then he stopped. 'What did you just say?'

Stu's face contorted into a mask of pain and his eyes filled with tears. 'Sarge, Laura is dead. Some kid found her body on a grave in St Mary's Church grounds.'

Will felt a surge of regret about the bad things he'd been thinking about her less than an hour ago. 'Are you sure it's our Laura?'

Stu nodded his head, sniffling into his hand. Tears were falling down his cheeks. He clearly couldn't bring himself to speak.

Will pulled a pair of trainers on and grabbed his keys off the table. 'I don't believe this . . . How? Are you in a fit state to drive because, if not, let me. I don't want you crashing on the way and blowing eighty-five on the breathalyser.'

'Of course I can drive. I came here to get you, didn't I? I never had that much to drink; it's just the shock of it all, you know. I mean we were with her until about half ten, when she left with the big bloke. Do you think he did it? He must have, but why? Why would he kill her?'

Will couldn't think clearly. One of his officers was dead. They sat in silence on the journey until Stu turned the car into the quiet road that led to the church. He felt sick and hoped the shock wasn't going to make him vomit. There were several police cars and vans abandoned all over the place, blue and red lights flashing. Stu stopped the car in the middle of the road and they got out. The familiar sight of Kav standing by the entrance to the church reminded Will of the events not that long ago, when the town had been turned into a killing field by a man obsessed with the old mansion in the woods and with Annie. Kav had also been on duty when the bodies were found last time. He looked ill now; his face was grey. One of the response officers brought Will a white scene suit, latex gloves, face mask and boot covers. He took them and whispered his thanks. The young officer offered another set to Stu, who shook his head and turned to look in any direction other than that of the church.

The officer spoke in a hushed voice. 'Sarge, the detective inspector said he would be here very shortly. CSI are ready; they are waiting for the go-ahead from you. They have just gone back to get a scene tent. That photographer from the paper showed up before with a kid in tow holding a half-dead bunch of flowers; the crafty bastard tried to keep Kav talking while the kid sneaked around the back with one of those little flip camera things that record video.'

Will felt his knuckles bunch into tight white fists. That man caused the same reaction in him every single time. 'Did you stop him?'

'Kav did – arrested the photographer and the kid for section five. The kid started blubbing like a baby. He dragged them both into the back of that van over there.'

Will felt a wave of relief because he knew if he saw that smug face he would knock him out. 'Thanks, Smithy.'

Will couldn't wait for the DI to arrive – he had to take a look now; just in case they all had it wrong. After dressing himself in the scene suit, he walked over to the gate that was the main entrance to the church and everyone on the perimeter turned to watch him. Claire, one of the PCSOs, was standing with the scene log and he nodded at her. The sadness in her eyes said it all. He felt as if time had stood still; the only sound in the area, which was full of people, was that of a small bird chirping and the crunch of the gravel underneath his feet. The sun was breaking through the clouds, and he had to force himself to look up from the ground and in front of him instead.

He could see her body a short distance away and felt his breath catch in the back of his throat. From where he was standing, she looked as if she was asleep. Whoever had done this had covered her body with twigs and leaves, just like the woman last week, and she was posed in a similar position. He forced himself to step closer, trying to stop his mind from associating his pretty blonde colleague with the cold, dead body in front of him, on display for the world to look at. There was no colour in her face and her lips were tinged with blue. Will knew that the minute they moved her the skin underneath would be mottled red where the blood had pooled, causing livor mortis.

He reached the grave and pulled on the pair of latex gloves that he had been clutching, then bent down. He could hear the sound of his heart thudding inside his head it was so loud. Her hands looked clean; it didn't look as if she had put up a fight against her killer. The perfectly manicured nails didn't have a chip on them. He took hold of one and gently turned it. From what he could see, there was nothing underneath the nails, but his friend Matt who was the local the pathologist would scrape them to make sure. He couldn't see any blood or marks on her skin. He'd have to wait for Matt to do a post-mortem to determine the cause of death, but at least Laura looked peaceful, as if she'd fallen asleep. Will knew that he would have struggled if there had been a lot of blood and the signs of a violent attack because it was hard enough looking at her now. He prayed that, however she'd died, she hadn't suffered.

Fuck, fuck, fuck. What happened, Laura? You're supposed to be in work, nursing a hangover and going on the dinner run for greasy bacon butties. Not lying here, dead.

He turned to see the detective inspector, Dave Martin, walking along the path. 'Jesus Will, what's going on? I'm supposed to be going on annual leave today; it's my daughter's wedding down in Northampton tomorrow.'

Will waited for it to register with him who it was that was lying dead in front of them and, give the man his due, it only took him twenty seconds before the shock registered on his face. 'No – tell me that's not Laura . . . our Laura! What the hell?'

Will knew that his boss wouldn't have listened to the phone call properly; he would have been expecting to see Laura here, working the scene, not lying dead and being the scene. Will often wondered how the man had got this far – he was a great guy and very clever but he didn't really listen to what anyone had to say; his mind would wander or switch off totally.

'I wish I knew, boss. She was with the rest of us until half ten last night in the Black Dog, when she left with some bodybuilder guy. She was drunk but happy to go with him and nobody noticed anything out of the ordinary.'

The DI, whose face was now the same colour as Laura's, unzipped his paper suit and loosened his collar and tie underneath.

'I can't believe it's Laura.' He shook his head. 'Right, everything by the book, not that we don't, but she's one of us and I want the bastard caught now, not three weeks later. Is this exactly the same modus operandi as the woman last week?'

'Yes, it looks like it. I'm not thinking straight. That's two women in just over a week, both murdered and left on show on top of old graves.'

'Then we have a serious problem, Will. Is Laura married? Oh, God, does she have kids?'

'No, boss, she's single. Her mum is elderly and has Alzheimer's and lives in a home on Abbey Road.'

The DI sighed. 'Good. I don't mean good that she hasn't got much family; I just mean that it's better she doesn't have a doting husband and three young kids who are waiting for her to come home.'

Will thought that maybe if she had, she would still be alive. Debs, who was duty CSI, walked down the path, followed by the new boy, who was carrying a white scene tent. Will had no idea what he was called but he looked about fourteen. He left them to it and turned to walk back out the way they had walked in. Time to let the experts do their part. Will knew that Laura was in excellent hands. Debs wouldn't leave until she'd checked every square inch for evidence. Matt appeared at the gate, carrying his heavy briefcase over to where the new boy was struggling with the tent. He nodded at Will, who was walking towards Kav. 'It's a sad day to see one of our own like this, Will. Why would anyone want to hurt Laura, let alone kill her?'

Will shook his head but wondered briefly how many relationships she'd messed up. Less than two hours ago he'd thought about killing her himself – hypothetically, of course. He wasn't a violent man, unless it was defending himself or anyone he cared about. The only exception would be the man who had wanted to kill Annie last year. Given the chance, Will would very much like to be left alone in a locked room with him for five minutes. 'I'm not sure, but we have a major problem. This is the second murder in just over a week and, as far as I know, Laura had no connection to the first victim, Tracy Hale, because she worked that crime scene with me. She would have said something if she'd known her.'

The DI began making his way towards them and his colour hadn't improved any. Fresh from his secondment at headquarters in Penrith, he was obviously figuring out the world of shit that was about to come crashing down on his shoulders. 'Will, what have we got so far? Anything that's concrete – witnesses, CCTV, anything?'

Will coughed into his hands as he felt his cheeks begin to burn. 'Nothing yet for Laura – a kid from the school found her.'

Kav spoke. 'I have two officers inside, checking the CCTV and taking first accounts from the teacher.'

Will carried on. 'The last victim was a bit of a loner, according to her work colleagues, very shy and didn't join in with much, both inside and outside of work. She had no close friends and didn't socialise with anyone they were aware of. She was single, no family and both parents dead. She hasn't got a record but did phone 101 a couple of weeks ago to report that someone had been in her house. A patrol went and checked the house and rear yard. There was no sign of anyone trying to gain entry and when she was asked why she thought someone had been in her house she said it was because the Sky remote control wasn't where she'd left it before she went to work. Understandably, the officers didn't really take much notice; you know how busy they are and short-staffed. There was nothing to substantiate that a crime had occurred so it was left at that. The next contact was when her body was discovered in St Mary's Church by the elderly housekeeper for the priest.'

'Jesus wept – has her house been searched from top to bottom?'

'Yes, CSI and Task Force went through it with a fine-tooth comb and didn't find anything; she wasn't killed there. Her house was immaculate. The day before she was discovered she had been to work and must have met her killer there or on her way home. Truthfully, we have nothing. The crime scene was relatively clean. There was a footprint on the soil near to the grave but it came back as a Magnum and you and I know it's the boot of choice for most response staff. Debs took a cast but most of the blokes in the station wear them so we can rule that out.'

'Anything else – blood, DNA, a bloody great fingerprint that leads us straight to the murdering bastard?'

Will shook his head. 'No blood, death by asphyxiation, nothing under the nails so she didn't put up a fight. We're still waiting on the toxicology reports, which Matt said he would fast-track but it still takes forever. It has to be the same guy because Laura looks pretty much identical to her and relatively peaceful for a woman who has just been murdered.'

'I don't suppose the church will have CCTV – there won't be much call for it – but what about the vicar? Has anyone spoken to him?'

'Boss, it's a Catholic church. We hammered on the presbytery door first thing and there was no reply. Stu and Laura spoke to the priest and took a statement after he'd reported finding the body last week. He's in his sixties and didn't have a clue why anyone would want to leave a dead body in his church grounds.'

Kav butted in. 'Father John is the priest for this church; my wife comes to Mass a couple of times a month. He's had to go and cover for someone at Windermere for a couple of weeks so he won't have been here. You'll have to get someone to go and speak to him up that end. The school does have very good CCTV, which is being burnt off as we speak.'

The DI cheered up at the thought of maybe having the killer captured on camera. 'Good – fingers crossed, it will all be on tape.'

Will decided not to piss on his chips and tell him that it was highly unlikely; the cameras didn't even look over to the church. The killer would have had to climb over the six-foot-high fence into the school playground carrying Laura over his back and gone through into the church by the gate they were standing close to. It would be amazing but the only person who would be that strong would be the bloody Hulk or someone who was off his head. If it was someone who was on one because they'd been up all night taking plant food or whatever, the crime scene would have been sloppy and disorganised. This was definitely the work of an organised killer.

Since the last murders, Will had become a bit of an expert on serial killers. His bedtime reading consisted of tales of Ted Bundy, the Yorkshire Ripper and almost every other serial killer that had ever been caught. He had promised himself should it ever happen again then he would be prepared; he just hadn't expected that it actually would. He needed to speak to Grace Marshall and fast. He didn't want to spoil her holiday but he would send her an email; that should be OK. He also wanted to wake up from this nightmare – right about now.

Chapter 15

Annie had no idea what she was doing but she seemed to be winging it just fine. The tourists weren't as bad as she'd thought they would be. She hated having her picture taken but she could live with it as long as she didn't have to look at the photos. The weather had been glorious and she couldn't have picked a prettier place to work. It was so different from the usual drunken chavs and endless domestics she was used to attending on a daily basis. She actually had time to think, which perhaps wasn't the best thing considering all she could think about was Will.

Today she was on foot patrol and she walked down the steep hill towards the busy town of Bowness. Everybody smiled and said hello and she smiled back. Passing the shops, she made her way towards the pier where the lakeside steamers docked. One full of kids was just coming in and they all waved at her; she waved back. She walked on towards the marina and the boat club. She had made it her first port of call the first day she was here, thinking it would be a great way to get to know some of the locals. She had spent a very pleasant hour with the club steward, who had showed her around, explaining everything to her. He had even taken her onto a couple of boats. She had never been interested in them before but now she was fascinated. It probably had a lot to do with the fact that they were moored on the most beautiful lake in England – in her opinion.

She had wondered what it would be like sailing around on one with Will, a picnic and a couple of bottles of champagne, then she kicked herself. *As if that's ever likely to happen, Graham. You've never been sailing in your life and Will probably won't have either, and aren't you forgetting the most important thing of all? You and Will are not together any more.* The pain in her chest was so intense it felt as if someone had just stabbed her through the heart.

She wandered along the jetties, admiring the huge boat that was now moored up and hadn't been there the last time she was here. An older man came out of the cabin with a half-drunk bottle of Coke in his hand and grinned at her. 'Good afternoon, officer, and what a fine one it is.'

'Yes, it is gorgeous. What a beautiful day to be sailing, especially on such a lovely boat.'

'Why, thank you; she is a beauty, isn't she. My wife doesn't agree but what the heck, you only live once.'

Annie nodded in agreement. He seemed so familiar. He had a thick shock of silver hair, bright blue eyes and a cheeky grin.

'I'm Annie, one of the local community officers. I'm very new to the area. Well, I'm not new to the area as such; I come here all the time on my days off. What I mean is I'm new to policing the area.' She shut up as her cheeks began to burn. Could she make a bigger fool of herself?

He put the bottle of Coke down and climbed down the ladder, as agile as any twenty-year-old. He turned to face her and held out his hand. 'I'm Tom and it's nice to meet such a lovely member of the constabulary.' He winked at her and she laughed. 'Would you like to take a look around my boat, Annie? My wife won't even come on it unless I'm dropping her off to go shopping. I'm dying to show it off to someone who might want to listen to me waffle on.'

She thought about it for all of ten seconds before she nodded.

'I'd love to.'

He climbed back up the ladder and she followed him up and onto the deck, where he proceeded to show her the cabin and below deck. It was gorgeous. It had two bedrooms and a galley-cum-diner. Before she could stop herself, she uttered, 'Wow, well, Tom, I am very impressed. I have to say, it's nicer than my house.'

He laughed and it was his turn to blush. 'Look at me, showing off; you know, I don't normally do that – I just couldn't resist getting the prettiest officer I've ever met onto my boat.'

Annie felt her already warm cheeks burn even hotter.

'My son's a police officer – not around here, though. It's a bit boring for him here; he prefers a bit of the action.'

A woman's voice called out for Tom and he grinned again. 'Oops, busted by the wife. Come on, she can make us something ice-cold to drink and we can sit on the deck and discuss the local neighbourhood policing priorities. That way, if anyone asks you have a valid excuse to be so blatantly taking a break.' He winked and she couldn't help laughing; she liked him. He turned to go up on deck and she followed.

Annie had to stop her mouth from falling open when she saw the woman who the voice belonged to. She had been expecting to see someone the same age as Tom. Instead, standing in front of her was a woman in her early thirties, the same age as her, and she was beautiful. She looked as if she belonged on a Hollywood film set and Annie felt a wave of embarrassment, standing there dressed head to foot in men's black combat trousers, a polyester shirt that was stuck to every inch of her body, Magnum boots and her luminous yellow body armour. Her hat was tucked under her arm because it was baking her head and her black curly hair was plastered to her head. Tom hugged his wife and kissed her cheek. 'Lily, this is Annie, our new community police officer. Annie, this is my wife, Lily.'

Lily smiled and held out her hand. 'I hope Tom hasn't bored you to death?'

'Not at all; it's very nice to meet you both.'

'Have you offered Annie a drink? She must be spitting feathers, wearing all that gear in this heat.'

'Sorry, I totally forgot. Sorry, Annie, would you like a cool drink?' He winked at her and she had to smother a laugh. 'Only if it's not too much trouble. It would be lovely. I am absolutely fried.'

Lily disappeared down into the galley and Tom pointed to one of the sun loungers on the deck. 'Do you want to take that stab vest off and make yourself a bit comfier? I promise that neither of us will attack you.'

'I better hadn't; I don't want to look as if I'm actually enjoying myself. Members of the public like to report us if we look too much like normal people.'

'Ah, yes, I know what you mean. I think most people think you come from an assembly line in Milton Keynes.'

Lily appeared, carrying a tray with three crystal glasses that sparkled in the sunlight and a jug full of fruit juice, ice and chopped fruit. Tom jumped up to take it from her, placing it on the table. He began pouring the juice and handed one to her; she thanked him and took a long sip. It was delicious. She looked around at the calm blue lake and the boats sailing on the water, the lush green hills and mountains surrounding it, and wished that Will was here; he would love this. What would it be like to enjoy life and not have to work for a living?

Lily broke the moment and began chatting about the new Laura Ashley shop that had opened and Annie joined in. She talked to them both for the next half an hour without having to think about much else. And then her radio burst into life, bringing her back to reality. The control room operator told her there was a minor road traffic collision, no injuries but the road was blocked and they needed some traffic control up by the church. Annie drained the last of her juice. 'Thank you so much; that was lovely and it was even nicer to have met you both. If you need anything at all you can contact me on this number.' She pulled a business card from her pocket, which had the constabulary crest on it and a list of telephone numbers, the police station address and her email. Tom stood up and took it from her, 'Thank you, Annie; that's very kind of you. I never know when I may need rescuing from Lily and her shopping fetish.' He winked and she laughed.

'Well, anything at all; if I can help, give me a shout.' She climbed down the side of the boat onto the jetty and began to briskly walk back up towards the church and the irate motorists.

Tom looked at Lily. 'Do you think that is the lovely Annie who has my son in such a fluster? There can't be that many policewomen called Annie. She reminds me so much of Elizabeth – similar features. It would figure that Will would fall in love with a woman who reminded him of his mum.'

Lily wrapped her arms around his waist and hugged him tight. 'Do you think we should do some digging, find some reason to speak to your inspector friend and get the background? I hope she is the same one; she seems so nice and down-to-earth. I can feel a spot of matchmaking coming on.'

Tom turned and kissed her. 'If she isn't Will's Annie, we should let them meet anyway. There is something about her I really like; I just can't put my finger on it.'

'Well, as long as we don't interfere too much it should be OK. Maybe we should invite Will up for a barbecue and ask Annie, as well as some of our other friends. That way, we can gauge their relationship, see if they know each other.'

Tom laughed. 'Lily, you are a hopeless romantic but I love you.'

Lily picked up the tray of empty glasses. 'You can take me home now – I have some planning to do – and then you can sail around the lake.'

'Your wish is my command.'

Chapter 16

Will and the DI followed the black Mondeo estate that carried Laura's body up to the mortuary when it was finally moved from the crime scene. Will wouldn't put any of his staff through watching their friend and colleague's post-mortem; he couldn't do it to them. He didn't want to do it but the feeling of guilt that had settled in his stomach told his brain it might be eased a little if he did as much for Laura as possible. Matt had said he would wait for them and do the PM straight away. Will had thanked him profusely, glad that Matt was one of the good guys. He didn't act like a pathologist; well, he didn't act like the last two Will had worked with. Matt was down-to-earth and didn't think he was better than everyone else, and he'd been in the pub with the rest of them last night for Stu's birthday. Buying the drinks and having a laugh. He had been as shocked as the rest of them when he'd got to the crime scene. He hadn't made them wait; he had come down as soon as he'd got the call and Will would be eternally grateful to him for that.

They arrived at the rear of the hospital and there, standing at the metal door that led into the mortuary, were a grim-faced Matt and Lisa – the coroner's officer – along with two technicians and two CSIs. No one spoke; they didn't know what to say. They just

112

began doing what they did all the time with no fuss or drama, simply an unspoken agreement that they would do everything they could to find Laura's killer.

*

Annie soothed her irate motorists and left the scene with an ice-cold white chocolate and raspberry milkshake, courtesy of the manager of one of the local coffee shops. It had taken an hour for recovery to come and she'd spent the whole time directing traffic. She felt a bit cheeky but she was dehydrated; the day was so warm and she was overheating. Who was she to say no to a free drink, so she shoved it down inside her body armour between her cleavage – one advantage of having a decent-size bust because, in her opinion, there weren't many. It was freezing and she had to walk slowly to make sure that she didn't dribble raspberry sauce everywhere.

Finally she got back to the station and coaxed the drink out. She placed it on the desk and unzipped her body armour, throwing it onto the floor. She took a big slurp of the drink and immediately thought of Jake; he would be missing her like crazy. Maybe she should convince him to transfer up here if another opening occurred, although it would probably be a bit tame for him; he liked the rough and tumble of a good old fight on a Saturday night outside the clubs. She missed him, though; it was quite lonely and she was often left to her own devices, which she liked, but she did miss the banter. The door slammed and a voice echoed, 'Only me. Anyone home?'

'Yep, just me; did you want something?'

Cathy walked into the office and smiled at Annie, her eyes lingered on the milkshake. 'Ah, I see you've been acquainted with Gustav. He makes a cracking milkshake but just be prepared for him to try and get into your knickers.'

'Pardon?'

'Has an eye for the ladies, does Gustav, and don't get me wrong, I'm all for a freebie, but I think I'm a bit old for him, although I'm pretty sure I could teach him a thing or two about where to shove those ice cubes.'

Annie managed to splatter milkshake all over her black T-shirt. 'Yes, he was a bit of all right.'

Cathy winked at her. 'Well, then, maybe a fun, flirty fling might just be the ticket for you, Annie.'

Annie felt her red cheeks burn even hotter. 'No, thank you. I'm over men for at least a year. Why don't you go out with him?'

'What, and put him out of his misery? No, I love to watch him fawn over my officers and me if I'm totally honest, and it wouldn't be the same, would it? The thought of it is always so much better than the reality, wouldn't you agree?'

Annie shook her head. 'Sometimes the reality is even better.'

Cathy nodded and changed the subject. 'I have some bad news for you; there has been another murder down in Barrow.'

Annie felt her heart skip a beat and she held her breath without realising.

'A primary school kid found a woman's body in a churchyard this morning. One of ours as well.'

Annie felt sick. Before Cathy could say the name she already knew; it had flashed into her mind as clear as day and a lead weight began to form in her stomach. 'Who was it?'

'Laura Collins – they found her naked, just like the other one. Poor bugger – what a way to go, murdered and left on show for all your colleagues to find.'

Annie shivered. A lump began to form in her throat and she didn't even like Laura, especially not after the trouble she'd caused her and Will. But the woman didn't deserve this – nobody did.

Cathy walked over to her and put a hand on her shoulder, squeezing gently. 'I've just come back from a meeting down in Barrow; afterwards, Kav filled me in. I didn't mean to pry, but he was concerned for you and he thought I should have an idea about some of the stuff that could affect one of my officers. Kav's a good man; we go back a long way. Remember what I said: if you need to talk, I'm always here.'

Annie smiled. 'Thanks, but I wouldn't burden anyone with the crap that happens in my life.' She kept thinking about Will and how terrible he must be feeling right now. She would give anything to be the one holding him, stroking his hair and telling him it would all be OK when he eventually finished work. He would be in a state and she couldn't help thinking that she wished she'd never heard of Laura Collins.

*

Cathy stuck her head into the ref's room, where Annie was sitting staring into space, her sandwiches unwrapped but untouched in front of her. 'I'm going now; can you let the night shift know to check the curfew folder and do some visits?'

Annie nodded. 'No problem; I'm going to have a wander around before I finish at ten.'

'Up to you, but you don't need to – you can just wait here and take it easy.'

'No, I get bored, but thanks. Goodnight.'

Cathy nodded. 'Goodnight.'

Annie stood up. She might as well have a wander around; there was nothing she could do. She left the station and heard the church clock chime seven. As she walked down the deserted street she couldn't help but smile; she loved it when the shops were closed and the crowds of tourists had moved on to other villages or back to their hotels for evening meals. Of course the Lakes relied heavily on the tourists to keep the businesses afloat but on a day shift it was a steady flow of dealing with irate motorists or posing to have her picture taken . . . which she hated.

She walked past the Pandora shop and thought she might treat herself to a new charm for the bracelet Will had bought her. It had been another gift for her birthday. When she'd left she did think about giving it back but then decided it was her little piece of him that would remind her of the good times. He had given it to her as a birthday present even though she'd never told him it was her birthday; Jake must have blabbed to him. It had brought a tear to her eye when she'd opened it; on the dark purple leather bracelet was a gold guardian angel charm, a gold love heart with a diamond in the middle and a ghost charm, which had made her giggle. She had never taken it off since the day he gave it to her. The first time she had popped into the shop to price the charms she had nearly passed out with shock to find out the value of hers. It was worth eight hundred pounds. She wouldn't have accepted it at the time if she had known that but, because it didn't look much, she had let Will wrap the bracelet around her wrist and delicately close the clasp. He'd lifted her hand and kissed it, telling her how much he loved her. *Ha, he loved you so much he couldn't wait to cheat on you with a super-skinny blonde.*

Annie blinked away a tear – all those years with Mike and she had never felt about him the way she did about Will. Even now it disgusted her how her heart would beat faster and she would flush pink every time she heard his name mentioned. She missed him so much but her pride had been hurt and it was hard to swallow and forgive him, although if he begged hard enough she would find him impossible to resist; that was the main reason she had asked for the transfer to Windermere station.

Will hadn't chased her or bombarded her with calls and texts asking for forgiveness since she'd left, though, which hurt almost as much as finding him comatose next to Laura. She knew he was giving her time to get her head together and she was grateful. Annie had been through so much this past year, a lesser woman would have been admitted to a mental hospital but she had soldiered on. Will had become her protector and lover and she had fallen so hard for him it had torn her apart when he had lived up to his reputation as a womaniser, and here she was. Alone, fed up and still seeing shadowy figures out of the corner of her eye whenever she didn't expect it.

The church loomed in the distance and she headed down the hill towards it to check the grounds and building. There had recently been a lot of metal plaque thefts from the cemetery in Barrow and she didn't know whether there were any plaques in the church grounds so she would check. That was the problem with society these days: no one had any respect for anyone, especially for the dead. What kind of person stole memorial plaques?

Costa Coffee was all in darkness – her favourite coffee shop before she began working up here. On the rare occasion that she and Will were off together they would come up for coffee and read the papers. *Bloody hell, when am I going to have some memories that are mine alone and don't make me want to throw myself into the lake under the first steamboat that comes along?*

As she neared the entrance to the church she saw the familiar figure of the little girl who she'd first seen standing on the steps to her house. The girl darted behind a gravestone and Annie's breath caught in the back of her throat. The girl was wearing the same white lace dress and black lace-up shoes as the last time; her hair was still in two plaits. Annie walked more quickly, wanting to catch up with the girl. It was chilly now and she could see her breath plume out in front of her when she exhaled.

'Hey, wait for me, kid. What are you doing . . .? I just want to say hello.' Annie was greeted by silence. She walked into the churchyard and felt as if she had stepped back in time to the eighteen-hundreds. The air was still and Annie walked towards the tall grave she had seen the girl disappear behind. She peered behind it but there wasn't anyone there. Impossible if she'd been alive; the churchyard was small enough she would have seen her leave. She felt tiny fingers tug on her jacket from behind and she turned but no one was there. 'OK, kid, it's just me and you now. You have my attention. What can I do for you? I won't hurt you. Please come and talk to me.'

In the distance she saw a glimpse of white flicker for a second as if the girl was trying to appear but struggling. Annie knew the girl was long dead but needed to tell her something and she just hoped that, whatever it was, it wasn't going to end with Annie fighting for her life again.

Annie checked every inch of the graveyard, which had some of the most ornate gravestones and memorials she had ever seen, but no brass plaques. As she rounded the corner she gasped, thinking there was a body on a grave but, on closer inspection, she realised it was a life-size stone angel and her heart rate slowed. There was no sign of the girl, not even a whisper in the air. She wanted something and there was no way she could ignore a kid who might be asking for her help; she couldn't live with herself if she did.

Her radio broke the silence as the mobile patrol requested a vehicle PNC for intelligence and Annie made her way out of the churchyard, closing the iron gate behind her. She continued her walk down to the lakeside to check the piers and boats, the whole time thinking about the little girl, which at least was a change from thinking about Will.

*

Matt had finished summing up Laura's post-mortem. He carefully stitched her back together again. Not that he didn't take care with all of his patients, but he did this much neater because he knew her, he'd worked with her and because she shouldn't be here on his table having her internal organs sewn back into her body cavity. Will hadn't spoken since he'd arrived and it had been almost three hours. There had been no discernible marks on Laura's body. No defence injuries and, judging by her bloodshot eyes, Matt's initial report concluded that she had died by suffocation or, to be medically correct, asphyxiation. But he wouldn't confirm it until the blood results were back; it was hard to say whether she'd been drugged or not until the samples were tested – the same for the amount of alcohol in her system.

They hadn't found one scrap of forensic evidence on her – no hair or fibres, no skin or DNA. Whoever had killed her was good; he knew exactly what he was doing and this worried Will more than anything because if he was so good at this there was a chance he wouldn't stop killing. Why should he? He liked it. There hadn't been a single drop of blood and Will had formed the impression that the killer probably wasn't very fond of it. There hadn't been a scratch on either of the bodies. Two dead women and not a drop of blood spilt, which was pretty unusual.

The DI had left to go back to the station and finish up what he could. He would leave it in Will's capable hands until he got back late on Sunday. Will and Matt left the sterile room as the technician was wheeling Laura across to the big bank of fridges. Will had to turn away; he would never get rid of the image of Laura being zipped into a black body bag and being pushed into one of the fridges. It was like something out of his worst nightmare.

They stripped off their boot covers, scrubs and gloves in complete silence. Matt was the one to break it. 'Coffee? I know I need something a lot stronger than bloody coffee but it's all I've got.'

Will nodded – his head was banging and he couldn't remember the last time he'd had a drink of anything; it had been hours ago. He followed Matt into his office and slumped down on the small black leather two-seater sofa at the back of the room. Matt made two mugs of strong coffee and took a packet of chocolate digestives from his desk drawer. 'I'm not hungry but my stomach's empty and I feel sick and I don't know if it's the shock of Laura or the lack of food.'

'I know what you mean. What the fuck is happening, Matt? I can't have another murderer running around killing women and, to make it worse, this one is personal. Why kill a copper?'

'Do you think it was that big guy she left with?'

'I don't know. I've never seen him before. I've had Stu go back to the pub to collect all the CCTV footage from last night to see if anyone in there knows who he is or where he lives.'

Matt nodded. 'He won't be that hard to identify. All you need is a couple of PCSOs armed with stills of the guy to visit all the gyms in Barrow, Dalton and Ulverston to see if he works out in any of them. Fingers crossed he will and you'll have a name and address for him before the morning.'

Will finished his coffee and took two more biscuits from the packet. 'I hope so, mate. It would be nice to end this now, before anyone else has to die. What's wrong with people? Why do they feel the need to kill others? And why the church? It's all so weird.'

'If I knew that I'd be doing your job, Will, not slicing and dicing dead bodies. I was never that good at puzzles when I was a kid, but I used to love that game, Operation – no one could beat me at that; I was the school champion.'

Will laughed and dragged himself up off the sofa. 'You sad git; don't go admitting that to anyone. It doesn't do much for that cool image you like to portray.'

Matt laughed. 'It could be worse; I could have been captain of the spelling team.'

Will shook his head and walked out of the door. He paused and turned back. 'I don't care how much it costs; rush those samples through. I'll pay for it myself if I have to. Don't let anyone moan about the cost. I want them as soon as humanly possible.'

'Will, I'd pay for them myself if anyone had the audacity to moan about the cost implications. As soon as I have the results I'll ring you, whether you're at work or not.'

Will walked from the pathology lab to the main entrance of the hospital to get some fresh air. It was still warm outside and it was so good to feel the sun on his face. He pulled his phone out and rang Stu. 'Get someone to pick me up if you're busy. I'm at the main entrance.' He ended the call before he could be asked a barrage of questions. He needed to think about the man who had been with Laura – he was distinctive because of his size. Surely someone would remember him or know him. He looked around at the people coming and going to visit sick relatives and his eyes began to water. No one would be visiting Laura ever again. His hands curled into tight fists and he kicked an empty can, which skittered across the pavement and bounced off the wheel of an ambulance. An old woman in a wheelchair smoking a cigarette looked at him. 'Bad day?'

Will nodded.

'It will get better, son – it always does.'

He smiled at her and hoped she was right because it couldn't possibly get any worse.

Chapter 17

Annie turned the car into her street. She couldn't remember driving home; her mind was so busy thinking about Laura and Will and what was happening. She wondered if Will was working the case and how everyone was in the station. She felt useless and frustrated. As she parked her car on the drive she picked up her phone to ring Jake.

'I take it you've heard, then? I've been dying to ring but I knew you'd be driving home. Can you believe it?'

'No, it's so unreal – how could this have happened? How can she be dead?'

'Listen, get a quick shower and come round. Alex is cooking so you only have to bring a bottle of that pink piss you drink.'

'Thanks, Jake, but I'm not that hungry.'

'Bah, you're talking to me now. There's no need to pretend you live off lettuce leaves and bottled water. Besides, he's cooking enough to feed Barrow Raiders rugby team so it would be rude not to.'

'Thanks, see you soon.' She ended the call and went into the house to strip out of her sticky uniform and have a cool shower. Fifteen minutes later, she was pulling up outside Jake's.

He threw open the door and hugged her. 'You have no idea

how much I miss you.'

'Thanks, but it's only been three days since I was last here.'

'Well, it feels like three months to me. I keep getting shoved in the van with Sean, who talks about nothing but football and women twenty-four seven – boring.'

Annie laughed. 'See, you didn't know how good you had it. Sorry.'

She walked in and straight through to the kitchen, where Alex was cooking up a storm. She walked over and kissed him on the cheek. 'Thanks for the invite. Something smells good.'

'Lasagne and homemade garlic bread, mini jacket potatoes and salad.'

'Please, will you leave Jake and come to live with me, Alex?'

Jake walked in, pushing his phone into his pocket and looked at them. 'You never get tired of trying to steal my boyfriend, do you, tart?'

'Worth a try, Jake; it must be like being married to a top chef.'

Jake opened the freezer and took a wine glass out and a tray of ice cubes. 'See how good I am to you; I chilled you a glass so you don't have to drink warm wine.'

'You are both just perfect; that's why I love you so much.'

She passed him the wine bottle and he twisted off the cap, filling her glass then passing it to her.

'Ah, what a day,' she said. 'So, are you going to tell me what's happened then or do you want to wait until we've eaten?'

'Don't be daft; I can't wait that long.'

Jake began relaying the day's events from when the phone call came in until Will escorted the hearse up to the hospital. Annie listened, transfixed.

'So what next – do they have any idea who it could be?'

'Apparently she left the pub with a man last night, so at the moment all fingers are pointing to him. They have the PCSOs going around the taxi offices, pubs and clubs with pictures of Laura and the mystery man, which were copied from the pub's

CCTV system. It's a bit blurry, though, and he looks like every single other guy in a tight white T-shirt with a shaved head.'

'I don't understand, though. Surely he must have realised she was with her workmates and there would be at least ten people who would be able to identify him?'

'Well, the bloke is either as thick as or it wasn't him, and if it wasn't him then who the hell was it?'

Alex put the food on the table. 'Dinner is served and no talking about murder or dead bodies. Some of us don't like it and are not as gory as the rest of you.'

'Sorry, Alex, I forget you're not one of us sometimes and that you have a respectable job that doesn't bring you into contact with the dregs of society. Although now I'm working Windermere it's a lot nicer.'

'I'm not sure about the dregs of society bit; I spend enough time with you two, don't I?'

They ate. Annie, who had found her appetite, tucked in and wished that Will was here, but he would be at work until God knows when. She was going to have to stop thinking about him so much – almost everything she did, she found herself wishing he was with her. It wasn't healthy and it wasn't going to make it any better. She finished eating and went to sit in the living room with Alex.

Jake stayed in the kitchen to clear up. He took a couple of plastic food containers out of the cupboard and filled them with food, ready to drop off for Will once he'd driven Annie home. He knew his friend wouldn't have had a chance to get something to eat and he still felt bad about the fight; even though he'd been man enough to apologise, it still didn't make it right. He wanted to let Will know that he wasn't a total idiot and still cared about him.

Chapter 18

When he arrived back at the station, Will made himself busy. He phoned Sally to see if they'd had any joy tracking down the taxi that took Laura and the man away from the pub.

'Sally, have you got anything yet?'

'I was just going to point you, Will; we've visited all the taxi firms. None of them have got a pick-up from the Black Dog at half ten on their books. So they either flagged a taxi down or jumped in one that had dropped someone off. None of them can check until after tea because those drivers are on nights and won't be in until seven. I've given each taxi firm a card and told them they have to check with every driver and then ring us straight away before they go to any jobs in case there is forensic evidence in the back of the taxi.'

'Bloody hell, you're good. You can come and be a detective any day if you get fed up of being nice to everyone.'

'Cheers, Will, but I'd only show you lot up; I wouldn't want to make you look bad. We're just about to start on the gyms.'

Will chuckled to himself for the first time all day. 'Thank you; let's hope our taxi driver is on duty tonight and not gone off to Spain for a fortnight.'

He ended the call. There had to be a link between the two

victims, apart from the obvious that they were both blonde and pretty. The room was silent; even Stu was quiet. Will stood up to address them. 'I'm just wondering how you all are. Does anyone need to go home or take a break? It's fine if you do. I don't expect you all to carry on like robots. It's been a big shock and a crap day for us all.'

Not one of his team of detectives spoke but they all shook their heads in unison. They didn't want to bail out, which was good. Will wondered if they would be allowed to continue with the enquiries anyway because Laura was one of them. The big men at headquarters might decide to pass it on to Kendal or Workington CID. Will would fight all the way if they did because he didn't trust anyone else with it. He wouldn't be able to concentrate if he wasn't working on the case; at least this way they were putting in a hundred and ten per cent and it was keeping their minds busy.

He looked at the whiteboard. There was a picture of the first victim: Tracy Hale. She looked as if she was fast asleep, apart from the blue tinge to her lips. Laura's death mask photo wasn't up yet; they would get it from CSI when they'd finished entering all the evidence into the computer system. He drummed his fingers on the desk. As soon as he had the results of the gym enquiries and he'd given the taxi firms a chance to ring in, he was going home to get something to eat. He wondered if he should phone Annie. It was bound to affect her, not just because of the situation that Laura had caused but because it wasn't that long ago she had been in a life-or-death situation with a killer. The relief that she wasn't blonde made him feel a little better. Whoever was killing these women didn't go for her type; she didn't fit his victim profile – thankfully. He took out his phone and sent her a text: *Need to talk xx*. He didn't think she would answer but it was worth a try.

*

He'd had a busy day. The thrill he'd felt listening to the call as it came over the radio was indescribable. With his blues and twos on he had rushed to the scene, excited that she had been found whilst he was still on shift. He had been the second patrol to arrive and had taken a cursory look before feigning shock like the first two officers had. His plan had worked a treat. They had never expected to see one of their own like that and it had thrown them all into turmoil. He'd even managed to set foot in the church grounds so if his footprints did come back he had an excuse for being there. As the day had worn on and more officers attended, he had really struggled to contain the gloating feeling he felt inside. It was getting harder, though. They were all traumatised and united in their grief.

He wasn't sure what he was going to do now; there was no way he could kill another colleague – it would be too obvious, but the thrill would be hard to beat. This was such a small town, it seemed as if everyone knew each other and if they didn't know you they knew your relations. Well, they wouldn't know his because they were dead; the only person who would care enough to remember was the priest, who could never forget. He would never be able to forget that he killed a nine-year-old and stood by whilst her mother slit her wrists. Did he really think that it had been finished with all those years ago, just like that? Technically, the man had got away with murder, and Sean would make sure he paid the price, one way or the other. Wait until the priest came home and found the surprise waiting for him in the bedroom. It had been a stroke of pure luck that the man was the priest's nephew and was staying with him. Sean hoped it wouldn't be for a few days, when the corpse in the bed would be bloated and rotting. Then he would hopefully get to relive today all over again.

When he'd been released from the crime scene by the DI, he'd gone back to the station to finish his shift, fill out his notebook and put his radio and gas away. There was a hush over the station; everyone seemed to be talking in whispers. He was trying to think of an excuse to go into the CID office, just to look at the shock that would be etched onto their faces, but he didn't have a justifiable reason. He didn't normally go in so he didn't want to arouse their suspicions; instead, he sat down at the computer terminal in the parade room and began to load the call logs. If he ever got the chance he would print it off and take it home to put on his noticeboard – a bit of bedtime reading whenever he was bored. For now, he would have to settle for reading it on the screen and basking in the glory.

June 29th 1984
13.00

John finished his telephone conversation with Father Robert and placed the receiver back on the cradle, then buried his head in his hands. He had no idea if he could do this, but he knew that he had to for Sophie's sake. His childhood fear was still there, lodged at the back of his brain like a splinter he couldn't quite reach to dig out and ease the pain. The memories of his life as a twelve-year-old boy before the shadow man consumed him were fuzzy, as if the shadow had emptied his mind of all the happy times – sucked it dry. The memories after were so awful he had to work hard to make his brain push them to some far, dark corner where the now-faded images were just out of reach.

It had been his mother's friend who had intervened back then and literally saved his soul and his life. She was a psychic, and on her last visit she had told his mum that the house had turned into a portal that led straight to hell. His mother, who truly didn't believe in God or the devil, had laughed and told her she was barking mad. It was the fear on her son's face and the fact that he looked so desperate that had been enough for her to let her friend do something to help him. He just wished he could remember what it was; maybe his belief in the power of God and the strength of his belief would be enough. After all, he wasn't a scared thirteen-year-old boy now; he was an adult who had given up everything to serve God. A voice echoed in his head: *No, you're not a scared schoolboy – you're a scared priest.*

He needed to perform a blessing on the house; that much was clear. He wouldn't take Sophie or Sean with him but he would have to ask Beth to come in case anything happened to him that he couldn't control; she could run for help. He pushed himself up from his chair. He was so weary that the slightest task seemed like a huge effort. He felt like a man in his sixties. He left the room to go and find Beth and followed the laughter that came from the direction of the kitchen. Opening the door, he saw Beth and her two children sitting around the table, the battered Snakes and Ladders board game spread out in front of them. Sean was giggling because he had sent Sophie to the bottom of the biggest snake on the board and she was sulking. Beth glanced at John and stopped smiling.

'Can I speak with you in private, Beth?'

She stood up and followed him out into the hall, the kids continuing to play without her.

'I'm going to go in and bless the house from top to bottom but I can't do it on my own. I'll need you to help in case something goes wrong.'

Beth stared at him, her eyes opened so wide he hadn't realised that eyelids could stretch so far.

'Of course I'll help, but do you think it's a good idea? I mean, what is that going to do? Will it make it leave Sophie alone?'

John dithered. Should he tell her a white lie or be truthful? He settled on the truth. 'I honestly don't know. I hope to God that it does, but I can't say. I don't know what else to do but it has to be better than doing nothing.'

'When are you thinking of doing it? I want to be ready; you know, try and build myself up to going back in. I'm terrified.'

129

He lifted his wrist to look at his watch. 'In half an hour. I'm going to the church for some holy water and to ask God for his help. Mrs Brown will watch the children. I want to do it while we still have plenty of daylight because I have no idea how long it will take.'

'Thank you, John. I appreciate everything that you're doing.' She stepped forward and wrapped her arms around him, hugging him tightly. John paused, unsure what he should do, but then he hugged her back – briefly. He pulled away first, his cheeks flushed pink, and Beth let out a giggle.

'It was just a hug; everyone needs a hug now and again. Even servants of God.' She winked at him and then turned to go back into the kitchen to play with her children until it was time.

Father John left the presbytery and walked across the freshly mowed lawn to the church, the scent of cut grass tickling his nose. He kept asking himself: would he give up God for the woman who had stolen his heart, and for her children? He should have told himself no, a short, sharp no. Instead, somewhere inside his head was a niggling thought that perhaps he could, that he might like to live a normal life, have a family and be loved.

He reached the church doors and went inside, where immediately an invisible cloud of guilt settled over his shoulders, weighing him down. He made his way to the altar and knelt down, apologising to God for his impure thoughts and asking for his help and forgiveness. Asking him for the strength to do what he had to do to get rid of the shadow man. When he finished he pulled the empty bottle from his pocket and walked over to the font. After blessing the water, he then submerged the plastic bottle, holding it down until the air subsided and it was full. He screwed on the cap and wiped it on the side of his trousers to dry it, then he walked to the altar and picked up the official aspergillum and filled the silver ball with more holy water; it didn't hold enough to bless the whole of Beth's house – that was why he needed the plastic bottle. He wasn't going to chance running out halfway through, leaving half of the house unblessed, because he had a feeling this was going to be one mean fight and the shadow man would object strongly. He was going to be prepared at all costs. He picked up the gold crucifix from the altar. It was heavy but it felt good in his hand. A true weapon of God, and if all else failed he could throw it and run.

When he got back to the presbytery, Beth and her children were still in the kitchen and had been joined by Mrs Brown, who was there with her sleeves pushed up to her elbows and flour spread all over the worktop. Sophie and Sean were both standing on chairs, one either side of her. They both had flour dust on their nose and all over their hands. They were engrossed in what they were doing and for that John was thankful. Beth looked at him and nodded. She walked across and kissed both her children on the tops of their heads. Then she followed him into the hall, gently closing the door behind her.

'Are you ready, Beth?'

'Not really . . . how can I be ready to go and bless my house against a shadow that shouldn't ever exist? I thought this kind of stuff was all made up to sell films and books.'

'I wish it was, Beth, I truly do.' He had to fight the urge to hold her again; he needed to start acting like a priest so instead he patted her on the shoulder. 'Come on, let's get it over with and then we can come home and eat some of Mrs Brown's delicious apple pie, smothered in fresh cream, and pretend that we are normal people.'

He walked out of the front door and she followed, closing it behind her. Neither of them wanted Sophie or Sean to follow them; they had both seen quite enough already. The sun was dazzling and it was hot enough to be sitting outside in the garden, sunbathing. John wished that was what he was about to do; it seemed such a tempting thought to do just that and forget about all it for a while. They reached Beth's house and a black shadow descended over them. The air cooled immensely and both of them looked up to see a huge black cloud in the sky, obscuring the sun and taking away its light and warmth. Beth gulped and looked up and down the street to see if there was anyone around. It was deserted.

John placed his hand on the metal gate to push it open but he snatched it back. 'It's freezing cold. How can it be so cold when the sun has been baking it for the last hour?'

Reaching out again, this time he pushed it open. Beth glanced at his white face and the blood drained from hers. He sprinkled some holy water onto the gate and stepped towards the front door, holding his hand out towards her for the key. She placed it on the palm of his shaking hand. He was terrified, longing to say: *Let's forget the whole thing and go back.* Instead, John continued walking until he was near enough to reach out and insert the key into the lock. It turned and the door swung inwards. Both of them gagged at the stench that was released into the air. It was just as Sophie had described; the house had gone bad and it was rotting from the inside. He stepped inside, closely followed by Beth. He breathed out and watched his breath fog up in front of him.

'In the name of the Father and of the Son and of the Holy Spirit.'

He crossed himself and Beth copied. A rumble underneath their feet made her let out a small shriek. She reached out and grabbed a handful of his robes. He had the cross from the church tucked underneath one arm and he thrust it towards her. 'Here, you hold on to this.' He sprinkled holy water onto the front door and the paint began to bubble and steam as if he had just sprayed it with acid, then he stepped inside the house. Beth followed, holding her hand up to her nose. John went through each downstairs room sprinkling his holy water and saying his blessing; the last one he blessed was the living room and when he stepped out back into the hall the air felt cleaner. The smell had faded and wasn't as eye-wateringly bad; it still lingered but it wasn't making their stomachs clench like before.

Beth grinned at him. 'It's working. Can't you feel how much better it is? And that smell isn't as bad.' She threw her arms around him from behind, hugging him tightly and completely breaking his concentration. Until that point he had been so focused on bringing in the power of good to fight the evil that it had been working. He had forgotten about his dilemma, about his feelings for Beth and how torn he was over his love of God.

He turned to look at her and a low voice laughed into his ear, and he felt every hair on the back of his neck stand on end. Pulling away from her, he began to climb the stairs. 'We're not finished yet, not by a long way.'

Beth followed behind him.

John struggled to climb each stair; his feet were so heavy that he had to drag them. As he neared the top he couldn't go any further. Two invisible hands placed themselves onto his chest and they were pushing him back down. He leant forward, turning to the side slightly, and pushed forward. His teeth began to chatter and he shivered, but he kept on pushing against them. The smell was worse than ever up here and he heard Beth groan behind him. He lifted the aspergillum, sprinkling water in front of him, and began praying. There was a loud hiss and the pressure lifted from his chest. He carried on. It was dark up here, even though the sun should have been shining through the windows. A blanket of darkness covered the entire place.

'I'm scared,' Beth whispered from behind.

John nodded his agreement, not daring to speak it aloud. He went into the first bedroom, which was Sean's, continuing with his blessing. As he sprinkled the water around, rays of sunshine began to filter through the window into the darkness, chasing the shadows away. Beth let out a small whoop of delight. John made his way out of the door and walked past Sophie's room – he would save that one until last. He knew that the thing was in there, waiting for him to go in and meet him face to face once more. If he blessed the rest of the house, filling it with God's light, he might just stand a fighting chance.

Beth's room was full of shadows and he saw movement in the thick black fog that filled the room. He walked in and carried on with his blessing, throwing holy water in the direction of whatever it was that was squirming in the corner. A low growl echoed around the room and terror filled John's mind as he imagined some huge demonic beast in the corner, waiting to pounce and rip his head from his shoulders. He made the sign of the cross and threw more water in its direction and it was gone. Sunlight began to pierce the darkness in here as well.

Two more rooms to go – the bathroom and Sophie's. As he led the way towards the bathroom he could hear someone splashing in the bath. A vision of Beth, naked and lying in a tub full of bright red water, filled his mind. Her eyes dull, glassy, dead. He didn't want to look past her beautiful face to see the gentle swell of her breasts but he did; he couldn't stop himself. 'Look hard, priest, because that is as near to the real thing as you will ever get,' a voice shouted down his ear. 'Unless you give me the girl. Let me have her and then you can have whatever your heart desires.' This time an image of Beth alive, standing naked in front of the bath, flashed before his eyes, her arms wide open, inviting him towards her.

John roared, 'Get your filth out of my mind, Demon.' Beth jumped backwards and he began praying harder than ever. Throwing water at the door, he stepped forward and threw it open, expecting the shadow man to be inside, waiting for him, but he wasn't – it was empty. The bath was also empty and he felt relief, although he had known it would be because Beth was standing right behind him. He turned to look at her but she wasn't there and he felt the skin on his arms begin to prickle with cold, hard fear. He knew this had all been too easy. *Fuck.*

He went back out. Sophie's bedroom door was ajar; it had been closed minutes ago when they'd passed. He stepped forward and kicked something hard. He looked down to see the cross he had given to Beth lying on its side. Stooping down to pick it up, he continued towards the door. Before he could push it open the smell overwhelmed him and he baulked. It was concentrated evil; if he had to say he knew what evil smelled like it would be this. He took the plastic bottle from his trouser pocket and unscrewed the cap, no time to mess around sprinkling tiny amounts; he might have to douse the bastard from head to foot in one go. John had never felt so terrified in his life. He made the sign of the cross and sprinkled the water onto the door into the same shape. There was a loud hiss as steam rose from the wood and the outline of the cross burnt itself into it.

He kicked the door open and then stepped inside. It was dark but he could make out Beth; she was cowering in one corner, her eyes fixed on the opposite corner. He rushed towards her and placed his hand onto her head; sprinkling water over her, he began to pray. She shook his hand from her head and let out a high-pitched screech. John spun around to see the shadow man who had haunted his dreams standing in front of him and he almost lost control of his bladder.

He stared in horror at the dark figure. Its body was formed from a black mass that was almost fluid. It rippled and rolled slightly as if it couldn't stay still, and it was much taller than him, almost seven foot, but the thing that scared him to the very core was its piercing red eyes. They were so bright he could feel them staring right through into the depths of his soul. He was frozen to the floor; he knew that he should be throwing his bottle of holy water straight into its face but there was something so horrifyingly hypnotic about it that he couldn't do anything but stare into its eyes, and it stared right back.

Beth let out a whimper, which broke his trance. John shuddered at the overwhelming stench that emanated from the thing and then he remembered what he had to do. He jerked back the hand that was gripping the bottle and watched in slow motion as the liquid travelled towards the thing. Then he lifted the heavy cross and began shouting his prayers to his God. The shadow opened its mouth, exposing a row of razor-sharp pointed teeth. The water hit its target, going straight into the gaping mouth and its eyes. The noise that came from it was deafening but the shadow began to disintegrate in front of his eyes. It started to fold into itself and then it disappeared.

Beth was on her knees, clinging onto John's legs; her whole body was trembling. John sniffed the air. The room felt clean and the sun's rays began to filter through, piercing the darkness, turning it from a black hole and back into a little girl's bedroom once more. John crossed himself then turned and made the sign of the cross on Beth's forehead, holding out his hand, which she clasped, and he pulled her to her feet. 'I think it's over. Come on, let's leave God to reclaim his house and fill it with light; we need to check on the children.'

She nodded and followed him as he led the way back to the stairs. He didn't look around; he wanted to get out of there to make sure that Sophie and Sean were OK. Beth ran down the stairs behind him. He pulled open the front door and they both stepped out into the brilliant sunshine. Neither of them looked behind and saw the two red eyes watching them from the gap in the attic trapdoor.

18.00

Sophie and Sean finished their tea and asked if they could go and play upstairs. Beth, who had almost recovered from the afternoon, nodded. 'If it's OK with Father John then you can, but go and ask him first. He might be tired and not want to listen to your racket.'

They ran off to find him. He had been in the church ever since they'd returned and discovered the children were fine. Sophie had heard him come back to the presbytery a short time ago and he'd gone into the office to make a phone call. He'd been speaking in hushed tones on the telephone to someone but it was all quiet now. Sophie knocked on the door.

'Come in.'

She opened the door and peered at the priest, who now had a thick white streak of silver running through the front of his normally dark hair. She stepped inside. Sean, who was bored of waiting, ran off upstairs to go and get his action figures from his room.

'What happened to your hair?'

Father John shook his hair. 'Nothing – what makes you say that?'

'Part of it has turned white.'

He stood up and walked past her to go into the hall and take a look in the mirror that hung on the wall above the sideboard. He lifted his hand and ran his fingers through his fringe. He didn't look too long at his face because he felt as if he had aged by at least twenty years and he wouldn't know what to do if his face looked exactly how he felt. 'I don't know, Sophie; I guess God thought I needed a different hairstyle.'

She giggled. 'Well, I hope he doesn't decide that I need a new one. I like my hair how it is.'

He winked at her. 'How do you feel now, Sophie? Do you think he's gone?'

She paused for a moment. 'I feel better. But I also feel the way I do when I'm watching television and I know something is going to happen but I don't know what.'

'I feel exactly the same. I think I managed to make him go away; he disappeared before my very eyes.' He wanted to tell her that everything would be wonderful now but he couldn't say the words because, in his heart, he didn't quite believe them. The images of Beth in the bathroom had had a profound effect on him, leaving him feeling unsettled. The shadow man had known all about his internal conflict and John was worried that it had left him open to something. When he'd walked back to the presbytery from the church he could have sworn he'd got a whiff of him but it had gone as quickly as it had arrived and he couldn't be sure.

Sophie walked over to him and stretched her small arms around him, hugging him tight. 'Thank you, Father John, you have tried to help me and I'm very glad that you did. I'll always be grateful that you cared that much.' She let go and turned and ran out of the room to go and find her brother to play with.

John felt a big, tear roll from his eye and down his cheek. It felt as if she had just said goodbye to him. Why were kids so accepting of everything? Well, he wouldn't ever let the shadow man hurt a hair on Sophie's head. He had refilled his bottle from the font just in case he needed it. He looked up to the ceiling: *Please, God, let this all be over. I beg of you, let that family be OK.*

John knew he needed to face Beth. He had been hiding from her for the last couple of hours but he didn't want to talk about the images he'd seen in the house or about what might happen next. He didn't need to go looking because Beth came and knocked on the door. He could hear the children running around upstairs, their laughter echoing throughout the house, and it made him smile.

She walked in. 'I don't know how to thank you, John; I know it must have been so hard for you.'

'You don't need to thank me, Beth; I would have done the same for anyone.'

She walked over and perched on the corner of the desk, directly in front of him. 'Your poor hair has gone white.' She lifted her hand to touch it and he felt as if an electric current had just passed through his body. Just being in such close proximity to her made him feel alive, truly alive. She moved closer until her face was inches away from his. He tried to contain himself and told himself to pull away. Instead, he groaned and reached out for her. He pulled her down onto his lap. She leant forward and kissed him so hard that it took his breath away. He had never felt this way before about any woman; he wanted her more than anything. She began to unbutton his shirt, the whole time kissing him, her tongue darting inside his mouth. He reached up and began to unbutton her blouse; the sight of the black lacy bra she was wearing was almost too much for him to bear and he buried his head into her cleavage.

An almighty scream and a deafening thud made John's blood run cold. Beth jumped off him and ran for the stairs. 'Sophie, Sophie, what's the matter?' John ran after her, taking the stairs two at a time, overtaking Beth. Sean was standing at the top, his face ashen and his eyes staring at something that they couldn't see. They were locked with fear and then he turned and ran for his room, slamming the door shut behind him.

'Sophie.' Beth ran towards her daughter's room and the stench hit her. She screamed in frustration. John passed her and threw the door open. His eyes watered. The smell was so bad, but it was nothing compared to the figure that towered over Sophie, pinning her to the bed. It turned to stare at him. 'I told you to give her up, priest. You are a disgrace to the God that you serve. Where was your God when you had your tongue down her throat?' It lifted a finger and pointed towards Beth. The thing's eyes were much redder than before and Beth ran towards her daughter. John followed, rushing towards the shadow. Sophie opened her mouth to scream and the shadow began collapsing inwards, making itself so small that it hovered above her head. John swiped his hand towards it but it disappeared into Sophie's open mouth and down into her throat. Sophie began to convulse; her eyes rolled to the back of her head until only the whites were visible and she began foaming at the mouth.

'Hold her arms now; we need to bless her. Has she been christened?'

Sophie was flailing her arms all over and, as Beth tried to grab one, she shook her head. Sophie was trying to claw at John's face. For a little girl, she had the strength of three grown men and

Beth had to fight with her to pin her arms down. John pulled out some rosary beads from his pocket and placed them onto Sophie's forehead. Her skin began to sizzle and burn where the cross touched and Beth began screaming at him to stop it. John withdrew his shaking hand. He wanted to throw up, shut his eyes, faint, die. He wanted to be anywhere other than here. He carried on praying and Sophie began to choke.

'Please . . . you have to do something to help her . . . it's killing her.'

John didn't know what to do; he needed divine intervention and he needed it now. Then the little girl, who had turned grey, began to choke even more. They tried to sit her up, one on either side, grabbing her arms, but it was impossible. She was a dead weight and it felt as if her body had been glued to the bed. She made a strangled sound and, just like that, her heart stopped beating, the choking stopped and the room was silent. Beth threw herself onto her daughter and began to sob uncontrollably. John felt gravity finally claim his legs and he stumbled backwards, falling to the floor. He kept tight hold of the rosary beads. 'We need to phone an ambulance, Beth.'

He pulled himself up on shaking legs and made his way to the landing. The phone was in the office and he began to run down the stairs on unsteady legs. He didn't care if he fell and broke his neck. His life had just ended along with Sophie's; there was nothing left to live for. His God had deserted him in his hour of need and he had failed Beth and her children, all because he had doubted his faith and fallen in love.

Chapter 19

2014

Annie had started yawning ten minutes ago and couldn't stop. 'Sorry, guys, I'm worn out and need my bed.'

Jake went to get his car keys. 'Come on, you hardcore party girl, I'll drop you off and then I'm going to take a food parcel to our friend Will. He's going to be in a bit of a state and I bet he hasn't eaten all day.'

Annie smiled at Jake. 'You're an amazing friend, Jake; that's really sweet of you.' She wondered if she should offer to run into the station with it but the office would be full and it might be a bit awkward. She felt her phone vibrate and read the text from Will – what was she going to do? She didn't know what to say so she didn't reply. She had put up with so much crap from Mike while they were married; there was no way she was stepping straight into another doomed relationship. The thing was, she knew that Will hadn't done anything wrong except get drunk and let Laura go home with him so he could snore down her ear all night. The fact was it hurt deep inside her chest, like a physical pain that she couldn't describe, but it was there. She wanted to stay friends with him but it would have to be just that, unless he proved himself otherwise. She also knew that he was going to be so busy now that he wouldn't have time for his own life, never mind her.

They drove to her house in comfortable silence. When Jake stopped outside her gate she leant over and kissed him on the cheek. ''Night, Jake, and thank you.'

''Night, Annie. Do you want me to come in and check the house?'

She laughed. 'No, thank you, I'm a big girl. I think I can manage. Anyway, who would be mad enough to break into my house?'

Jake didn't reply, just smiled, and she had to stop herself from thinking about last year, when a man had got into her brother's house when she was looking after it. A man who had wanted to kill her. She shook herself and lifted a hand to wave at Jake and turned to walk along the path to the front door. Jake didn't drive away until she got her key out and let herself in, locking the door behind her. He still didn't drive away until the hall light, then the living room light came on. Satisfied that she would have been out on the front street screaming by now if anything was amiss, he drove down the street, making his way to the police station to see Will.

Her house was cool and it was a welcome relief after today; her forehead and chest were still burning. Annie checked the downstairs was secure then kicked off her flip-flops and made her way upstairs. As she got near to the top stair she got a whiff of rotten vegetables and wondered if next door had burnt their tea. It smelled like school dinners, back in the day when she was nine years old and life was such a breeze.

She went into the bathroom and began cleaning her teeth, splashing cold water onto her face. She looked into the mirror above the sink and froze; there was someone standing behind her. She whipped around to face them but no one was there. Her heart was racing. She'd definitely seen the figure of a man.

Picking up the heavy glass tumbler from the shelf, she felt the roof of her mouth dry up as she edged closer to the shower curtain. *Please don't let there be some freak standing behind it.* Her left hand shaking, she tentatively reached out and grasped the plastic, whipping the curtain aside and screeching as she did so with part fear and part relief – there was no one on the other side. That horrible smell seemed stronger in here. With legs that felt like jelly, she made her way out of the bathroom. The door to the master bedroom was ajar and she couldn't remember whether she had left it that way or not. She should ring Jake and ask him to come back, but then she knew it was probably her imagination playing tricks on her so she carried on.

Too scared to step into the room in the dark, she reached her hand and arm through the gap, feeling along the wall for the light switch. *Please don't let anything grab my arm.* A vision of Pennywise the clown from her favourite horror story when she was a teenager filled her mind, ripping poor Georgie Denbrough's arm right out of its socket with its sharp pointed teeth. She found the switch and the room was bathed in light. She pushed open the door and stepped inside. It was empty but the smell was strong in here. It was so strong that she lifted her hand to cover her mouth and nose. She walked further in, across to the window to open it a crack and let some fresh air in. It smelled as if something had been left to rot in here but she hadn't used this room since she'd come back.

Although she was afraid to bend down and look under the bed, she forced herself to do it. The only things under there were the plastic storage boxes that were filled with the books that wouldn't fit onto her bookshelves. Feeling braver now, she walked to the wardrobe and flung open the doors – no smelly man hiding inside. Looking into the mirror, she thought she saw a dark shadow flit across it and she turned to the space behind her where it would have been. The room was empty – a trick of the light, perhaps.

Satisfied there was no one there, she turned off the light and shut the door until the latch clicked shut. Annie then opened the small cupboard where she kept her bedding and towels. That was OK so it just left the other bedroom. Her legs were not shaking quite so much but she did the same and stretched her arm through to switch on the light. Once the room was lit up, she stepped inside. It was empty and this room was so small there was nowhere for anyone to hide. The bed was a divan with drawers underneath it. There was an antique church pew that was currently an antique clothes horse and an old dressing table she had painted a chalky white colour, with a stack of magazines and books on it. Nothing was out of place and she was thankful the smell was only very faint in here because she was knackered and wanted to go to sleep.

She went back into the bathroom to get the air freshener and began spraying it around, hoping to mask the smell. Just to be on the safe side, she ran back downstairs to check that she'd locked up and then she checked each room again. The house was empty and she was all alone. At least she hoped she was because something that smelled so bad couldn't be a good thing, could it?

Once upstairs, she got undressed into her favourite pair of faded pyjamas and then climbed into bed, leaving the nightlight on. She picked up her book and began to read about the sordid life of a celebrity escort. No longer able to read anything remotely scary before bed, she would read a couple of pages of some biography or other to keep her mind free from the horrific images that all too often wanted to take over.

*

Will was sitting at his desk. The office was empty. He had told his detectives to call it a night and he would see them bright and early to continue their hunt for Laura's killer. How had this happened? He didn't understand it. They had all been together two nights ago in the pub. They needed to find that guy she'd left with because it was a pretty good bet he had been the one to kill her, but would he have killed her if he knew she was a copper? Surrounded by twelve other coppers? Will wasn't sure if anyone could be so stupid. Guilt gnawed at his insides and he felt sick; his body was fuelled by nothing more than caffeine and it was making him feel ill. He lifted his hand, which was shaking like an alcoholic's. He needed food to take away the wired, nauseous feeling in his stomach but he didn't know what to eat. *What a bloody mess; how could one man fuck up his life to such a degree in the space of a couple of weeks?*

He glanced up at the whiteboard with a picture of Laura's face looking back at him. Her lips were smiling, but her eyes were staring at him, accusing him, and he looked away. He had let her down, just like he had let Annie down. He felt his eyes sting with tears. The door opened and he blinked several times to clear them – he couldn't let anyone see what a mess he was; it wasn't exactly professional. Jake strode through the door and Will breathed out in relief. Jake wouldn't care if Will threw himself on the floor and howled, although Jake *would* tell the whole station about it.

'I come bearing gifts.'

Will looked at the plastic containers. 'Please tell me that's home-cooked food – I'm starving.'

Jake passed them over. 'Alex's lasagne made from scratch, a box of salad and jacket potatoes. I'm running a feed-the-fucked-up-couples kitchen. Annie came for tea.'

'Thanks, Jake – how is she, does she know?'

'She seemed OK – shocked, but everyone is. She managed to eat a full plate of tea and drink three glasses of wine so that's her fed, watered and hopefully tucked up in bed for the night. What's up, Will? You look like crap.'

Will screwed his eyes up. 'You really need to ask, or are you just being polite in case I have toothache or a migraine? And, by the way, I do have a migraine.'

'Look, we all know you're a total fuck-up; there's not much

145

point in beating yourself up about it. You're just going to have to get a grip and move on. I can't be bothered with you feeling sorry for yourself and all that.'

Will felt his mouth drop; he couldn't help it. Jake had a way of rendering just about everybody speechless.

'Let's face it, you had your chance with Annie and screwed it up by getting leathered and sleeping with Laura, who is now dead and in a fridge in the morgue. You're losing your touch, Casanova.'

'Why don't you piss off, Jake?'

'Because I've come to cheer you up, my friend. You know, I never thought I'd hear myself say this, but you and Annie make such a good couple. You are both so right for each other and I don't like seeing the pair of you like this, hurting and lonely.'

'Me neither. I feel as if my heart has been ripped from my chest. Last year I didn't think I would ever feel this way about a woman. I used to look at my dad and Lily and wonder if I would ever be that happy. Now I realise more than ever that Annie is the one for me. I just wish I knew how to make it up to her.'

'Space and time, mate. She's missing you just as much but you have to understand where she's coming from. She was in a terrible relationship and then she left that one and started a new one with you – someone who has the worst track record for relationships out of all the men in the station. She's bound to be a bit edgy and pissed off with you.'

'I know that – thanks for reminding me. I just hope she realises that I could never find a woman to take her place.'

Jake slapped his back. 'No, I totally agree with you there; you won't ever find someone like Annie and her amazing gift of seeing dead people.'

Jake turned to leave and Will followed him. He needed to go home and shower then eat and hopefully go to bed and fall into a coma for the next six hours.

*

146

Annie tossed and turned in her sleep; it wasn't a restful slumber by any means. She could hear a little girl's voice calling to her and she kept pushing it to the back of her mind. It sounded as if it was coming from the mirror. She mumbled, 'No, go away.' Several times in her dream she was in her old bedroom that she shared with Mike. The oval antique mirror she'd had since they'd got married was in the corner. It looked as if a bright light was shining from inside it but she knew this was impossible because the bedroom light wasn't on.

The girl's voice came from inside the glass. 'Please help me, Annie. You have to. He won't let me go and I know Sean is killing those poor women. He used to be a good boy. I need you to help me make him stop and then you must set me free. I don't want to live with the shadow man anymore. I want to be free and go into the light to see my mum.'

A high-pitched shriek made Annie wake from her sleep and sit bolt upright. Something was wrong. She swung her legs out of the bed and picked up the first thing she put her hand on, which was her Kindle. *Nice, Annie, are you going to read the nasty man a story?* The smell was back and it was so strong that it made her gag. Lifting a hand to her nose and mouth, she covered them as best as she could and pushed open her bedroom door. She was terrified but had no choice; she had to look into the mirror. As her fingers touched the switch she stared in the general direction of the corner of the room where the mirror stood and felt her knees threaten to give way. There was no bright light but she saw two red pricks of light, either reflected in the glass or inside the glass, glowing red. Two eyes and then they were gone.

She flicked the switch and the light burst into life. The room was empty – no kid, no smelly man and no animal with glowing red eyes. There was just her and that awful smell. She wondered if an animal had got trapped in here while the house had been empty and was decomposing somewhere. Eugh, she needed a man to poke around under the floorboards and behind the wardrobes just in case. Tomorrow she would be extra nice to Jake and see if he would come and take a look for her. As tough as she was, she didn't want to find half a rotting pigeon in her house. Seeing dead people she could handle as long as they weren't too scary, but dead animals freaked her out.

She pushed the two red eyes to the back of her mind or else she'd never sleep in her own house ever again. She went into her bedroom and closed the door. As she climbed back into bed she said a prayer because it made her feel better, but she knew that, whoever the kid was, she needed help and she had better find a way to help her because she was beginning to scare her. The poor little thing wanted to be with her mum – she wondered how long she had been dead. Her clothes weren't that old-fashioned but then Annie wasn't very hot on kids' fashion. She remembered the plastic toy she'd thrown into the drawer that the girl had left the very first time. If she could find out who it was or what film it was based on, that would be a start.

*

Will walked into his empty house; he didn't like it. He had got so used to Annie being here it was strange now that she wasn't. He locked the front door and took his plastic boxes into the kitchen, where he set about emptying them onto a plate, except for the salad, and put the plate in the microwave. Running upstairs, he stripped off and then went into the bathroom, where he had the quickest shower ever, three minutes, and he was towelling himself dry and slipping on a pair of clean boxers. It was almost eleven and he was only just eating his tea. He took the plate from the microwave and sat down at the table to eat. Alex was an excellent cook. He cleaned his plate, mopping up the last of the sauce with a slice of thick bread and even thicker butter. Then he got a bottle of water from the fridge and went upstairs to bed. He put his iPod on, managing to switch playlists before Adele had a chance to rub his nose in it once more.

Throwing himself onto the bed, he thought about Laura again and then he thought about Annie. He wondered if she would be able to do her thing and speak to Laura, like the other dead people she had spoken to. Imagine if Laura could somehow communicate with her; it would be amazing. She could even tell Annie what had happened and save months of investigation. Then he realised that Annie would probably be the last person she would speak to if that sort of thing was even possible and he couldn't exactly go around and ask her to try and contact the dead spirit of the woman who had split them up. Annie would probably punch him in the balls for even thinking about it, but it happened in that film *Ghost* with Whoopi Goldberg.

That was a film, you moron. This is real life. Still, it might be worth asking Jake to ask her because they both knew that Jake was that crass he would and she wouldn't think anything of it, coming from him.

Chapter 20

Father John couldn't settle; he didn't like being this far from his own church. He knew it was a part of his job to cover whatever parish was in need, and over the years he had moved more times than he cared to remember, but he felt as if he should be there. Especially with the discovery of another woman's body in his church grounds. Was there some connection to him or was it just a coincidence and whoever was killing them either liked or hated Catholic churches? He had a week-long course of special Mass, three funerals and the wedding of a prominent business-man's daughter to perform so he couldn't go home yet, even if he wanted to.

He would phone his nephew Ryan later to see if the police had told him anything about what was going on. He was surprised that Ryan hadn't already phoned to tell him about the body, but then again he might not even know about it. Ryan lived the life a younger John could only dream about, often staying at some girl or other's house, sometimes not coming home for days. It did leave him a little envious but he could cope with that; he was past it now anyway, or so he liked to convince himself. The only woman he'd ever really loved had been Beth and she had shaken his faith to his very core; on more than one occasion he had asked

God if he had purposely taken her away from him. He was still waiting for his answer, which he didn't think he would get any time soon, but as the years had gone on he had learnt to forgive and forget. He had never looked at another woman again with a hint of passion for fear of God striking them down; he couldn't live with any more deaths on his conscience.

He lay in bed and thought about that fateful day back in 1984. He had been young, so naïve, but all he'd wanted had been to help. Not to cause any distress. Sophie had been such a beautiful child and he had failed to save her from the shadow man. John shuddered. The thought of that shadowy figure filled him with dread. To this day he couldn't stand the smell of cooked cauliflower. If the thing ever came back, next time John would banish it for good; he would seek help from Father Rob and together they would send it back to wherever it had come from.

A loud bang as the wooden crucifix that was above his head fell to the floor and made him jump out of bed. It had narrowly missed his head. How on earth had that happened? His heart began to pound in his ears as he bent down to pick it up. He turned it over in his hands. It wasn't broken so he hung it back on the nail and waited to see if it would happen again. He began to repeat his prayers and watched the cross but nothing happened. He sighed and got back into bed; something was going on and he was too afraid to find out what.

*

He had gone home from work and run himself a bath; he had stayed in it for almost an hour, topping up the hot water whenever it started to get cold. Today had been better than he could have imagined and he replayed every single minute of it over in his mind. He needed to pick his next victim; there was no point hanging around. He wanted to do it while they were knee-deep trying to solve the first two murders and not give them any

151

breathing space. It was turning into a game and he was beginning to think that he could win if kept his cool and followed the ground rules that he'd set. All day he'd tried to come up with a plausible excuse to go into the CID office and failed. Tomorrow he would offer to help out with the house-to-house enquiries, tell them he wanted to help in some way. They never said no to anyone else helping them out and they were in shock so they wouldn't think anything of it. When he'd towel-dried himself he wandered naked into his office and picked up his most recent photos of Laura. He studied her for a long time; she had been beautiful and still looked beautiful, even in death. He pinned them onto her noticeboard; he was very proud of what he had managed to achieve and now it was time to put Operation Anael into action.

He turned to the third noticeboard, which was empty, but in the next few days it would fill up to match the other two. He already had a girl in his sights. When he had been watching Laura he couldn't help but notice the girl who worked in the hairdressers below her flat and he had a bit of a crush on her. She looked about twenty-one and had beautiful long blonde hair. He knew it wasn't natural as he seen her sitting in the chair, her hair covered in pale blue bleach, flicking through the pages of a magazine, but he'd realised she was perfect.

Opening the wardrobe, he stared at the two outfits hanging up. He reached out to stroke the sleeve of Laura's suit jacket and a whiff of the perfume she wore was released. He inhaled – *Goodnight, ladies*. He pushed the door shut and walked to his bedroom across the hall; he was tired. The last two weeks of running a double life were hard work. Before long he was under his duvet. He didn't notice the little girl standing at the edge of his bed, her eyes moist with tears. If he had he would probably never kill again but he couldn't see her, even though she visited him often. He could see the black shadow that was never far behind, with its creepy red eyes, but he wasn't afraid of it. He knew it from a long time ago; it was the shadow that had scared

Sophie in the days before she'd died. It had spoken to him a few weeks ago and told him if he wanted to set Sophie's soul free he should do what it asked and kill the priest.

Sean had already been pondering this for a while but he had started his own plan of revenge against Father John and would not deviate from this until he was satisfied it was finished. Only then would Sean kill the priest, in one of his beloved churches, under the watchful eyes of God. He would sacrifice the priest's soul to the shadow man and set Sophie free. Laura would be a hard act to follow; there would be a media frenzy tomorrow and it would probably even go national. Sean would be famous but he wasn't in it for the glory; he was in it to make sure that priest wished he had never set eyes upon Sean's family.

Sean ran his hands over his head and chuckled. There wasn't much hair but he would go and get it cut tomorrow and make friends with his next victim. He turned on his side and smiled to himself; it was amazing when a plan came together.

Chapter 21

Annie spent her two days off work gardening, reading and doing nothing much. She had dragged the sun lounger out from the back of the shed and felt obliged to use it. The weather was gorgeous; it had been sunny and dry for a whole week now, which was a record. The hosepipe ban would be coming into force soon, even though it rained for three hundred and sixty days last year. She sprawled on the sun lounger in her shorts and strappy vest top and hoped that Jake wouldn't turn up with someone in tow wanting a cold drink and somewhere to hide for a while from the public. Her shifts had changed and she didn't work the exact same times as him anymore. She'd kept herself busy so she wouldn't think about Will but he would creep into her thoughts when she least expected it. If he came back tomorrow and begged her forgiveness she would cave in and say yes, but she wouldn't make the first move; she was far too stubborn. She wondered if he had moved on already. She didn't think he would have had the time but there would be someone at work all too ready to offer him some comfort and a bed to share. She growled and threw the book she had been reading without looking.

'Is that how you treat all your visitors?'

Horrified, she pushed her sunglasses to the top of her head to see Will standing there, holding the book she had just launched.

'Sorry, I didn't see you there or hear you come in, to be honest.'

'Oh, that's OK then. Is there a particular reason you threw it then – was there a full stop in the wrong place or something?'

She laughed. 'Just practising my throwing skills; you never know when you might need them. Anyway, what brings you here?'

'I just needed a break for a bit before I go to search Laura's flat again, see if there's anything we could have missed. Have you spoken to Grace lately?'

'I did last week; she was very excited about her holiday. Are you going to phone her?'

He dragged one of the cast-iron garden chairs over and sat down next to her. Annie began fiddling with her vest top and wondered why she hadn't brought a T-shirt out with her in case of emergencies.

'I want to. I need some help now but I feel bad about bothering her while she's away.'

'Come on, Will. You and I both know that she would kill you if you didn't. She loves it and has been desperate to prove to everyone just how good she is; she never got the chance last time.'

'Do you think I should?'

'Yes; why don't you email her copies of everything and the case reports? Is that why you came to pay me a visit? Did you want me to make you feel less guilty about interrupting her holiday?'

He paused. 'Of course not. I was passing and saw your car and just wanted to check you were OK.'

Annie mentally begged him to say that he also couldn't stand living without her and would she please have him back. 'I'm fine, thanks; I haven't really done much except pull a few weeds out and sunbathe. I'm back in work tomorrow. I don't suppose you'll get a day off until all this has calmed down a bit. Have you got any leads? Jake said that you haven't been able to trace the man Laura left the pub with. That's a bit suspicious, to say the least. Why would he not come forward if he was innocent?'

'I don't know; he's either left town or hiding from us. All the taxi offices and gyms have been checked. Someone from Body Fit Health Studio thought they recognised him but not through going to the gym, and they couldn't tell us his name or where he lived or worked. Between you and me, it's turning into a total disaster. I'm terrified that whoever it is has already got his next victim and there is nothing that I can do to stop it.'

'What about the church? There has to be some connection, don't you think? I don't understand why he would want to put a naked dead woman on a grave and make her look like she was asleep; that's some pretty serious fucked-up thinking, Will.'

'You're telling me. It's a Catholic church and the priest is a man named John Trelmain. He was in town and phoned up about the first body but he has been sent to Windermere to cover for a priest who has been taken ill so he wasn't even here when Laura was discovered. Laura and Stu both spoke to him and took his statement after the first body was found and they both said he was genuinely distressed by what had happened. In Laura's words, he was a nice man and she didn't think he had anything to do with it. I wondered if you could go and speak to him again next time you're on duty, see if he can think of any reason why St Mary's is being used as a dumping ground for dead bodies. Make it a friendly chat and ask him if he has any crazy parishioners that he's upset, if anyone has a grudge against him. See if he recognises the man from the CCTV still – it has to be worth a try.'

'Do you think he could be the killer?'

'Oh, God, no, I hope not. If I did, there is no way I would send you to speak to him. I'd never knowingly put you in any danger, Annie. He's in his sixties; I remember him from a funeral I went to last year. He came back to the wake and was really nice; he had us all laughing and a few of the older women were clearly lusting over him. I just hope his memory might be jogged and he might be able to point us in the direction of a psychopathic parishioner.'

'I'll go and see him tomorrow; as soon as I've spoken to him I'll ring you.' She stood up. 'Come in the house and I'll get you a cool drink; your polyester suit must be making you burn up from the inside out.' She winked at him and he laughed, following her into the much cooler kitchen, where she opened the fridge door and produced a jug filled with fresh fruit and juice. She filled two glasses with ice and topped them with juice.

'That's a bit posh for you; I expected you to throw me a can of Coke.'

'I do have some class, you know. Actually, I copied from a lovely woman I met at the boat club in Bowness. Her husband invited me onto the most beautiful boat I've ever seen and then she produced a jug of juice like this and it was divine and, you know, even though they were clearly loaded, they didn't act like they were. They were so nice and normal.'

'Look at you, mixing with the rich and wealthy already and you've only been there a couple of weeks. I take it you're enjoying it then, not missing the Saturday night free-for-all brawls.'

'Yes, up to now I am. It's been lovely and a lot more cultured than Barrow town on a Saturday night. I think I did the right thing.' She saw Will's cheeks flare with red streaks and felt a small sigh of relief inside her. *He feels really bad about it, Annie, so that has to be a good sign – right?*

'I'm sorry that your hand was forced; it doesn't make it any better, but if you had gone because of me and hated it I would feel even shittier than I do right now. At least that's one thing I can tick off my conscience.' He finished his drink and rinsed the glass in the sink. 'I'd best get going; I've been putting this off for far too long. Thanks, Annie, it was nice to see you again.'

He turned to leave and she felt her heart sink. *Nice to see her.* Bloody hell, was that the best he could do? In her mind she wanted him to kiss her and never stop. She followed him to the door. 'Bye, Will, be careful. I'll ring you after I've spoken to the priest.' He nodded and then turned and walked down the path, but his shoulders were slumped and he walked slowly. Annie scolded herself for being so harsh but she shut the door so she wouldn't go running after him. Why did life have to be so tough?

As she walked into the kitchen a shiver ran down her spine, making her break out in goose bumps. Annie saw the girl standing next to her sun lounger and she ran out of the door towards her. 'Wait, please, I need to talk to you. Please don't go.' The girl's image wavered in the sunlight like a mirage and then, with a ripple, she was gone. Annie no longer felt as if her body was on fire; instead, she felt as if her insides had turned to ice. She looked down on the lounger and saw the plastic figure that she'd placed in the drawer. The canvas fabric was freezing to the touch but she sat down, clutching the figure, afraid to go back inside her house in case she had any visitors who weren't from this lifetime. She should have asked Will to come back and check her bedrooms but deep down she knew that the smell wasn't from a dead bird or mouse. That smell was from something that was bad to the core, but she didn't want to think too hard about it because she still had to go into the house on her own and sleep in there.

She lay back and squeezed her eyes shut, trying not to think about the dead girl. There was one thing, though. Will could have asked anyone to go and speak to the priest; he could even have sent Stu to do it because he'd spoken to him previously, but he had used it as an excuse to come and see her and she was grateful because it now gave her a reason to keep in contact with him. Even if it was just on a professional level. It was good of him to give her the time and space to think things over but it looked as if he felt the same way that she did. Pride was such a painful thing and she wished she could forget what had happened and start over.

*

Will drove to Laura's flat with a heavy heart; it had almost killed him not begging Annie to have him back and now this. He'd avoided coming here up to now by sending Stu along with some Task Force officers to do a thorough search for any evidence. The DI was back tomorrow from his daughter's wedding; he would be expecting that Kendal CID would have taken over running the case but they were, in their own words, short-staffed and up to their necks in it. Workington were in a similar situation so he'd had a long chat with the chief superintendent about whether they would be able to run both cases without external help. In one way Will would have loved to be able to hand it all over to someone else but he wouldn't know what to do with himself. It would drive him insane trying to look for petty burglars when another team were trying to solve his murders, and they *were* his because he felt partly responsible for Laura's death. So he'd told the super that as long as he could investigate it fully and in a professional manner then he would very much like to be the lead – well, until they caught the bastard or Will cracked and had a nervous breakdown.

He found himself outside Laura's flat and parked up. There was a patrol car on the opposite side of the street. Will got out and walked up towards it. Sean was sitting inside with his head bent, writing in a notebook. He knocked on the window and Sean visibly jumped, his face white, and Will laughed as Sean put the window down. 'Bloody hell, Sean, you're supposed to be a fearless copper. I might have been an old lady wanting directions. What were you going to do, draw your taser and red-dot me?'

Sean snapped the notebook shut and put it down on the passenger seat. 'You gave me a heart attack. I was right in a world of my own then. Just making sure my book's up to date. Kav has been randomly checking them at the end of each shift. Smithy's was three days out of date and he made him stay behind to bring it up to date in his own time. Smithy was right pissed off; according to him he had a hot date he was late for.'

'I bet he was – good old Kav. I'm just checking Laura's flat to

159

make sure we didn't miss anything.'

Sean looked solemn. 'It's terrible – poor Laura. I hope you get the bastard that did it.'

Will nodded. 'Oh, I will. I promised her that I would. I don't care how long it takes; I will find him and bring him to justice.'

'Good luck. I best get off. I've got shit-loads of jobs to catch up on.'

Will turned and walked towards the small door at the side of the hairdressers. He glanced inside the shop; it was busy. A hairdresser with long curly hair looked across at him and smiled; he smiled back and walked on towards the flat door.

*

Sean was shaking so much his mind felt all fuzzy and he thought he was going to pass out. He drove a short distance away and parked up outside the Italian takeaway that didn't open until five. He was furious with himself – careless, he'd been so careless. He should have seen Will park up, not let him catch him blatantly taking notes about the hairdressers and the girls who worked there. Will hadn't acted strange and he didn't think he could possibly have seen what he was writing; he didn't look as if he'd paid that much attention. At least if he checked he would see that Sean was the area cover for the town centre, so if Will did ask Kav about him it would be OK, but it had unnerved him. He was panicking too much; he began taking deep breaths to try and get a grip. Will didn't have a clue and they were all so focused on finding the big man Laura left with they weren't even considering any other suspects. That little unexpected detail had worked out very well in his favour.

He finally began to control his shaking and the butterflies inside his stomach stopped fluttering. His radio burst into life as the control room operator passed him a job, a shoplifter at Debenhams. Good, he could focus on work and forget about everything else for a while. He told them he was practically on scene and drove around the corner to the back entrance of the shop, which was favoured by almost every shoplifter in town. A man in his early thirties came running out of the door and Sean was out of the car and grabbing hold of him before he'd even realised. The man struggled to break free from Sean's grip but then he realised how much bigger he was than him and stopped dead in his tracks and held out his wrists.

'There's a good boy, Mickey. You know it makes sense; it's far too hot to fight.'

The man, who was cuffed in seconds, rolled his eyes. 'I hate you lot. You're always skulking around. Do you not have anything better to do?'

Sean began to laugh. 'And what exactly have you been doing inside that shop for the last ten minutes?'

The security guard who had followed the man out looked at Sean. 'He's taken two bottles of aftershave, stuffed them down his shirt.'

Sean patted Mickey down and felt the two square boxes at the top of his trousers waistband. 'You can pull those out. I'm not sticking my hands down there.'

He watched him struggle to lift up his shirt with his hands cuffed; he eventually managed it and passed them to Sean. 'It's too bloody hot to be banged up today. If I go guilty, will you get me in and out?'

'I would have thought it was pretty obvious you were guilty, but yeah, you're right, it is too hot to be stuck in custody for hours and I'm not on about you. I'm thinking about me.' Sean marched him over to the patrol car and opened the back door, shoving him inside.

Chapter 22

Annie was in a deep sleep and was surprised when the alarm on her phone began vibrating. She opened her eyes and felt completely refreshed. She hadn't smelled anything bad or had any visits from the girl. She got out of bed and went to have a shower. The house felt clammy; it was going to be another warm day. There wasn't any point putting much make-up on or spending time doing her hair because within twenty minutes of being at work and wearing her uniform the make-up would have melted and her hair would be a wet, sweaty mess – nice. She loved the summer but not when working ten-hour shifts. Winter was much better for her appearance. She went down to make herself a bowl of cereal, then she made herself a packed lunch, took a bottle of cold water from the fridge and left the house, getting into her car. It was stifling inside so she pressed her finger on the button to let the roof go down. Her drive to work was through some of England's finest countryside and she never got tired of the views.

As she reached Bowness she drove slowly; it was busy. Lots of tourists and cars. She drove to the station and got out of the car. The church was her first point of call this morning, regardless of what other jobs the control room had lined up for her. As she opened the door she was greeted by the aroma of burnt toast.

She followed it to the kitchen, where there was a PCSO waving a magazine around and an officer wafting the tiny kitchen window open and shut. Annie smiled. 'You two are just about as good as I am at cooking.'

They both nodded. 'Dimwit here said that you couldn't burn toast in this toaster; he said it had a special cut-off button. Isn't that right, Eric?'

Annie looked at the basic stainless steel toaster. 'Did you dream that last night? That toaster is almost as old as me.'

Another two slices of black toast popped up and all three of them laughed. She left them to it and went to the locker room to get her kit on. She zipped up her body armour, then fastened the heavy black belt around her waist; technically, she didn't need the belt because of the new state-of-the-art stab vests but she found them heavy enough without adding a baton, handcuffs and CS gas to it. Not to mention the assortment of fine books, pens, latex gloves and first-aid kit. She was ready for any eventuality; well, almost – she had declined the taser training that some of her colleagues had been keen to do. She was naturally clumsy and didn't have the best track record when it came to safety. Jake had been convinced the only people she would actually hit with the taser would be either him or her, possibly both of them at the same time, but definitely not the target. After picking up her hat from the top shelf of her locker, she walked back down the corridor and out of the station, the smell of burnt toast following her.

The church was a short walk from the station and she hoped that the priest was in; if not, she would knock at the presbytery next door. If Annie had enough money she would like to buy an old church and renovate it into a home; there was something so peaceful about them that it might be easier to switch off from the dearly departed if you lived in a house that once belonged to God. Coach after coach of Japanese tourists drove past, their heads bobbing and hands frantically waving. She waved back and grinned. Kav would bloody hate it up here because he wasn't much of a people person. Annie, on the other hand, liked it; in fact, she was beginning to love it.

She reached the old wooden gates to the churchyard and walked through, along the path to the church, and tried the door handle. It was locked. She walked around to the rear of the church just in case the priest was pottering around on such a lovely morning. There was no sign of anyone so she went back out of the gate and walked the short distance to the presbytery. It was a beautiful building and built in the same style as the church, from limestone which would have been from a local quarry. There was a lot to be said for devoting your life to God; priests got the most amazing houses to live in and call home! She opened the much smaller gate and stepped onto the path. The scent of old English roses filled the air; it was beautiful and so was the front garden. Annie stopped next to a bush filled with pale pink blooms. She lifted one of the flowers to her nose; the aroma was divine.

'You can't help but stop to have a sniff, can you? I do it every time I go in and out of the gate and I don't think I could ever tire of it.'

Annie turned to see a man with a shock of thick silver hair and crinkly blue eyes standing on the front step to the house. He was wearing a pair of three-quarter denim shorts and a faded Rolling Stones T-shirt, trainers and no socks.

'They are gorgeous. I don't suppose you know what they're called? I'd love to plant some in my garden.'

'I don't, but I think Father Simon might. He's in hospital at the moment but you could always ask him when he comes out. I'm sure he would be grateful for a visitor who didn't want to know about whose turn it is to arrange the church flowers.' He winked at her and she laughed.

'I might just do that.'

'Please forgive me; I'm stopping you from carrying out your duties. I'm sure you didn't come to discuss the roses. Do you have a more pressing matter?'

'I'm looking for Father John Trelmain. I just need to have a quick chat with him.'

'Would you advise that I tell you that I'm him or should I have told a white lie and said he wasn't in either?'

'I'd rather that you admitted to being you. It's nothing for you to worry about, but it is really important. Do you have five minutes?'

'For an officer of the law I have all morning if I'm not in any trouble. Please come inside and we can chat without the local residents paying too much attention and it's much cooler inside. These big houses are lovely and cool in the summer but a bugger to keep warm in the winter. Still, you can't have it all.'

She held out her hand to shake his. 'Annie Graham.' He took hold of it, shaking it firmly, then opened the door and walked inside. Annie followed. The hall had a beautiful original mosaic floor, and a huge oak sideboard, which was ornately carved to depict the Last Supper. Everything was pristine and immaculate but then she supposed that it would be: no kids had ever run wild in this house to cause any damage. She followed him into the kitchen, where a huge table filled the middle of the room.

He pointed to a chair. 'Would you like a drink?'

'Coffee would be lovely, thank you. I haven't had one this morning because I didn't want to be late for work.'

John laughed. 'Well, that's no good. I can't have you running around all morning with no caffeine in your veins – you might not survive. I know that I wouldn't.' He made two mugs of coffee and put some chocolate biscuits onto a plate, placing it onto the table in front of her. 'I think I can guess what this is about – I believe they found another woman's body in the churchyard three days ago.'

Annie picked up her mug. 'Thank you. Yes, and to be honest we are still at a loss as to why. I've been asked by the detective sergeant in Barrow to come and have a chat with you to see if there is anything at all you might know that could shed some light on the matter. Do you know of anyone who may hold a grudge against the church or you?'

'There are probably millions of people who hold a grudge against the church; religion is not everyone's cup of tea. But personally, to my knowledge, I can honestly swear on the holy Bible that, as far as I know, I have no enemies as such. Don't get me wrong, there may be the odd jealous Mothers' Union woman who I haven't given much attention to but these women are even older than me. As far as I know, I have no parishioners who have displayed psychotic tendencies, if that's what you're thinking. In fact, I don't have many parishioners full stop. The church is in decline and the majority of people who bother to turn up for Mass are my age or older, although there has been an influx of Thai people lately, who are the most gentle, beautiful souls that I have ever met. I would never point my finger at any one of them. I would be surprised if whoever is killing these women has ever come to a church service.'

Annie picked up a biscuit and nibbled at it before sipping her coffee. 'I think you may have a point. Maybe they should start checking with local hospitals to see if any patients who hold a fascination with the church have been released. Did you know that the last victim was a police officer?'

'No, I didn't. That must be terrible for you all – how do you even begin to cope with such tragedy?'

'I didn't know her very well but I feel sorry for her colleagues and friends. She was last seen leaving a pub with a man who we haven't managed to identify as yet.' She realised that she didn't have a picture of the man to show him. 'Damn, I can't believe I didn't print a copy for you to look at, in case you recognise him.'

Annie realised she had just blasphemed in front of a priest but he didn't look in the least concerned that she had.

'I'm going out to do a couple of home visits to sick parishioners in the next half an hour but I should be back after two if you want to pop back with it? I could get the housekeeper to rustle up some lunch and you can sit and have a proper break.'

'If you don't mind that would be great, but don't bother going to any trouble. I don't want to put you out.'

'Annie, it would be my pleasure. It's nice to have some company; it's very lonely up here. It's even nicer to have a conversation that doesn't revolve around how much you've sinned this week. It drives me mad; yes, I'm a priest and it's my calling but I have a life as well. I love to read, listen to rock and roll, and I'm partial to the odd bottle of wine, but that's between you and me. I don't want to tarnish my image as a pillar of society.' He winked at her again and she grinned.

'Thanks for the coffee, Father, and the biscuits; you certainly know the way to a girl's heart.'

He bowed. 'At your service, officer.'

Annie stood up, sad to be leaving the cool, peaceful kitchen to face the burning sun. She could have stayed all day. If she ever got fed up with working for the police she might just look into becoming a vicar . . .

'I'll look forward to seeing you around two. If you're busy don't worry. Just come when you can.'

Annie made her way down the path and past the gorgeous roses and began to walk back towards the police station so she could email Will and get him to send her a copy of the photo of Laura and her mystery man.

*

Will finished the last line of his email to Grace, which he had read twice over to make sure it all made sense. He pressed the send button and hoped that whoever she was on holiday with would forgive him for just spoiling it. He looked up at the whiteboard, which was above Laura's desk. The desk was just as she'd left it. No one had wanted to be the one to move her things so they hadn't. They had left it, including her mug and empty lunch box.

The pictures of the two women were very similar; there were pictures of them when they were alive and two larger ones of them before they had their post-mortems. They definitely had a look of each other. Same long blonde hair, thin, both pretty, although not so much on these photos because these were death masks. Laura was the prettier of the two, but they both looked relatively peaceful, which was the only saving grace. It would have been terrible if they had been sliced open like the girls last year. Those images were the last things he saw most nights before he closed his eyes; he could never forget them.

He walked to the far corner of the room where the kettle was and switched it on. He was waiting for the DI to arrive. The office was empty, which was nice. Will liked his own company; it gave him the chance to think without any interruptions. He took his mug of coffee back to his desk and began checking his emails. He had one from Annie and his heart skipped a beat. He opened it and read down; she'd talked to the priest and he definitely had no suspects. She wanted him to email the picture to take and show him and he cursed himself. Had no one sent out a global email with the picture of the man to see if anyone recognised him? He was just hitting the send button when his phone began to ring; he looked at the display and cringed but answered immediately. 'I'm so sorry to bother you, Grace.'

'Will, I can't believe it and, to be honest, it is very nice here but it's ever so boring. I was about to resort to buying a new book to read but this is much better.'

Will paused.

'Oh, my . . . I'm sorry, Will. I didn't mean that how it sounded. Poor Laura, poor you . . . I'm home in three days but I'll go over everything you've sent me and get back to you; is that OK? Because if not I can come home sooner, but whatever, as soon as I'm back in England I'll grab some clean clothes and come straight down.'

'Thank you, Grace, that's really kind of you. I hope I haven't ruined your holiday too much.'

'Don't be soft; you know I love my job as much as you love yours, even though it takes over. I want to help and I'm glad that you asked me.'

She ended the call and he felt a little bit better, knowing that her input might be able to make the difference, because up to now they didn't have a bloody thing. The church was just a body dump. Matt had told him that they had died elsewhere because of the livor mortis on the small of their backs and necks, yet they had been found lying on their sides. He just had no idea where to start looking. If only they could track down this mystery man. Will had a feeling that he might be falsely pinning all his hopes on this guy as the killer but it was all that they had for now, along with a boot print they couldn't say wasn't from one of the uniformed officers who had attended the scene.

Chapter 23

Annie went straight back out on foot patrol after emailing Will. She didn't want anyone catching her moping around in front of the computer like a lovesick teenager waiting for him to reply. She wanted to make a good impression and get to know the locals and the best way to do that was by walking around and meeting them. She headed through the town and towards the pier and the boat club. There was something about the place and it was the ideal location to fantasise about being rich. Bowness was busy today; she got stopped to have her picture taken at least six times. She smiled, nodded at them and continued on her way.

The *Teal* had just docked at one of the piers and there were quite a few passengers waiting to board. Annie waved at the crew members who were busy on deck and they paused to wave back. The hills and mountains that surrounded Lake Windermere were a luscious mixture of almost every colour green you could imagine. There were lots of small rowing boats out on the water and a couple of sailing boats that were gently bobbing on the calm surface of the lake; she stood for a moment to take in the view. It was one she could never tire of and she wished she knew how to write poetry so she could describe how lucky she felt; but literature had never been her strong point. She wouldn't have a clue where to begin.

'Annie.'

The voice broke into her daydream and she turned to look behind her in the direction that it had come from. She smiled to see Lily making her way towards her.

'I'm so glad that I've seen you; I wanted to ask if you would like to come to our barbecue on Friday night. Tom gets this unearthly desire to cremate every piece of meat in a three-mile radius when the sun shines for more than two days.'

Annie didn't know what to say; she was touched that they had thought to invite her, but she hated anything like that. 'I would love to, thank you. I'm working until six but I could come after, if that's OK?'

Lily squealed and then stepped forward and hugged her. 'Marvellous – it will be a good opportunity for you to get to know some of the locals and it would be the perfect chance to introduce you to Tom's son; I think you two would really get on.'

'Do you need me to bring anything with me?'

'Just yourself. Tom has a complete shopping frenzy and empties the shelves of the supermarket. I think he drives them mad, to be honest, but it keeps him out of trouble.'

Annie felt a little overwhelmed by the thought of it; she couldn't remember the last time she had done something or been invited anywhere on her own. As if Lily was reading her mind, she whispered, 'And don't worry about getting all dressed up; clothes don't make the person. You could be dressed from head to toe in Chanel and be a total bitch, or you could be wearing Primark and sparkle like a diamond. Trust me, I know, just be yourself and don't worry that anyone is better than you. We are all the same, only each of us has a different purpose in life; some work hard for their money and others are handed it on a plate.'

They began walking in the direction of the boat club and Lily continued to chatter away. 'If we get the chance to have a good old natter on Friday night I'll tell you my secrets and how I ended up marrying Tom. I know how it looks because he's much older than me but it's not like that at all. I would love Tom if he lived in a two-man tent at the top of Coniston Old Man. Don't get me wrong, I hate camping but I love him so much it wouldn't matter where we lived.'

Annie found herself grinning. Lily was funny and nice and they chatted about anything and everything until they reached Tom's boat. 'Please come and have a drink and you can let Tom bore you for a bit while I hide my shopping.' Annie followed her up the ladder and onto the boat.

Tom was below deck and smiled when he saw them both. 'To what do I owe this pleasure?'

Lily patted his arm. 'Annie was on her way down here. She told me that she couldn't wait to see your boat again.' With a wicked grin, Lily ran down the steps to the galley below, leaving her with Tom.

'Did Lily invite you to our do on Friday?'

'Yes, she did, thank you. I'm looking forward to it.'

'Good, I'm glad about that. It will give you a chance to get to know a few people.' He lowered his voice. 'I think Lily has her heart set on matchmaking you with my son, so don't be offended. Just tell her to mind her own business if she drives you mad.'

Lily appeared with another jug filled with juice and fruit. 'Non-alcoholic Pimm's.'

Annie couldn't be offended by Lily; she was too nice and it was very sweet of her to try and get her fixed up but she was off all men – well, almost all men. She finished her drink and said goodbye. There was a shoplifter at one of the jewellers who had been detained so she made her way back up the hill towards the shop. She walked in and was surprised to see a little old lady sitting on a chair with a glass of water in one hand and a security guard standing beside her. She looked at the guard. 'What happened?'

'Mrs Fitz was looking at the watches. She felt a bit faint and asked for a glass of water and then put one of the watches into her handbag when the shop assistant went to get her a drink.'

'Where's the watch now?'

The elderly woman began to sniff into her handkerchief, then rooted around in her bag and pulled out a white watch that had a crystal-studded face and strap. 'I don't know what I was thinking. I was looking for a gift for my granddaughter and knew that she would love it. Then I started to feel a bit faint, the lovely girl went to get my drink and I must have put it into my bag. I'm so embarrassed; I've never done anything like this before – I swear. My Albert will be furious.'

Annie patted her shoulder. She felt sorry for her. 'It's OK, Mrs Fitz. What's your full name and date of birth? Let's see if we can sort this out. You wait here while I speak to the manager.'

'Margaret Alma Fitz, twelfth of October 1931.'

Annie went through into the back office to speak to the manager, who didn't look a day over twenty-five and had red, flushed cheeks.

'It's company policy to prosecute all shoplifters, but I feel terrible.'

Annie nodded in agreement. 'Well, technically she didn't leave the shop; let me do some checks on her to make sure she isn't a master criminal.' Annie passed the details over the radio for a PNC check; if she came back no trace she would do her best to make sure the manager let her off with a stiff warning. After a minute her radio burst into life. 'No trace on those details.' Annie let out a sigh of relief and turned to face the manager. 'She isn't on any of our systems and she's getting on a bit; it looks as if it was a mistake. Would you be OK if we don't press charges?'

The man bit his bottom lip then sighed. 'Yes, I would. I'd never sleep again if she got marched from here in handcuffs. I can't talk to her, though; can you take her outside and talk to her? Just tell her not to come back in and I'll smooth it over with the staff.'

'Wise decision; the publicity wouldn't help – she looks like everyone's favourite nana.'

They went back in and Annie bent down to talk to Margaret on her level. 'Good news, Margaret. The manager thinks that you made a mistake and is happy for me not to take this any further as long as you don't come back in. Do you understand?'

The woman dabbed at her eyes and patted Annie's hand. 'Thank you so much. I'm sorry to have caused you any trouble, dear.'

Annie straightened up and offered her hand to Margaret. 'Come on, Margaret; let's take a walk in the fresh air and let these nice people get on.' She helped her up and walked her outside. As she reached the door she turned and smiled at the manager. 'Thanks.'

'Do you need a lift home?' she asked Margaret. 'I can get one of my colleagues to come and take you.'

'Oh, gosh, no, thank you. I've caused you quite enough trouble for today. I will be fine; I'll go and get the bus. I'm so grateful to you. I don't know what my family would have said if they found out.'

Annie squeezed her shoulder. 'You do have good taste, though, Margaret; that watch was lovely.' They both laughed and Margaret turned to shuffle off towards the bus stop.

Annie turned the other way and began to walk up the steep hill towards the station. She needed to see if Will had emailed her that picture. Her stomach let out a loud rumble; it was almost two and she was starving. The station was empty when she walked in and the smell of burnt toast still lingered in the corridor. She shut the door and made her way to the office. It was dark inside. Very little light came through the window because of the large trees and shrubs planted directly outside it. She didn't bother to turn the lights on; instead she sat down at a computer to log on and check her emails. There was one from Will with an attachment, which she opened. She felt her stomach drop to her feet to see a grainy black and white photo of Laura with this mystery man. It was probably the last photo of Laura alive and it gave her a cold shiver.

A door banged somewhere in the building. Annie turned her head and caught a shadow flitting past the open office door. 'Hello?' There was no answer and her skin began to prickle; someone had shut that door. She pressed the print icon and then stood up to go and investigate. She checked every single room but the building was empty. Unsettled, she walked back into the office to collect the picture from the printer, picked up her hat and went straight out of the door that she had not long come through. Her heart was racing and she had no idea why. Within five minutes she was back at the presbytery and once again she was greeted by Father John, who this time actually looked like a priest in black chinos with a pale blue shirt, dog collar and a large gilt crucifix around his neck.

'Perfect timing – I've just got back myself and I'm starving. Absolving people of their sins doesn't half give you an appetite.'

Annie laughed. 'If I'm honest, so am I.'

'Good, we'll eat first and then talk shop, if that's OK with you. At my age I have to eat regularly or I'll pass out.' He opened the door and she followed him once more into the cool hallway, relieved to be out of the sun for a while. He unclipped the starched white band from his collar, then pulled the heavy cross over his head, placing it on a silver platter on the sideboard. Then he undid the top three buttons of his shirt and sighed. 'That's better; I can breathe now. Your turn. I've practically undressed myself in front of you. Get that stab vest or whatever you call it off and let your body breathe.'

Annie did as she was told, first unclipping her heavy-duty belt and then unzipping the vest.

'Tell me, officer, do you always strip on a first date?'

Annie felt her cheeks begin to burn but he laughed so loudly it echoed around the hall. 'Sorry – sometimes my sense of humour is not entirely appropriate for a priest.'

Annie began to laugh and followed him into the kitchen, where an invisible housekeeper had cleared away the mugs and plate from earlier. She took a seat and watched as he went over to the fridge and began pulling plates and bowls out. Soon he had put plates, cutlery and napkins on the table. He added a huge dish of salad, a plate of homemade quiche and an assortment of mixed sandwiches. It looked delicious and Annie had to check her chin to make sure she wasn't drooling.

'Help yourself, my dear. I have to say one thing for Simon's housekeeper; she knows the way to a man's heart. I think the reason he may have had his heart attack is because she is killing him with kindness, but what a way to go.'

Annie totally agreed with him. She loved her food, as her less than perfect figure showed, but she was beginning to feel comfortable with it. Will would tell her how much he loved her just the way she was and it had done wonders for her confidence. 'Thank you, John, this is wonderful and it's very kind of you.'

'My pleasure, Annie; never believe what you hear about priests. We're not all a bad bunch/ I suppose it's a bit like police officers. Some of them are total . . .'

'Pricks.'

He grinned and nodded in agreement. 'You took the word right out of my mouth. But some of them are wonderful, just like you. I bet you are brilliant at what you do and I get the impression that you actually care about people as a whole.'

'I do try, although sometimes it's very hard. I like to treat everyone the same, regardless of their past or upbringing.'

'And that, my dear, is a very rare quality. Far too many people are so consumed in themselves they rarely have time for anyone else, but you are different. I knew that straight away.'

They ate the rest of their lunch in silence until John stood up and went to the fridge again. 'Would you like a cold drink?'

'Yes, please.' He passed her a can of ice-cold cola and put one down next to his plate. Annie was full; she had eaten some of everything and a large plate of salad. She normally hated eating in front of strangers but there was something about John that made her feel as if she'd known him a lot longer than four hours. 'That was lovely. I'm so stuffed I don't think my body armour will fasten.'

He shook his head. 'I'm quite sure it will. Now, what have you come to show me?' He pushed his plate to one side and pulled a pair of gold-rimmed oval reading glasses from his shirt pocket. Annie stood and pulled the folded-up piece of paper from the deep pocket of her combat trousers then passed it to him. 'Sorry it's not very good quality but it's the best that we have. We believe the woman was killed not long after she left the pub with the man but no one has a clue who he is. It's a total mystery.'

John bent his head and lifted the picture nearer so he could study it. Annie watched as the colour drained from his face and she felt a prickle of excitement. He knew who the man was – bloody brilliant. Will would be well chuffed. John held it a bit further away then brought it up close again. He whispered, 'I know that man; in fact I know him very well. It's my nephew.'

Annie felt the excitement disappear as fast as it had come. 'Really? I mean are you sure? It's not a very good quality picture.'

John nodded. 'It's Ryan. He came to visit last week. He got a job that starts next week at the local gas terminal so he's looking after my house while I'm up here. Have you tried knocking at St Mary's presbytery? He should be there.'

Annie assumed that whoever had been tasked with the house-to-house enquiries would have knocked. 'They will have. He can't have been in when they tried.' John pulled a phone from his trouser pocket and rang his nephew; it rang out. It didn't even go to voicemail, just kept on ringing. He ended the call and tried again, still no reply. Then he tried his house phone, which rang and rang. He looked at Annie. 'I'll try his mum, my sister. Hello, Maureen, I can't get hold of Ryan. Has he phoned you in the last couple of days? No, oh, OK, it's not important. I just need him to do me a favour; I'll send him a text. Bye.'

She noticed that his hand was trembling. 'Something is wrong. He phones his mum almost every other day without fail and she hasn't heard from him for three days. I need to go back to Barrow now.'

Annie nodded. 'Let me ring my colleague down there who asked me to come and speak to you. Then I'll go get a police car and we'll blue-light it all the way.' She stood up and dashed into the hall to put her gear back on. She rang Will, who answered on the first ring. 'I know who the man is; it's the priest's nephew Ryan Trelmain and he's living at St Mary's presbytery. No one has heard from him for three days.'

'Right, thanks, Annie. I'll get a task force team and we'll go and search the house. Thank you so much.'

'I'm bringing Father John through; he thinks something has happened to Ryan and wants to see if he's OK.'

'Shit, what if this Ryan is our man? It might totally mess things up.'

'I know, but if I don't bring him he's going to come down himself anyway. At least if I bring him I can keep an eye on him. Oh, and Will, go easy on John; he's a really nice guy.' She ended the call and turned to see John standing in the doorway and felt a wave of embarrassment. 'I'm really sorry, John, but you do understand how serious this is. We have to cover every eventuality.'

'Yes, I do and I understand that you need to do your jobs. I'm just a little overwhelmed to think my nephew could be involved in any of this. He's always been such a good boy. This will kill my sister – she dotes on him.'

'Well, let's hope it's all a huge mistake. It doesn't mean that he's involved. You wait here and I'll go and get a car.'

'If you don't mind I'd rather walk down with you. I need some fresh air.'

They left the house and walked briskly down to the police station. John perched on the dry-stone wall that bordered the car park. 'I'll wait here.'

Annie went inside and heard Cathy's voice coming from her office; she knocked on the door and walked in.

'Ten o'clock and if you're a minute late I will know because I have an officer stationed at the bottom of our street just to keep an eye on you.' She ended the call. 'What's up?'

Annie launched into a condensed version of the last ten minutes.

'Shit, really – the priest's nephew? Bloody hell, that's one for the books. Take the panda. No one needs it tonight so it won't matter if you don't bring it back until tomorrow. You'll just have to park it outside your house when you finish – oh, and Annie, you be careful.'

Annie nodded and ran into the office to get the keys off the hook. She felt terrible for John and that lovely lunch was now sitting in the pit of her stomach feeling like a lead weight. She went back outside. His face was grey and she hoped that he wasn't about to keel over. She got into the car and he followed. No sirens because it wasn't technically an immediate response but she did put the blue lights on to get through the busy traffic.

Chapter 24

For once luck was on Will's side. Task Force, the armed response unit, were actually in Ulverston, which was only eight miles away and they would be armed and here for the briefing in fifteen minutes. The DI was running the briefing and Will was glad that he was here to take over; it had been a long few days. He wasn't too happy about Annie bringing the priest but the man deserved to know if his nephew was involved and it was his home they were going to be storming into with rifles, tear gas and tasers. He just hoped that none of them were needed and the man would come in without any hassle. They didn't know if he was the killer or not, but he was the closest thing to a lead they had and they weren't taking any chances.

Will walked into the large briefing room on the first floor, which was almost full and would be once the armed officers arrived. The thunder of footsteps coming up the stairs signalled their arrival and he began to feel better than he had in days. They came into the room dressed from head to toe in black and looked a formidable sight. They all wore black baseball caps, black jump-suits and black body armour; they lined up along the back wall, ready for their orders. Will nodded at them and got a collective nod back. This was serious and everyone knew that. There was no laughing and joking like at any other briefing; everyone was eager to get on with it.

Thirty minutes later, they took their positions surrounding the presbytery. Will had walked the perimeter of the church and house, uncomfortable in his stab vest under his shirt and suit jacket. There was no sign of life from the house. Two of the men in black had practically given one old woman an instant heart attack as she had come out of the church with a bunch of wilted flowers. They had escorted her away from the area and placed her in the back of a marked police car until it was over. Officers had closed the road at either end to stop traffic and members of the public strolling down and getting caught up in anything. The atmosphere was tense. Will walked back and gave the all-clear over the radio.

The entry team moved in, the heavy red battering ram held securely between them. Four loud bangs and the wooden door splintered, giving way, and then they were in. The first officer inside gagged at the smell, it was so bad. One of them waved Will over and lifted up his mask. Will jogged over towards the door and felt his stomach lurch; someone or something was dead in there and it stank. He lifted his hand to his nose and nodded. Stepping back, he waited until the entry team did a sweep of the building. He wasn't sure what to expect but he knew it was going to be bad; maybe the killer had topped himself and would save them the trouble of putting him before the courts.

The three officers who had gone in came back downstairs and removed their hats. The sergeant spoke. 'There's a dead male in the upstairs bedroom. Looks like he's been there a few days; decomposition is quite advanced. Probably due to the fact that someone turned the heating up full in the room. It really stinks in there, Will, but from first impressions it looks like he's your guy.'

'Bollocks – thanks, guys. We'll take it from here.'

Will turned to the DI, who had been talking on his phone the whole time, giving a running commentary to the control room inspector. 'It's time to get suited and booted, sir.'

A car drove into the street, blue lights flashing. Annie's familiar figure got out of the driver's side and a grey-haired man got out of the passenger side. *Double bollocks.* He was glad to see Annie but not so glad to see the priest. He watched as she turned to the man and must have told him to stay put because he ran his fingers through his hair, then shrugged and leant against the bonnet of the car.

Annie walked towards Will. 'Anything?'

'Dead man in the upstairs bedroom. I haven't been up there yet but Task Force said he looks like our guy. We can't let him in.' He nodded in the direction of the priest.

'Really? Bloody hell! I suppose that would explain why no one has seen him since that night. OK, I'll keep John out of the way but he's not daft. What do I tell him?'

'You're going to have to tell him that we've found a body but we don't know any more than that at this moment in time. His house is now a crime scene and it will some hours, possibly days, before he'll be allowed access to it. Is there anywhere you can take him? You know how long this is going to take; he could be here until tomorrow.'

Annie shrugged. She'd never had to babysit a priest before. 'Can he not go inside the church, or is that a crime scene as well?'

'Not as far as I know. I want him near in case he has something to do with it but not too near that he's going to get in the way. I'll get Scott and Ian to give inside the church the once-over and then you can both go and wait in there. Thanks, Annie. I appreciate everything that you've done today.'

Will turned and walked across to where the team of armed officers were huddled; for the time being they had been stood down and were in the process of putting their weapons back inside the armed response vehicle.

Two of them headed in Annie's direction. 'It stinks in there. It's going to take more than some fabric freshener to make that house smell as fresh as a daisy again.'

'Is it that bad? This is turning into a living nightmare when bodies are turning up in churchyards and presbyteries. It's just not right.'

Both of them nodded in agreement with her and all three of them walked towards the church. It was open, thanks to the flower-arranging old lady, who couldn't have noticed anything amiss or she wouldn't be alive and breathing. But it was better to be safe than sorry. Annie waited at the church door while the two officers went inside and checked the building. Five minutes later they came out.

'All clear. Maybe you should let that old woman out of that car and send her on her way. She's been in it since we came.'

Annie looked across at the car and the woman, who was staring earnestly at John. *Shit, two for the price of one.* She walked over and opened the car door. 'Would you like to come back inside the church? It's a bit warm to be cooped up in here.'

The woman nodded and got out of the car, making a beeline for John. Annie saw him grimace and she followed her over. 'Actually, if you give me a quick statement you can get off home now and if we need anything someone will be in touch.' Annie had interrupted the woman's interrogation and John threw her a look of thanks.

'Oh, are you sure? Do you not want me to wait here with Father John? It's no trouble; we can have a nice catch-up.'

'No, it's OK, thank you. This is a crime scene and we need to keep it closed for some time, probably hours, so you will be better off going home.'

The woman told Annie what she knew, which amounted to nothing, and Annie wrote it all down. Then she escorted her to the end of the street. 'Thank you.' Annie watched her walk away, her head in the air and obviously put out that she had just been told to go home. Heading back to the church and John, she felt sorry for him; he looked defeated and grief-stricken.

'Thank you, Annie. I fear an interrogation from Hilary more than I fear God himself. Are you going to tell me what's happening? Or do I have to wait?'

'I'm sorry, John, but we don't know an awful lot ourselves at the moment. All I can tell you is they have found a man's body in the upstairs bedroom.'

His hand flew to his mouth and he shrank before her very eyes. 'Do they know who he is . . . is it Ryan?'

'They can't say at the moment; the search team went in and only took a cursory look around. I'm sorry, John, but this is going to take a while for them to process, but as soon as they do know something they will come and talk to you. Is there anywhere you want to go? Should I drive you back to Windermere?'

'No, thank you, Annie. If there is a dead man inside my home and the only other person to live there is my nephew who no one has spoken to for three days, then I think it's pretty clear who the dead man is.'

'It does look that way but you never know; there's a slim chance it could be someone different.'

Annie spotted the photographer from the local paper across the road and took hold of John's elbow. 'Come on; let's get you inside the church, away from prying eyes.' It was thirty seconds too late, though. The photographer had already taken a picture of the harrowed-looking priest, head bent in deep conversation with Annie. The picture would make the front page of the local paper tonight and the nationals the next day with the headline: 'God's House of Death' in bold black print.

Chapter 25

Detective Inspector Dave Martin led the way up the steps to the house, closely followed by Will, both of them rustling loudly as they walked in matching white crime scene suits, face masks, boot covers, hoods pulled up and latex gloves. Will thought he was going to pass out he was so hot. As they stepped through the door to the house Will heard his boss dry-heave into his face mask. Will did his best not to inhale but the smell was terrible and it filled the whole house. He wasn't looking forward to meeting Ryan Trelmain, if it was him.

They went up the stairs, staying close to the wall, Will mirroring Dave's footsteps so as not to trample everything. The less disturbance, the more chance the CSI would find some evidence. He forgot and inhaled, which made his eyes water. They went into the bedroom with the door open. Scott had told him all the bedroom doors had been closed and they had checked each room, shutting the doors as they left until they found the one with the body, which they had left ajar so they knew which one to go in. The room was stifling. Will looked at the radiator; it was turned up as high as it would go. He didn't want to touch the dial in case there were fingerprints on it but he needed to locate the main central heating control and turn it off.

The heat was unbearable, combined with the smell and the heat from outside. For the first time ever Will worried he might pass out and that was before he looked at the body on the bed. Steeling himself, he looked over to the double bed. One side of the cover was thrown back over the body and he thought about Laura; it would have been the last place she slept. He surveyed the room, taking his time. There was an almost empty bottle of water on the floor. At the foot of the bed were a crumpled pair of jeans and the white T-shirt that the man she'd left with had been wearing. Will felt uncomfortable, like a voyeur. He was seeing things about other people's lives that he had no right to see.

Dave turned to him. 'Shit for sugar, it looks like we've found our man and it looks like he was killed the same night as Laura, judging by the state of decomp.'

Will stepped closer to the bed to take a close look at the man he'd spent the last three days searching for: the duvet covered his bottom half but his boss had lifted the top part back, exposing his chest. Due to the heat in the room and the temperature outside, it had sped things up a lot; the chest and lower abdomen had inflated with gas and were tinged green with marbling all over. His eyes, which were open, were covered with a milky film and one eye was covered with bluebottle larvae, as were his nose and mouth. Will looked at the huge butcher's knife, which was protruding from his chest; a trickle of blood had run down from the wound, not as much as he would have expected but the knife was buried to the hilt and the blood could be underneath his body or it could have bled internally. Whatever it was, Matt would be able to confirm at the post-mortem.

Will was surprised the killer had resorted to more extreme violence but the man on the bed was big, with lots of muscles. So he'd gone for a swift kill. What did this tell Will? That he had killed this way so there was less chance of a fight. Maybe he wasn't scared of blood but just preferred not to kill that way. The heat and the putrid smell got too much and Will pointed towards the door. Dave nodded and this time it was Will who left first.

When he finally made it out into the fresh air, he ripped off his face mask, struggling for breath. He began to take deep breaths, not caring who was watching because right now he was very close to losing it for the first time in eight years. A hand on his shoulder squeezed hard and he turned to look at his boss who, once he'd pulled his mask down, looked as green as Will felt. Matt arrived and Will nodded at him. 'It's bad.'

'I'll go in and do the preliminaries, and then you can get it processed.'

'I'll come back in with you.' He snapped his mask back over his nose and followed him. He would be quite happy to never have to set foot in this house ever again but he felt responsible. He knew that Laura had been flirting in front of him to try and make him jealous and he'd stuck his head in his pint of lager, letting her leave with a total stranger, and now they were both dead.

*

Sean was off work but he had heard on the radio that the police had sealed off St Mary's Road, the church and the presbytery because a body had been found inside. His normally calm exterior didn't look so calm today. His stomach was rolling and he felt as if he was on a boat that was sailing across the choppiest of seas. He hadn't shaved for a couple of days and had dark stubble on his face. He had to keep reminding himself that he needed to keep it together; it was OK. They would take hours to process the scene. He had worn gloves the whole time so he hadn't left any prints but still something was niggling away at him. He was pacing up and down his living room and needed to do something but he had no idea what.

He might go and sit outside the hairdressers for a while and watch his next girl to keep his mind busy. He wanted to check out the next church but he didn't know how good Will was. Had he figured out that it was all the priest's fault? If he had then he would more than likely have plain-clothes officers watching the other two churches the priest sometimes worked from. He couldn't risk it in daylight; it would be much better to go when it was dark.

He picked up his keys from the coffee table in the living room and went outside to his black truck. Once inside, he drove to the car park opposite the hairdressers and parked in a space where he could see in through the huge glass window. He even took what change he had from the drinks holder and went and bought a ticket from the machine and a paper from the shop nearby. He wound the windows down, spread his paper across the steering wheel and leant back, watching the woman inside the shop. He wished that he'd brought his radio home with him to listen to what was going on but that would have been a bad idea. The minute he turned it on it would show up at the control room at Penrith that he was on duty and it would have raised suspicion. But it would have been nice to have heard exactly what was going on.

He wondered again how good Will actually was and if he would have him arrested before he even got chance to kill girl number three. For the first time he realised that it could come to that – he could end up handcuffed and put in the cells. Bollocks . . . he had been so obsessed with the thought of getting his revenge on the priest he had never really given much thought to what might happen if he got caught. They hated cops in prison. Being on his own didn't bother him; he'd been on his own since the day he'd found his mum dead and he'd never really got close to anyone. Always afraid they would leave him. It was better to be alone than live with the constant fear. He supposed if faced with the choice he'd probably kill himself – maybe his mum and Sophie would be waiting for him, but then again he had killed innocent women and a man so he didn't deserve to go to a better place.

He would wait and see what today brought and there was always the Mental Health Act. He could convince them he was insane and get put into a secure hospital; at least then it wouldn't matter who he was.

*

When the crime scene had been thoroughly processed and they could leave it guarded by PCSOs, Will had gone back to the car to strip off. The paper suit was stuck to his back and even more difficult than normal to get out of, but he finally managed it and put everything into a brown paper evidence bag. He wished that he could get rid of the smell as easily but it was still there. Lifting his shirt sleeve up, he sniffed. It smelled terrible, a combination of sweat and dead body. That was one scent that was never going to be bottled and be available to buy in the shops in time for Father's Day. He needed to go home and shower, change his clothes. It was almost six and he was knackered.

Matt had arranged to do the PM first thing in the morning so at least he didn't have to go through that tonight. Will didn't even want to go and face Annie, he smelled that bad, so he waved an officer over and told him to take him home. They got into the patrol car and the officer immediately put both front windows down full. Will put his head back and muttered, 'Sorry.' When he got to his front door he heard the house phone ringing and ran to answer it. 'Hello.'

'It's Dad – just checking up on you. I've rung your mobile a couple of times.'

'Sorry, I've been at a murder scene all afternoon and couldn't answer. Is everything OK?'

'Fine, everything's fine. Sorry, son, I should have realised you were busy. It's a mess, isn't it? I'm phoning because Lily keeps pestering me to remind you about tomorrow night. Please say you can still come; she'll kill me if you don't.'

Will laughed. 'I will try my best; tell her I promise.' After tomorrow's post-mortem he wasn't sure how he would feel about eating charcoaled animal flesh but he needed a break.

'Good lad, you know it makes sense for the both of us if you turn up. She means well. Most people are coming for six but you just get here when you can. If you're late I'll save you a couple of nice steaks and I've got you a case of your favourite lager chilling in the fridge. Why don't you stay the night? Have a night off, turn your phone off.'

'I think I might; it sounds like heaven. Tell Lily thanks and I'll see you both tomorrow and can you please tell her from me that I don't need fixing up with some rich businessman's spinster daughter; I'm OK in that department.'

His dad laughed. 'Yep, will do, but you know Lily; she can't help herself, she sees it as her role in life to get you settled down and married.'

Will put the phone down and went upstairs to shower, then he was going to bin the clothes he was wearing and put on his comfy jogging pants and a T-shirt. If he had to go back to work he was going relaxed for once.

Chapter 26

Annie sat with Father John whilst Stu took a statement from him and she listened to the man answer every question Stu asked, whilst looking him in the eye and never shying away once, even though he was clearly distressed. Annie knew that until they knew better John would be a suspect but she didn't believe for one minute that he had anything to do with the murders – and she trusted her instinct a lot more than anyone else's judgement. When Stu had finished asking the questions it was John's turn.

'I need to know who the man is inside my house because, as far as I'm concerned, the only people who have access to it are myself and my nephew. As I'm sitting talking to you that must mean that the body inside is Ryan. Who else could it be?'

Stu looked across at Annie. 'Can I have a word?'

Annie stood up and put her hand on John's shoulder. 'Give me a minute. I'll find out exactly what's going on.' She walked towards the back of the church and Stu followed. 'Look, I know you can't say much but the man has a right to know. What was he wearing or can you not get a picture of his face for him to look at? It's not fair – he's been here for hours and he's sick with worry. He needs putting out of his misery one way or another.'

Stu shrugged. 'You're right and I totally agree with you. It looks as if it is his nephew but that's not for me to say. I'll go and see if Debs can nip in and show him a picture of the man's face, but it's not nice; it will be a bit of a shock for him.'

'Thanks, Stu. I'll go and prepare him, let him know it's bad. He will be the one who is going to the hospital for the official identification anyway.'

Annie walked back towards where John was sitting and Stu went outside. 'John, we are going to get a photo of the man's face so you can take a look and see if he is Ryan. I have to warn you, though, it isn't very nice; he's been there a couple of days so there will be some swelling and possibly some insect larvae on his face.'

'I don't care . . . I need to see. I need to know if it's Ryan and then I can figure out how to break it to my sister before it's all over the news.'

The church door slammed shut as a gust of wind took it from Stu's grasp; Debs was in front of him. Annie wanted to throw up as she waited for them to approach. Debs lifted her face mask up and nodded at John. She lifted the camera and after a couple of seconds of flicking through the pictures found one that was the most suitable. She held it towards John, who stood up to take a look. He pulled his glasses from his shirt pocket and slipped them on. Then he took one look at the mottled green face on the screen and sat back down. He whispered, 'Thank you, dear, I'd like to confirm that is my nephew Ryan.'

Annie sat next to him and put her arm around his shoulders. She felt a lump in her throat and couldn't speak so she just rubbed his back. He nodded at Debs. 'I'm really sorry for your loss,' Debs said. Then she turned to go back and finish what she had been doing.

Stu looked across to Annie. 'I'll let the DI know.' Then he turned and followed Debs out of the door.

Annie turned to John. 'I don't know what to say. I'm so, so sorry.'

'I don't know what to do. I can't let my sister find out about this on the news but I don't think I can manage the drive down to tell her.'

'We can contact the local police station nearest to your sister and they will despatch a family liaison officer to go and speak to her. These are highly trained officers who will be able to support her in every possible way. Would you like me to arrange it and once the officer is at your sister's house you could phone and speak to her then?'

He nodded. 'Could you do that? It would be most appreciated, thank you, Annie.'

Chapter 27

Sean ran his hand over his head. His hair was pretty short but it gave him an excuse to go inside the hairdressers and break the ice, make an appointment with his next angel. He might get it all shaved off, totally bald. They would probably take the piss out of him at work for weeks, though, if he walked in looking like a thug. He had a clear view of her through the window because her workstation was next to it. She had worked solid since he'd got there. His stomach let out a loud growl: lunchtime, and if he was hungry then she must be too. He hoped she'd need to leave the salon to go and get some lunch. He folded the paper and watched intently. Ten minutes later, he was rewarded as she came out of the shop wearing a pair of dark sunglasses. She had tied her long hair up into a high ponytail and looked quite stunning.

He got out of the truck and followed her from a safe distance. She walked thirty seconds up Dalton Road – the main shopping street – turned left and walked into the new delicatessen. He followed her in, standing behind her in the queue. She asked for a chicken salad on a brown baguette, no butter and a little bit of light mayo. Sean wondered if she'd known this could be her last meal would she have gone the whole hog and had butter and full-fat mayo. Another assistant asked him what he wanted and he repeated her order. The girl turned to look at him with a look of sympathy on her face.

'You too? Bloody diets.'

He smiled and nodded. 'I know, I seem to spend all my time dreaming about food.' The assistant passed her change and she smiled at him before she left the shop. The girl serving him began to slice his baguette. 'Actually, I've changed my mind; can I have chicken mayo, no salad and two sausage rolls.' He paid for his food and then casually strolled back to his truck.

*

Annie got off the phone to the DI. She hadn't been able to get hold of Will and suspected that he'd called it a night. He'd been working solid since Laura's murder and the DI was fresh from his weekend away. 'John, I know that you don't want to leave here but there is absolutely nothing you can do here tonight. The house is a crime scene and is likely to be sealed off for a couple of days. There isn't any way you will be allowed inside. Do you have anyone you could stay with?'

He shook his head. 'No . . . yes . . . well, probably, but I don't want to. I want to be on my own. I'll stay here in the church if it's OK with you. There's a blanket in the vestry and a blow-up bed that no one claimed at the summer fair. I'll be fine. I'd like to stay close by and I also have a long and meaningful conversation that I need to have with God.'

He was trying to joke but it didn't sound as funny as it should. 'Are you sure? Can I get you something to eat, a sandwich, or something to drink?'

'No, thank you. I don't seem to have much of an appetite and if I have a drink it will be of the spirit kind and not orange juice. I may just raid the Communion wine. There is a whole case of the stuff, which was sent by mistake. It's far too strong to give out at morning Mass. I meant to send it back and didn't get around to it, thank the good Lord for something.'

The sarcasm in his tone was biting and Annie felt terrible for him. 'I'm going to let whoever is guarding the scene know that you'll be in here, then they won't get scared and wonder who is wandering around in the church, and then I'm going to have to go home. I should have finished work a couple of hours ago and I need a shower.'

Father John stood up and hugged her. 'Of course, thank you, Annie, but you shouldn't have hung around here to keep me company. You have a life to go home to, but I do appreciate you being here. I hope whoever the lucky man is truly appreciates how special you are.'

Annie laughed. 'I can stay a bit longer if you want me to; it's no bother.'

'No, you go home, I insist. I'll be fine, just let your officers know so they don't come and taser me in the middle of the night.'

She walked towards the door and felt her heartstrings tug at the sight of the man who was now kneeling down and praying at the foot of the altar. As she opened the church door she got a whiff of the smell that had filled her house and she grimaced. She looked across to the house and street outside the church. Both were sealed off with blue and white police tape. There was no one around except for two PCSOs who were standing either end of the street to stop people walking all over the crime scene. Annie headed towards Sally, who she used to work with. 'Hiya, the priest is still in the church. He said he has nowhere to go and he wants to be close by. I've checked with the DI, who said it's OK as long as he doesn't try to get into the house, so can you keep an eye on him, please?'

'It's awful, what a shame. He was only a young lad. There is some messed-up stuff going on in this town. I bet you're glad that you don't have to work it all.'

Annie looked down at her bright yellow stab vest and laughed. 'How do you figure that one out? I transfer to the Lakes to get away from all of this and by my second week I'm knee-deep in another bloody murder case. What a nightmare this is turning into.'

'Gawd, Annie, what is it with you and mad axe men; you attract them like flies to shit.'

Annie bent her head towards Sally. 'I honestly don't know, but I swear this is as involved as I get with this one. Father John is a lovely man and I'll help him as much as I can but I'm keeping well away from anything remotely dangerous.' She began to walk towards the panda car she'd parked up hours ago, then turned to Sally. 'Did you smell that awful smell before? Like rotten veg or a dead animal.'

Sally shook her head. 'Nope, nothing; were you near a sewer drain or something? It's not coming from the house, is it? Apparently it's really bad inside.'

'No, I don't think so, the windows and doors are shut. It can't come from in there and it was near to the church, right where I stepped out of the door.'

'Must be an old drain; this weather does nothing to improve the smell.'

Annie smiled and continued walking up the street to the panda car. She'd forgotten all about the terrible smell in her house that kept coming and going and now she didn't know if she wanted to go home in case it was still there. She could sense something but had no idea what it was; all she knew was that it was bad. She got into the car and started the engine. As she pulled her seat belt across she glanced in the rear-view mirror and screamed. The dead kid was sitting directly behind her; the air in the car crackled it was so cold. The girl lifted a finger to her lips to shush Annie and then she whispered, 'Please don't make a noise. He will hear you and know I'm here. I'm not allowed to talk to you but I need you to help me. I don't want my brother to kill anyone else, but I can't do anything to stop him. I'm stuck here and have been since the day that I died.'

'Who's your brother and why are you stuck here?'

The girl faded into thin air but her voice whispered directly into Annie's ear, freezing the tiny hairs inside. 'Sean Wood is my brother's name and I'm Sophie. The shadow man won't let me leave and you will know when he's around because he smells really bad. I have to go; he's coming.'

And she was gone, leaving behind a trail of frost on the inside of the window next to where she had been sitting. Annie was shaking. Who or what the fuck was the shadow man? She turned on the engine, wanting to get far away from the church before he put in an appearance. She drove home and parked the panda car outside her house. Well, if the neighbours hadn't figured out she was a copper they would now. Still, it should make them all feel safe. She couldn't help but smile – if only they knew that she was actually a bloody liability.

She got out of the car and went into her house, finally booking off duty with the control centre. She stripped her body armour off in the hall then opened the small wall safe she had in the hall cupboard and locked her radio in there. She sniffed the air; the house didn't smell of anything bad tonight, just the faint aroma from the various air fresheners she had dotted about the place. She took her phone out to ring Will; there was no reply. She needed to tell him about Sean Wood; there wasn't anyone else she could tell. They would want to know how she had come by this information and what was she going to say – that a dead nine-year-old girl told her in the back of a police car? She would definitely be detained and taken up to the hospital for a mental health assessment. *Poor Annie – it finally got too much for her* was what they would be saying at work.

She had no idea who this Sean Wood could be; she needed more than a name. If she could find out more about Sophie then that could help. She tried Will's phone again; still no answer so she left him a voicemail and tried to sound relatively sane while she spoke. There was nothing else she could do except have a cold shower and make herself some tea, read for a bit and try and get some sleep.

Chapter 28

Annie checked her reflection in the mirror then walked to the door of the women's locker room, turned around and then checked it again. Her stomach was churning and she didn't know if it was nerves or hunger. She hadn't eaten all day because she felt nervous so it was probably a bit of both. She was looking forward to seeing Tom and Lily but she hated social events; they were always low on her list of priorities. Her plan was to show her face and then sneak away after a couple of hours. She didn't intend on staying long but she didn't want Lily to think she was rude after she had been so kind to her. Cathy walked out of the inspector's office looking very glamorous. She took one look at Annie then laughed. 'Are you going to a barbecue at Tom and Lily's, by any chance?'

'Yes, is that OK?'

'Of course it is, you daft bugger. Where do you think I'm heading off to? Please, can I have a lift and then I can get drunk and forget about my own crappy life for a couple of hours.'

Annie laughed. 'Yes, of course you can; it will save me the embarrassment of having to walk in on my own looking like a fish out of water.'

They left the station and got into Annie's car. It was a beautiful evening, the air was still warm and it was perfect. They chatted about the weather, Laura's murder and everything apart from Will.

'How do you know them?'

'Oh, I only just met them, the first day I started working here, and we hit it off; they seem like such a nice couple. You wouldn't think they were well-off.'

'Apart from the huge boat and the mansion on the lakeside, you wouldn't know at all.'

They both laughed. 'They are a really nice couple and very supportive of the police. I'm surprised you haven't met them before if you have been going out with Will.'

Annie turned to ask her what she meant when Cathy shouted, 'Next right – sorry, I forgot that you haven't been here before.'

Annie made a sharp turn and drove through a pair of huge metal gates; the drive was narrow to begin with, evergreen rhododendron bushes on either side, but then it opened onto one of the most breathtaking houses she had ever seen. It was huge, not as big as the mansion she had managed to burn down last year, but it was close. Built from slate and limestone, with the render in between whitewashed, it had a huge set of steps leading to the front door, which were flanked on either side by very realistic stone lions. The trees were lit up by hundreds of fairy lights and bunting was strung from tree to tree. She parked her Mini in a tiny space next to a huge Mercedes and didn't realise her mouth was open until Cathy began to laugh.

'Not bad, eh? Now, who lives in a house like this?'

Annie smiled. 'Oh, wow, can you imagine? It's beautiful.'

Cathy jumped out of the car. 'Come on, I'm thirsty; let's get this party started.'

Annie followed her. She didn't go near the front of the house but followed the strings of bunting around the path which led to the back. As they rounded the corner the smoky smell of barbecue coals wafted around to meet them; whatever Tom was cooking smelled good and her stomach rumbled. There were already at least twenty people congregating around the huge drinks table that held every bottle Annie could name, along with a fridge full of soft drinks and lager and a separate one filled with wine.

'Bingo, we're in luck; they haven't drunk everything in sight yet.'

Annie followed Cathy towards the bar, still in shock at how beautiful the house and gardens were. A hand touched her arm and she turned to see Lily, who looked stunning. She hugged Annie fiercely and whispered in her ear, 'Remember, you are just as good as anyone here and you look gorgeous.'

Annie felt her cheeks begin to burn and hugged Lily back. 'Thank you – you look amazing, Lily.'

'Thanks, Annie; welcome to our home.' She waited until Cathy had poured two glasses of wine and passed one to Annie. 'Come and say hi to Tom; he's been telling everyone about you. To be honest, I think he may have a bit of a crush on you, so just slap him if he gets too much.'

Annie, who had just taken a huge gulp of the crisp, cold wine, spluttered all over. Lily winked at her and led her by the hand through the crowd of people to the biggest barbecue she had ever seen, where Tom was proudly flipping burgers.

He turned to see them both and grinned; putting down his fork, he stepped towards Annie and hugged her. 'I'm so glad you could make it; you can rescue us from the boring I'm-so-rich brigade. When they start the annual I'm richer than you are competition in approximately an hour's time.'

'Well, I can try but I have no idea what I could do to top that.'

Lily pulled her hand. 'Come on, I've saved the best table for us. Tom's son should be here soon; he's promised me faithfully that he'll be here, regardless of what's happening at his work.'

They sat down and Cathy wandered over to join them with a bottle of wine in one hand and a glass in the other. Annie sat and listened as Lily chattered on, telling her a condensed biography of each person present. She sipped her wine slowly, wanting to be able to drive home. She had nowhere to go if she got drunk and didn't fancy sleeping in her car. An hour later, when the food was being served and the wine was flowing freely, Lily screeched and then stood up. She ran towards the side of the house, excited to see whoever it was that had just arrived. Annie turned to speak to Cathy about how amazing it all was when she was interrupted by Lily. She turned to see Will standing next to her, grinning.

'Well, fancy seeing you here, of all places – it didn't take you long to get in with the locals.'

He winked at Annie and Lily squealed with delight. 'Eek, tell me you two know each other, but in case you don't, Annie, this is Tom's son, Will.'

Annie felt her cheeks begin to burn. She wanted the floor to open up and swallow her whole – what an idiot. Why had she not figured out who Tom's son was – Will was practically the model of his dad? Annie smiled at Lily. 'Yes, we do know each other, quite well. Isn't it a small world?' She was trying her best to keep her composure but it was increasingly difficult and it made her realise just how little she knew about the man who had stolen and then broken her heart.

Cathy began clapping and chuckling to herself. 'Well, bugger me, if it isn't the lovers reunited.'

Annie glared at her but she was too busy laughing at her own joke, which was fuelled by her fourth glass of wine.

Lily began to drag Will away. 'We'll be back in a minute; I just have to show Tom that Will made it away from his desk.'

Annie stared after them, horrified. She looked across at Cathy.

'Sorry, kid, but I didn't want to ruin the surprise. I realised that you had no idea and thought it might make you turn around and drive straight home if I told you.'

'I feel like a complete fool – how embarrassing. I had no idea. I really should get going.'

She stood up to leave and Cathy shook her head. 'You can't leave now; he's only just arrived. This whole thing was probably done to set the pair of you up.'

Annie turned to see Will, who was being kissed rather

enthusiastically on the cheek by the wealthy, skinny daughter of one of Tom's friends and that was it; she couldn't take it anymore. It wasn't jealousy; it was humiliation. She would never fit in here in a million years. Tom was laughing at something Will had said and Annie began walking back the way she had come with her head down. She had to get out of there. Go home to her modest house, sink a bottle of wine and cry herself to sleep. She almost made it to her car when footsteps came running up behind her and she smelled Will's aftershave before he gently placed his hand on her shoulder to turn her around.

'You can't leave now; I've only just got here.'

She shrugged his hand away. 'I'm sorry; did you think I was here to see you? I had no idea you were coming or I wouldn't have bothered.' She pulled her car key from her pocket and pressed the button to release the lock.

'Annie, please don't go. I want you to stay. It's so nice to see you; I miss you more than words can say.'

She shook her head and got into the car, slamming the door but putting the window down enough to speak to him. 'I came because Lily and Tom have been so nice to me. I had no idea they were your parents. Six months I lived with you and you never thought to tell me anything about your dad. Instead you've let me make a complete fool of myself. I'm going home, Will; enjoy the rest of your night. You were coming here without me anyway so it doesn't make the slightest difference whether I'm here or not.'

She started the engine and began to reverse. Will shook his head and stood behind the car until she had to slam the brakes on.

'Move, Will, I want to go home.'

'I don't want to move. Why are you so pissed off? Because I never told you my dad was loaded? What would you have said if I'd told you? It isn't important and it has nothing to do with you and me, so what's the big deal?'

She couldn't answer him truthfully because she didn't really know what was wrong with her; apart from the fact that she needed to go home and cry all over the place like a right girl. 'Nothing's wrong; it just proves that you and me are not cut out to be together. There's no trust and I'll never be the girl you want me to be.'

Defeated, he stepped to one side to let her leave. He lifted his sleeve to wipe at the corner of his eye. 'But you are already the girl I want you to be. I just want you, Annie Graham.' He whispered it after her, watching her leave, then he turned to face Lily, who was watching with her hand over her mouth.

'Oh, Will, I'm so sorry; I shouldn't have interfered.'

He walked towards her and wrapped his arm around her shoulders. 'Don't be daft, Lily; it's me who has messed this up beyond belief. Thank you for trying and she isn't mad at you; she's mad at me. Last year she went through a really tough time after her husband tried to kill her. Then she managed to get kidnapped by the man who killed those girls last year and he tried to kill her.'

Lily squeezed his hand. 'Dear God, Will. Poor Annie! But I don't understand; why is she so angry with you?'

Will felt his cheeks begin to burn. 'Because I messed up a couple of weeks ago and ended up sleeping next to one of my work colleagues on the sofa. Annie walked in to find the pair of us nearly naked. I swear I never did anything, I wouldn't have, but I've totally fucked it all up, Lil.'

She hugged him. 'You need to sort this out; it's pretty obvious how much she loves you and I've never seen you act this way over a woman, so I think it's safe to say that she's the one, Will. Come and have a drink, something to eat and talk to your dad. Then tomorrow you are going to send her the most exquisite red roses and declare your undying love for her. She needs you but, more importantly, I think that you need her even more.'

Lily led Will back around to the rear garden, where the laughter was louder and the smell of food was too much to bear. He sat down next to Cathy, who was working her way through a plate full of food.

'Well, well, you're not doing a very good job at getting back into our Annie's good books, are you? Did you really not tell her about all this and that one day you'll be a millionaire living the high life? Leaving the rest of us behind, dealing with the same old shit?'

'Get stuffed, Cathy; she would have run a mile. I wanted her to love me for me.'

Cathy spat bits of bread and chewed up burger all over the table. 'Fuck me, you're even more screwed up than I am. Seriously, though, you need to sort it out. She's a good kid and, as much as it pains me to say this because I'm not into all this soppy shit after I caught Dan shagging around, you two make a good couple and I don't want you upsetting my officer. I promised Kav I'd take care of her and you're not helping.' She poked him in the chest.

'What do you think I should do then, seeing as how drinking two bottles of wine has made you the expert of the day?'

'Ask her to marry you, prove that you're serious and don't bring out a prenup agreement for her to sign. I reckon if you fuck it up again she's entitled to go after every penny you have. It might just make you think twice next time temptation jumps in your way.'

A hand patted Will's shoulder and he looked up to see his dad smiling at him, holding two bottles of beer. He handed one to Will and nodded at Cathy. 'That's pretty good advice, Cathy, spoken like a true professional.' He winked at her and she pushed herself up from the chair.

'Excuse me; I need to pay a visit to the ladies' room.'

Tom sat down in the chair next to Will. 'I'm sorry to hear about it, son. It sounds like you have a lot on your mind. Do you want some good advice from an old man?'

Will took a long swig of his beer and nodded.

'As much as I hate to agree with Cathy, she does have a point; after everything Lily has just told me about Annie, if you are serious about her maybe you should take the plunge. You could have a long engagement. It doesn't have to be one of those get yourself married in six weeks jobs, but it might convince her how much you love her.'

*

Annie was furious with herself. She had just acted like a jealous teenager and she was old enough to know better. Why did Will Ashworth have that effect on her? She was going home to bed; maybe in the morning she'd feel a bit better about the whole balls-up. She would need to apologise to Lily and Tom – could she embarrass herself much more?

As she arrived at her two-bedroom semi she burst into tears. It wasn't much but it was hers and she'd worked hard to pay for it. Movement at the bedroom window made her look up, but she couldn't see anything – a trick of the light. She sat in the car for five minutes, staring up at the window to see if anything else moved but it didn't. Her heart was racing and she was expecting the dead kid to press her face against the glass. When Annie was satisfied there were no ghosts in her house she got out of the car and walked around to the back garden, unlocking the door. If she got a whiff of cabbage she was out of there, but it was the sweet smell of vanilla that greeted her from the plug-in air freshener by the back door.

She went in and dumped her bag on a kitchen chair. Opening the fridge, she thought about a bottle of wine but settled for water. Taking her laptop off the worktop, she made her way upstairs to bed. She was going to do some research to see if she could find out who Sean Wood was and where he was now. Then she could approach Will professionally with everything she had, and probably apologise to him for being an idiot whilst hopefully saving the day.

Chapter 29

Grace Marshall had spent the last three days solidly working on a profile good enough to present to Will and his team; she wanted to prove to him just how good she was. Two women found on graves inside the same church grounds and one man found dead in the presbytery adjacent. It wasn't rocket science that the church was the key thing; St Mary's was a Catholic church led by a priest named John Trelmain. It was his nephew who was found dead inside the house. Will had run him through the system and there was nothing: no records for him at all. The priest had lived a quiet life of servitude with no major scandals so it was highly unlikely he was the killer. But Grace did think he was the link; he had to be, she just had to find out how.

She was on a train, which gave her time to think. She was too tired to drive and needed to be able to concentrate on what she was doing. She hadn't told Will she was definitely coming but she wanted to go and visit St Mary's first thing in the morning and put all the information into the software programme she used, called RIGEL, which would work out the parameters using a computer algorithm, which in turn would work out the distance of decay, which meant in a nutshell that many offenders did things that bit closer to home and it could hopefully bring up the area in which the offender was likely to live. It would at least give them something to work from, which would be better than the nothing that they had right now.

She went through the reports again. The footprint sat heavy on her heart as if it was pressing down directly onto her chest. The same footprint was found at both crime scenes and yes, it was a Magnum boot and she knew they were the footwear of choice for most of the coppers and PCSOs, but why was that the only one found? Shouldn't there have been several footprints if that was the case? Of all the officers and technicians who'd visited the scene, the same one stood out. It was more than a coincidence, she was sure of it.

*

Will had slept in his old bedroom on the king-size luxury bed that moulded to your body shape. That and the beer had given him the best night's sleep since Annie had left. He woke up bright and early, showered and got dressed and went downstairs to the sound of the Hoover and the smell of bacon frying. Lily was busy hoovering the hall and Will pecked her on the cheek as he passed. That was one of the reasons that he loved her and, although she would never take his mum's place, she was a pretty good stand-in. She insisted on doing her own cleaning even though they could afford to hire someone to come in and do it. She never pretended to be anything other than herself. He walked on down the hall to the kitchen, where his dad was doing the cooking. He passed Will a huge bacon and sausage bun.

'Here, I'll be eating sausages until Christmas. I bought far too many; at least it will set you up for the morning. Did you sleep well?'

'Yes, thanks, but I need to get going soon. Still got a madman killing people and I have no idea who he is.'

Will bit into the bun and felt brown sauce dribble down his chin. His dad passed him a paper towel.

'Scary stuff that, son; you take it easy out there.'

Will nodded, he gave his dad a hug then made his way to the front door and past Lily, who paused to say goodbye. As he was getting into his car, his dad came running out of the front door after him.

'Will, I've been thinking about the Annie situation. I think that my son the born-again bachelor who was never going to settle down has fallen in love. Stop me if I'm wrong. Do you want to spend the rest of your life with her?'

'I wasn't sure if I could, you know, commit to her in that way but now that she's gone, yes . . . yes, I do. I want to come home to hear her singing along to the radio out of tune. I want to walk in to the smell of freshly baked cakes, even if they are burnt around the edges. I want to kiss her goodnight and sleep with her in my arms every single night and it hurts so much that I've thrown everything that I ever wanted away.'

'I get the feeling that she still feels exactly the same about you but you've hurt her pride and that, Will, is never a good thing to do to a woman.'

Tom pulled a small black velvet ring box from his trouser pocket and handed it to Will. 'That was your mother's engagement ring and it was my mother's before that. Your poor grandad worked for three years solid to pay for that ring but he said that your gran was worth every single penny. Maybe it's time to put it to some good use again; your mum would love that and she would want to see you settled down and happy. The only person who can make that change happen is you.'

Will pocketed the box. He remembered his mum wearing the ring every single day. It was a big diamond, which was flat but in the shape of a flower with smaller diamonds around it like petals and Annie would love it. He smiled at his dad and then hugged him before turning and getting into his car, silent tears falling down his cheeks for his mum who had died too young, for Annie, Laura and himself.

Annie had showered and was back in her car, ready for another day at work. She hoped that Cathy wouldn't be in today; it was too early to have to begin grovelling. The way she had been sinking them back last night made Annie think that she would either be off or on a late shift. Annie's sole purpose today was to find out who Sean was. She thought about the times she'd seen the girl and wondered where she was buried. The church grounds might be a good place to look if she could remember which grave it was she had disappeared behind. She wasn't even going to go out in her uniform because she didn't want to get stopped for a photo opportunity every five minutes.

The small station was quiet, not one person in sight, which was good for her; it meant she didn't have to explain what she was up to. She turned her radio on and clipped it to her shirt and left to go and have a mooch around the churchyard. She didn't know if Father John was back up here or still in Barrow and she felt a bit guilty that she hadn't bothered to check up on him but she was busy. This afternoon she would pay him a visit and see how he was.

She reached the church and walked along the uneven rows of graves, searching the headstones for a girl called Sophie Wood. She had just about given up when she turned a corner by the side of the church and let out a squeal. She'd forgotten about the life-size monument of the angel and had thought it was another dead body. Stepping closer to take a look, she saw that it was a beautiful grave – the angel was lying on her side, her wings tucked neatly behind her and she looked fast asleep. There was an inscription that ran around the stone plinth it was resting on, which read:

Sophie Wood aged 9 years 6/5/1975–29/6/1984
Elizabeth Wood aged 34 years 1/1/1950–30/6/1984
Mother and daughter reunited, safe in God's arms

Annie felt the hairs on the back of her neck prickle. It was true, Sophie had existed and if she had then so must her brother. Annie needed to check the parish records and the registrar's office to see what she could find out. She didn't know if there would be any information on the police computer but she'd check that as well. She should really tell Will and let him or one of his officers do it but she still had her doubts in the back of her mind. She knew that he would believe her and not question her motives but she didn't want him to get a hard time because of her message from the other side. Coppers were relentless with the piss-taking. She also needed to speak to Father John. Although he was only covering for the usual priest, he might be able to help her.

*

Will arrived at work and made his way to his office, where he was pleasantly surprised to be greeted by Grace Marshall, who was sitting behind his desk, her laptop open, typing furiously.

She looked up. 'Morning, Will – don't ask; I had to come. Do you want to get cracking or is there something you need to do first?'

He looked around at his team, who were all busy on the phone or the computer. 'Am I glad to see you; let's get cracking.'

'Good, I was hoping you'd say that. Is there somewhere we can talk in private?'

He raised an eyebrow at her but didn't say anything; instead, he turned and left the office with Grace close behind, carrying her notebook and laptop under her arm. He didn't speak until they had climbed three flights of stairs and were sitting in one of the third-floor empty offices, as far from anyone as possible.

She shut the door behind her. 'I'm sorry about the drama but you need to hear what I've got to say, think about it and then decide what we're going to do, without an audience listening in.'

'Go on then; I have to admit you have me intrigued.'

'Well, I've been through everything that you sent me twice over. I've studied it in great detail and every time it comes back to the same thing.'

'Which is?'

'The boot print; it has me stumped. I've thought about every single scenario and it just doesn't fit. Why, of all the people to attend a crime scene, is there the same Magnum print at both scenes?'

'I would have thought it was pretty obvious, Grace; you, of all people, must know that most police officers wear them so it will belong to one of us.'

'OK, and yes, I do know that. Let's try this then. How many people, other than officers, wear size-twelve Magnums and would have a legitimate excuse to be at a crime scene?'

Will thought about it. 'Erm . . . nobody. Well, maybe the CSI but I'm pretty sure Debs, who attended both scenes, isn't a size twelve. Why.'

'I know this is a scary thought, Will, but it's almost as if it was planted there, staged. Look at me; I left my boot print by mistake because I was one of the first on scene, which makes it obvious that I'm not the killer.'

She watched his face as realisation began to take over. 'Shit, no fucking way. Are you telling me that the killer is a police officer and he left it there on purpose so we wouldn't think anything of it if we found any trace evidence that pointed back to the owner of the shoe?'

Grace nodded. 'I'm sorry but yes, I think the killer is a police officer or someone who has legitimate access to the crime scene. I think he is very organised, a meticulous planner and will have planned everything down to the last detail. These killings are not sexually motivated; they are more about revenge or anger. I'm interested in why he chooses suffocation as a means of death. It could be because he doesn't want to ruin their faces but I'm still working on that one. I also think he is just a normal guy, not too loud or brash. He will get on well with most of his colleagues but he doesn't have any close friends or a girlfriend; he's a loner. In my opinion he's a narcissistic sociopath, which means he kills because he wants to and not because of some primal urge or compulsion. From the detail and the time he's taken to stage his victims, it appears he is quite the perfectionist.'

'But Ryan Trelmain wasn't staged; he was killed and left there.'

'That's because Ryan wasn't a part of his plan. He was in the way and stopping him from getting to who he really wanted – Laura. He went for a swift kill because he needed him out of the equation. He's clever; he knew that you would automatically discount the footprints because you would never in a million years believe that the killer would be one of the good guys. We need to go through the logs and scene logs and list every male officer or member of staff, male and female, who have size-twelve feet and attended, and then you need to cross-reference it with the other two crime scenes to see if they were on duty or in attendance. As organised as he is – and we'll assume it's a him because of the shoe size and the fact that most serial killers are male – he can't keep away and is getting a massive kick out of being at work when the bodies are discovered. If there isn't one person who was at all three crime scenes then we need to check the duties and see how many of the same officers or staff have been on duty each time a body was discovered.

'Oh, and Will, you can't let this out of the bag because I have a feeling that if he finds out you are onto him he will flip and go out in a blaze of glory if needs must. It could get messy. We know that he has no conscience and I don't doubt for a minute he will kill as many people as possible, including himself if he's faced with that option. If I'm right then he doesn't have anyone waiting for him each day when he finishes work and no reason not to finish on a high. Please, Will, we can't give him the chance because he will take it personally once he realises that you are onto him and he may come after you and what's yours, which includes Annie.'

Will, who had been sitting bolt upright listening to her speak for the last five minutes, slumped forward. Putting his elbows on the desk, he buried his head in his hands and sat like that for a couple of minutes and then peered at her through his fingers. 'What the hell are we going to do, Grace?'

'Who can you trust or, more importantly, who doesn't have size-twelve feet?'

'Up to now, that's me. I don't think anyone in my office does but I couldn't really say for sure. What if they just borrowed someone's size-twelve boots and they are really a size nine?

Grace chewed her thumbnail for a few seconds. 'Then, my friend, we are fucked.' She went through the pictures she had tucked away in the back of her notebook until she found the one of the footprint and studied it. After a while she smiled and then held it towards Will. 'Nope, they have to be his boots; you see where it's worn a bit on the heel and the pattern is not as distinct. If the boot was too big it wouldn't have made that impression in the soil. That was where the full weight of the body pressed down into it.'

'Phew, thank Christ for that. So if I go and print off the duties and the logs and photocopy the scene logs we can go through them together. We won't mention it to anyone if he's as much of a ticking time bomb as you think. Why is he picking blonde-haired women?'

'I would say because he has a grudge against someone from when he was younger; they must have blonde hair and be pretty because I would bet that whoever pissed him off once upon a time looked very similar to both victims. It could have been a mother who left him or a sister he was extremely jealous of. It could even have been a previous girlfriend who left him.'

'Do you want to go down and get your stuff and I'll drive you to my house?' He looked at her long blonde hair, which was piled into a loose bun on the top of her head, and her delicate features.

She fitted the victim profile so he couldn't risk her being in the station and he wondered if she'd worked that one out as well.

'If that's what you want to do . . . Oh, and Will, we need to speak to the priest. He is the key to all of this, even if he doesn't know it.'

They left the room and stepped into the deserted corridor, walking along until they passed the staffroom, which was empty. Will felt on edge and couldn't get his head around the fact that one of the good guys had turned out to be not so good after all and that it could go from bad to worse in the blink of an eye. He waited in the corridor while Grace went back into his office to collect her things off his desk. When she came out he walked her to where he had parked his car down a little back street.

'Wait here and I'll go and print the stuff off that we need, then we can go back to my house and see what we can find. The fewer people we tell the better, although I'm tempted to tell Jake and Annie, but I'm scared of dragging them into it. I know for a fact that it won't be Jake, even though he does have size-twelve feet, he's definitely one of us and Alex would be the first to ring me or Annie if he thought that Jake was cracking up. The killer must live alone or have access to somewhere that no one else does because the first body dump wasn't the primary scene and we still have no idea where the first murder took place. We only found the second one because we were searching for the man who Laura left the pub with. The first victim's house has been searched several times by CSI and Task Force and it was clean.'

'Did I read that Tracy Hale phoned up because she thought someone had been inside her home?'

'Yes, you did, but the only reason she thought that was because the Sky remote had been moved.'

'Can you tell me if it was taken away and checked for prints after her body was discovered?'

'I don't think so . . . shit. I didn't even think of that and I doubt anyone else has; we need that control. If the killer stalked her

216

then he could have been in her house and touched the control; his prints could be on them. It's a long shot, but what have we got to lose?'

Grace nodded. 'I'd say so; anything at this point is worth a try. The quicker we can identify the killer the less chance there is of anyone else being hurt.'

Will slammed the car door shut and jogged back to the station, adrenalin making his hands shake a little; a fine sheen of sweat broke out on his forehead, which he wiped with the sleeve of his jacket. Now wasn't the time to screw up; people's lives depended upon him. He rushed into the station and back to his desk. He couldn't even look into the parade room, he was so on edge and frightened he might give something away. CID staff didn't wear work boots so he was pretty sure it wasn't any of his team, but that didn't mean they didn't still have a pair tucked away at home or in the locker room. Every one of them had begun life as a response officer. The office was busy; his team had all been allocated tasks at the morning meeting to be following up on. He sat down at his desk and logged back on to his computer, where he set about printing out the duty rotas for the days the victims were found. He then took the crime scene logs and went to the photocopier. If anyone wondered what he was doing, they didn't comment; in fact they didn't even give him a second glance and fifteen minutes later he had everything that he needed. Without saying a word, he gathered his papers and left the office.

Kav came through the back door just as Will was about to leave. 'How's it going?'

Will found himself instinctively looking down at the man's boots and then snapped his head back up. 'Not so good. What size feet are you? I've got some boots at home that I've only worn a couple of times; you can have them if they'll fit.'

'I don't think my feet will fit in your boots Will; I'm a thirteen.'

'No, these are elevens but they are massive so would probably fit someone who's a size twelve. Do you know anyone who they

217

might fit? I'm having a clear-out and it would be a shame to let them sit there.'

Kav shrugged. 'Jake, probably, one of the bigger men. Do you want me to ask around?'

'No, it's OK. I'll stick a notice on the board; cheers, Kav.'

Will walked out of the station, relieved it wasn't Kav. That would have tipped him over the edge. He hadn't thought about that; it would be one of the bigger guys so that was another thing they could use to cross-reference when they had their list. He couldn't wait to get home and work through what they had and hopefully find the murdering bastard and bring him in before Laura's funeral.

Chapter 30

Annie knocked at the presbytery door quite a bit louder than she had meant to but it was a big house and she wanted to make sure if Father John was in there he would hear her. She waited and was rewarded by hearing footsteps on the other side. She hoped it would be John and then smiled to see him standing on the other side of the now open door. 'Hi, how are you?'

He stepped to one side to let her in. 'I've been better. My sister arrived late last night so one of your kind officers drove me back to meet her. She's been in a bit of a state so I had to phone the doctor. He's not long been and gave her some sleeping tablets; they knocked her right out. I wish there was something that I could take to block this whole nightmare out.'

'I'm so sorry, John; I really am. I hate to bother you, but I was wondering if there is any way to find out who the parish priest was in 1984. Would you know where they keep the records? It's really important.'

'I don't know about the records but I can answer that question because I do know exactly who it was. It was me, a lot younger and ever so keen. Why did you want to know that?'

Annie was shocked and took a minute to consider her reply. What if the man standing in front of her was the killer? But then her relatively new sixth sense told her that he was a good guy and it wasn't him. She hoped that she was right and wasn't walking straight into the arms of another madman. 'Well, this is really hard to explain but I believe it to be true; do you believe in ghosts?'

It was John's turn to pause for a second and Annie felt a bit awkward, wondering if she had just asked him the ultimate no-no in questions that you should never ask a priest. He studied her face and then slowly nodded. Taking her by the elbow, he gently led her through to the kitchen and shut the door behind them.

'What I am about to tell you is between you and me; is that OK? I can't bring the church into any disrepute and I don't want it to become public knowledge, do you understand?'

Annie, lost for words, nodded.

He took a deep breath. 'I do believe in ghosts and when I was a lot younger, and by that I mean thirteen, I kept seeing one that scared the living daylights out of me. It was the main reason I turned to God. I believed that if something like that existed then so must the Almighty. But why do you ask and what has it got to do with 1984?'

She wasn't sure just how much she should disclose to him about herself but then decided that honesty was the best policy; lying was too complicated. 'I had an accident last year where I sustained a serious head injury and ever since then I have occasionally been able to see ghosts. At first I thought I was having hallucinations, but then some really strange things began happening to me and I met a medium who told me that I had developed a sixth sense. Apparently some people do after such injuries.' She waited for John to laugh but he didn't; he just nodded for her to continue. 'I have been seeing a little girl but at the same time I have also seen a man . . . well, he is more of a shadow of a man, but he smells really bad.'

The colour drained from John's face and he looked as if he was going to be sick all over the table. He dropped down onto one of the pine chairs. 'Do you know what this little girl is called?

Is it Sophie?'

'Yes, she told me that her name was Sophie Wood; she also told me that she doesn't want her brother to keep on killing. But the shadow man does and he won't let Sophie go to the light; he keeps her with him in the dark.'

Annie didn't think she had ever seen a living person look the colour that John was right now. His face was ashen.

'I haven't thought about little Sophie Wood for a long, long time. Do you think it's her brother who is killing these women, who killed Ryan? Oh, dear Lord; he thinks it's my fault, he's blaming me for what happened back in June 1984. I swear to God it wasn't my fault. I only wanted to help. I almost gave up my priesthood for Sophie's mum Beth and those children but it all went terribly wrong and now Sean has come back for his revenge.' John crossed himself and began relating the tale of what happened all those years ago. When he'd finished he began reciting a prayer.

Annie took out her phone and rang Will. 'Don't ask the details but I have a name for the killer; at least I'm ninety nine per cent sure he's the killer.'

'What's his name, Annie? I'm at home with Grace. She's come up with a profile and it's not good news. It all points to the killer being a copper.'

Annie made a sound in the back of her throat that sounded like a squeal. 'The name I have is Sean Wood; his sister was called Sophie Wood and she died back in 1984 when Father John Trelmain tried to help the family and I think because of this he has one massive grudge against John. Will, there's a response officer called Sean but I'm sure his second name is Black.'

'Thanks, Annie. I'll look into that now and get some background checks done. For the time being, we need to keep John safe. Grace said that he was the link and once Sean realises that we're onto him he might want to go out in a blaze of glory. Is there anywhere you can take him and keep the both of you out of the way until we find him? I don't want to involve you, but I don't have many people I can trust at this end.'

'I can't take him anywhere, Will. Ryan's mum is here and she's out for the count; the doctor had to sedate her. Whoever this Sean is was orphaned at an early age and, according to John, put into foster care in Manchester or somewhere near to there.'

'Thank you and tell John thanks; we should be able to narrow it down within the hour and not days. I'll ask Jake to come up and stay with you both. I'm really sorry, Annie, I've managed to drag you into something dangerous all over again. Secure the building and you know the drill; don't let anyone, and I mean absolutely no one, in except for Jake.'

Annie felt sick from her stomach to the bottom of her feet. 'I won't. Will, please be careful.'

Chapter 31

Sean was on his rest days – no work for three days – and he'd taken up his usual position outside the hairdressers to watch her. He liked her more than he'd liked the other two. From the salon's Facebook page he knew that she was called Sophie, which was quite fitting. He watched her come out to get her lunch. This time he stayed where he was. When she came back he was going to go in and ask for an appointment with her. He knew that there was no CCTV camera in the shop because there had been an attempted break-in a month ago and he had dealt with it. As she came back around the corner he got out of the truck and headed towards the salon, not giving her a second glance but walking so he got to the front door of the shop at the same time that she did. He knocked her slightly and looked up. 'I'm so sorry; I didn't notice you there.'

She smiled. 'It's OK.'

He opened the door and walked in, holding it open for her, and she gave him a smile that almost melted his heart. He grinned back and headed for the small counter where another girl was on the telephone. Sophie disappeared into the small staffroom at the back but came out almost immediately. 'Can I help you?'

'Sorry to be a complete pain. I'm just after a bit of a tidy-up. Is there any chance someone could run the clippers over my head? I can't do it myself; I always manage to cut myself.'

'I can do it now for you, if you want?'

'I don't want to ruin your lunch break; I can wait until you finish.'

'No, it's fine; it's only a chicken salad baguette, very boring, and I'm not that desperate.' She led him over to her workstation in the window and he sat down. As she tied the gown around his neck he felt a cold shiver run down his spine. She smiled at him in the mirror. 'Did someone just walk over your grave?'

He laughed. 'I hope not.'

'Number two all over?'

He nodded and marvelled at how light-fingered she was and so gentle. It was all over too fast and as she began to brush the hairs off he couldn't resist. 'I know this is a bit cheeky but I was wondering if you fancied a drink when you finish work. It's my day off and I'm fed up of spending it on my own.'

Sophie blushed and let out a small laugh. 'I'm not sure. I mean I want to but I'm supposed to be working late tonight. It's my turn to clean the salon so I won't be finished until seven.'

'Seven is great by me. Do you want me to pick you up or I could meet you at the Railway.'

'If you don't mind, I'll meet you there, thank you.'

Sean offered her his hand. 'I'm Sean. You don't remember me out of my uniform, do you?'

She shook her head.

'I'm the police officer who came a few weeks ago when someone tried to break in.'

He saw her visibly relax. All the stress of accepting a date with a total stranger had been taken off her shoulders. Everyone knew the police were the good guys.

'I thought you looked familiar but I couldn't place you. If it starts to rain will you pick me up from here? Now it's my turn to be cheeky but I'd hate my hair to get wet.' She winked at him and they both laughed. He pulled out his wallet and she pushed him away. 'On the house; that was the quickest haircut and, to be honest, the best chat-up I've ever had. I'll see you at seven.'

Sean said goodbye and walked out of the door and across the road towards his truck, the excitement building inside his chest. He wanted to shout at the top of his voice how bloody wonderful he was but he didn't. He got into his car and drove straight home. He needed to decide where this sleeping angel was going to be laid to rest. He was thinking about taking her to Father John's doorstep. How fitting that the priest was back at the church where it all began and how kind of the local press to tell him. It had been a long time since he'd paid a visit to his mother and Sophie's grave.

As he drove home he decided that this was exactly what he was going to do and he liked it – he liked it a lot. He had taken a few risks today but it was all going to be worth it. He wanted to see the priest's face when they were reunited and he had decided that as long as the priest suffered then he would be done with all this. His mission would be finished.

*

Annie stood up and stretched. 'I need you to show me the location of every window and door; we need to make this place as safe as we can until they capture him. They are on the verge of narrowing it down but we can't take any chances. Once Sean realises they are onto him he may just come looking for you and I promise I won't let him hurt you. Then I want you to start at the beginning and tell me exactly what happened in 1984.'

John led her around the house from room to room, where they secured the windows and locked all the doors. In the lounge were two huge patio doors and Annie knew they were the weak point. If Sean did come here it would be through them that he would try to gain access. She double-checked they were locked

225

and then began dragging the heavy chesterfield sofa over to put in front of them, as well as anything else she could find. By the time they had finished they were both sweating and breathing hard. 'If he does come in this way, at least it makes it awkward and we should hear him.'

She turned and checked the internal door to the room to see if it had a lock but it didn't; only the bedrooms did. When they went back into the hall Annie dragged a chair over from the small writing desk in the corner and propped it underneath the handle. She had no idea how big or strong Sean was; if it was the Sean she sometimes worked with then yes, he was tall and fit. He wasn't married but she had no idea if he was in a relationship or not. She'd always got on with him and would find it hard to believe if it did turn out to be him. What a mess this whole thing was. One thing she did believe, though, was the man was on a mission and he would do anything to finish what he'd started. She didn't say any of this to John; he was distressed enough. They finished checking every room, except the one his sister was asleep in.

'I don't want to disturb her. Would you go in and check that her window is shut?'

Annie nodded; she opened the door slowly so it didn't squeak then tiptoed across the wooden floorboards to the open window to close it. The woman on the bed let out a small murmur but didn't open her eyes. Annie left as quietly as she'd entered and shut the door behind her.

'My friend Jake, who is also a policeman, is on his way from Barrow so everything will be just fine.'

John nodded and began to walk towards the stairs. Annie felt a cold hand touch her arm and she turned to see Sophie standing behind her. The little girl lifted her finger to her lips and this time Annie understood. The girl walked into the bathroom and she followed her in.

'I won't be a minute; just need the toilet.' Annie's heart was racing and the room was so cold that the mirror had fogged up.

'Sean is going to kill again. He already has a victim and the shadow man is coming here. He wants you, Annie. He said he will take Sean's soul as soon as he's killed Father John but he also wants your soul because he said you were very special. John tried his best to help me but he wasn't strong enough to win. You need to tell him that he has to fight the shadow man and banish him for good this time because he is getting stronger and won't stop. You must tell John if he can put an end to it I will be able to go into the light and be with my mum; it's been so long since I saw her and I'm tired of being in the dark.'

'How can he stop him, Sophie? What does he need to do?'

'John will know; he's always known. He was just too afraid to do it, but he must this time or you'll both die and be stuck in the shadows forever.'

Sophie handed her the broken toy figure that Annie had put in her kitchen drawer. 'Sean used to love the A-Team; he gave me this the day I died. Give it back to him and tell him that I want him to stop all of this.' A faint smell of rotten cabbage entered the room and Sophie's face turned into a mask of horror. 'He's near; I have to go. Tell John that I said thank you but this time he must fight his very best if he's to save us all.'

Annie watched as Sophie's image faded before her. One minute she had been talking to the ghost of a dead girl and the next she was shivering in a room that had turned into a walk-in freezer. Annie felt a heavy ball of dread lodge in the base of her throat. She didn't want to die – the shadow man could get fucked. But she also didn't know how to stop him. Her face as white as Sophie's, she ran down the stairs to the kitchen to find John.

He looked at her face and shook his head. 'No, please, I don't want to know. This has got to stop.'

Annie sat down on the chair opposite him. 'Sophie died while you were trying to help her, didn't she?'

He nodded in slow motion.

'She told me to tell you thank you, but that he's back and you

227

have to banish him for good this time because he's on his way here and he wants me. He's keeping Sophie prisoner. Please, John, tell me you know what she is talking about because I'm just about keeping it together. I have no idea how to fight a shadow man that wants my soul. Sophie told me that you know how but that you've always been afraid to do it.'

John buried his head in his hands and sobbed, not for himself but for Beth and Sophie and little Sean who had blamed him all these years with so much hatred that it had turned him into a cold-hearted killer. He cried for his nephew and the two women who had been killed, all because his own faith hadn't been as strong as it should have been in 1984. He had lost the only woman he had ever fallen in love with because of his relationship with God. Annie leant over and grabbed his hand, squeezing it tightly. She let him cry until the tears dried up and there were no more left inside him, then she handed him a tissue and waited for him to blow his nose.

'Right, I want you to start at the beginning and then I want to know what we can do about this shadow man. I'll help you fight him because, as far as I'm concerned, no more people are dying because of him, especially not me.'

Chapter 32

Will and Grace sat at his kitchen table, heads bent over the sheets of A4 paper he had printed out, with a bright yellow highlighter each. He had narrowed it down to three men who were all, as far as he was concerned, excellent police officers. There was Sean Black, who was the obvious choice because of his first name; Smithy, aka Steve Smith, but he wasn't a big man and Will doubted he would have size-twelve feet; he had also been in the job as long, if not longer than Will and he definitely wasn't the brightest man in the station. There was also Joe Parker, who was tall and could well have the right size feet. Joe was the one with the least number of years' service and the one they knew very little about. They both agreed that it was between Sean Black and Joe Parker as they were on the same shift; Smithy's shifts crossed over. Will's gut instinct told him it was Sean Black but he didn't want to make assumptions and screw it up. Joe and Sean were on their days off, which gave him a little time.

He rang Annie again. 'Can you ask Father John to describe what Sean looked like; ask him if there were any distinguishing features – scars, moles, birth marks, maybe 666 behind his ear. We've managed to narrow it down to Sean Black and Joe Parker.'

There was a pause while Annie asked, 'John said that Sean has a scar on the left side of his cheek; he fell out of a tree onto an action figure. Of course it will have faded by now but it should still be there. I know for a fact that Joe doesn't have a scar on his cheek; he's the one who is so vain he spends more time grooming himself than he does doing jobs. The last briefing I went to, I remember staring at him and trying to figure out why on earth he loved himself so much; I'm positive it's not him. I can't remember about Sean, though. I've never paid much attention to him, really.'

'Thanks, Annie; it looks as if Sean Black is our man. I'll get someone to run some background checks on him. I don't really know him and I haven't got a clue where he is or what he's up to. It goes without saying if Sean or Joe Parker turn up, hit your red emergency button and don't let them in. I'll ring the boss now and ask him to get the ball rolling at this end. As soon as we know what we're doing I'll ring you back.'

'Good; try and make it soon because he already has his next victim lined up. I don't think he'll do anything while it's daylight but once it gets dark it's a whole different game.'

'How do you know so much, Annie?'

'If I told you that a dead girl told me, would you believe me?'

The phone went silent. Finally Will found his voice. 'Yes, I would believe you, Annie, and I do believe you. Please be careful.'

'You too, Will.'

He ended the call and looked at Grace. 'I'm sure that Sean Black is our man, from what Father John has said, but until we get those background checks done we can't be positive. According to Annie, he already has another victim lined up.'

He dialled the DI's number, relieved when he answered it on the second ring, then he spent the next ten minutes relaying everything to him. Will had to hold the phone away from his ear while the DI had a complete shit-fit on the other end. After a minute he put the phone back. 'So, boss, how are we going to play this? We don't have much time; he needs picking up before he kills again.'

'I'm not disagreeing with you, Will, but seriously, one of us – how, or even why? This is going to cause the biggest scandal since the Yorkshire bloody Ripper. Have we got enough proof to bring him in? Grace's profile is all very well but if we bring him in and there is nothing concrete his solicitor is going to walk all over us and he'll be let out again to kill, not to mention lodge a complaint for harassment. I admit a matching boot print puts him at the scene but it will get dismissed; CPS will throw it out. They will want more evidence than a boot print and a hunch and you know it as well. Unless there is any forensic evidence at his house – we need to go in and search it. Let me get hold of his personnel file and think this through for a bit. I'll get back to you soon.'

Will put his phone down on the paper-strewn table. 'Well, that went better than I expected but not as well as I'd have liked. We really do need to find something concrete that ties him to the scene but time's running out. It's going to be hard to keep this quiet. The more people find out about it, there's a greater chance he'll realise that we're onto him. We need someone to keep tabs on him but it can't be any of us. He'd recognise us; it needs to be someone from another area.'

'I could do it.'

'No way; it's kind of you to offer but you're not trained for any of this and you have blonde hair and would be just his type. I can't let you put yourself in danger, Grace.'

'Yes, but you could give me a radio and show me how to use it. I could park up near to his house and watch for while; you could be around the corner with backup and run around to save the day if need be.'

As tempting as it sounded, he couldn't do it. 'Thanks, but no thanks; we'll think of something.'

*

John finished telling Annie about the terrible time back in 1984. He didn't leave anything out. He told her about the awful time he'd had choosing between Beth and God. It was about time he confessed to someone. 'If I had been a real man I would have turned my back on God and taken Beth, Sophie and Sean away from here but I was too scared. I think that's what Sophie is trying to say, that because of how I was feeling my faith wasn't strong enough to fight the shadow man back then.'

'What about now, John? How strong is your faith now?'

'It has never been stronger; the older I get, the stronger it becomes. The thought that sooner rather than later I will meet my maker strengthens it every day.'

'Good, because what do we need? I can feel him hanging around, although I only keep getting a faint whiff of him now and again, but I know he is waiting for the right moment to make his move.'

John went into the lounge and returned with an old leather Bible and a crucifix. He placed them both on the table and laid some rosary beads on top of the Bible and then he began to pray. When he had finished he crossed himself and then he turned and placed his hand on her head and said a different prayer; this one was to St Michael:

> 'Saint Michael the Archangel,
> Defend us in battle.
> Be our protection against the wickedness and snares of the devil.
> May God rebuke him we humbly pray;
> And do Thou, O Prince of the Heavenly Host,
> By the Divine Power of God,
> Cast into hell Satan and all the evil spirits
> Who roam throughout the world seeking the ruin of souls.'

He made the sign of the cross on Annie's forehead and placed the rosary beads around her neck.

'I can be strong, Annie. This time I won't let him win and, no matter what happens, you have to let me get on with it. If this is my time then so be it but I will not die and go to the darkness. I refuse and, as God is my witness, I will not let him hurt you.'

Annie lifted the hands she had been sitting on to stop them from shaking and squeezed his hands. She hoped Jake would arrive any minute now because John had gone into serious priest mode and if she was honest she was terrified; the atmosphere in the house was charged like static electricity and she was waiting for it to start crackling.

'I need to go into the church, Annie; I want to meet him on God's ground. He pretends that he can't come inside but he can and he will. Tonight he means business.'

'I'm sorry, John, but we need to stay here. The church is far too open and I can't watch your sister and you. It's not just the shadow man; we have no idea where Sean is or what he's planning.'

'It's OK; I understand – you're right and that's fine. He's waited almost thirty years for this; another hour or two won't make much difference, but I do need to be on my own somewhere. Do you mind if I go into the lounge to gather my thoughts and pray?'

'Of course not. I'm sorry, John. I understand and when Jake gets here we can reassess the situation.'

She watched him pick up his Bible and the crucifix. His face was grim and he looked much older than he had the first time she'd met him less than forty-eight hours ago. He meant business and she felt terrible for him. He went into the hall, moving the chair from the door handle, and then turned to face her. 'I will call you when I'm finished; please will you make sure that my sister doesn't come in and disturb me. I really, really need to concentrate.'

'I will. Do you want me to knock on the door when Jake gets here?'

'No, once I've said my prayers and prepared myself I will come and get you. Thank you, Annie, for everything. I'm so sorry we had to meet under such terrible circumstances but I'm glad that we did.'

Annie smiled then left him to it. She didn't feel right about what had just sounded like a goodbye and she didn't feel very good about leaving him to it, but she wasn't a priest and didn't know what they did in these situations. She didn't have a clue what she should be doing in this situation either and not for the first time she wondered how on earth she got herself mixed up in these kind of scrapes. She went into the kitchen and texted Jake: *Hurry up, the priest is freaking out and I'm scared. I think you may finally get to see your ghost.*

Taking out her pocket notebook, she began to write everything up. This was way beyond the call of duty but she was doing it for Will. She hoped he was safe and they had managed to locate Sean down in Barrow. She was engrossed in writing, leaving out the visits from the dead girl and anything to do with the shadow man. A loud knock on the front door made her jump up from the chair. She withdrew her baton and went to peer through the spyhole. A sigh of relief escaped her lips as she saw the man mountain called Jake standing on the other side, blowing her kisses. She opened the door and he stepped in and hugged her. 'Woman, how do you do it? How do you manage to get involved in all this madness? There is one advantage, though; life is never dull with you around.'

His phone beeped and he pulled it from his pocket to read her text, which had only just arrived; he looked at her. 'Are you kidding me? Seriously, don't tell me you're seeing dead people again.'

Annie blushed. 'Not through choice. I don't exactly pick and choose when to see them – they just appear. Come through to the kitchen and I'll fill you in on everything.'

'Where's the Holy Father?'

Annie elbowed him in the side. 'Shh, he'll hear you. He's praying in the lounge and this is no joke. He's preparing himself to do battle with a shadow man.'

Jake rolled his eyes. 'Oh, this is getting better and better. Who is the shadow man?'

'I don't know exactly, but he smells really bad and he collects people's souls and keeps them with him in the darkness. He has a young girl called Sophie trapped with him and it's her brother who is killing everyone.'

Jake flopped down onto one of the kitchen chairs. 'Have you started on any medication that I should know about, Annie?'

She sat down opposite him. 'I'm being serious; apparently this shadow man wants my soul and he's coming to get me. I'm freaking out. Father John has known him for a long time and he is going to save the day and my soul – I hope.'

'Good, I hope so. I mean I'm here to defend you but if all I can smell is someone with a case of bad wind whilst you're doing battle for your soul what am I supposed to do – stand next to you waving a cross around?'

'I don't know. I'm waiting for John to tell me. Do you think I should go and check on him? He's been in there for a while now.'

Jake shrugged. Annie went and pressed her head against the wooden door. If he was still praying she'd leave him to it. The room was silent; she listened for any sign of movement but there wasn't a sound. For the second time in thirty minutes she withdrew her baton. Jake, who was watching from the kitchen door, did the same and stepped behind her. She turned to him and whispered, 'It's too quiet.' He nodded and then pushed her to one side, taking hold of the door handle. Annie felt her heart hammering so loud she couldn't hear herself think. He pushed it down and slammed the door open, stepping into the room. It was empty but the patio doors were wide open. Annie looked around. 'Fuck, he's gone to the church. Now what? His sister's asleep upstairs. I'm supposed to be watching her.'

Jake climbed over the sofa and pulled the doors shut, locking them. 'Sleeping Beauty should be just fine. If what you say is true, then it's John the killer wants. I bet he won't even know about his sister. We'll lock her in and go to the church.'

Annie knew he was right; they had no choice, but she felt uneasy leaving the house. Will had told her to stay put but he didn't know about the shadow man. Jake opened the front door. She looked around and then followed him outside, taking the key and locking it from the outside then pocketing it inside her body armour.

'How far is the church?'

Annie pointed to the massive building next door and he laughed. 'Well, thank the good Lord for small miracles. I didn't fancy running a mile in this heat.'

He took off and she followed close behind. As they reached the door to the church there was a terrible smell, which made Annie gag. 'He's here . . . oh, God, I don't know what to do!'

'Who's here, Annie – the killer or the shadow man? Please don't say both.'

'Can't you smell him?'

The colour drained from Jake's normally tanned face, which made her feel even worse. 'No, I can't, but I guess we go in and face the music or whatever it is.' He grabbed hold of the black iron ring and turned it to open the wooden door, and they stepped inside.

Chapter 33

Will heard someone hammering on his door and looked at Grace. 'Stay in here, shut the door and if you hear me shout, run like fuck out of the back door and don't stop until you find someone to help you. If it's a policeman then keep on running.'

He opened the kitchen drawer and pulled out a claw hammer that Annie kept in there for emergencies. Holding it behind his back, he cautiously approached the front door and looked through the tiny pane of glass to see his boss, Dave Martin, standing on the other side. He opened the door. 'Dave, what are you doing here?'

'I've come to try and work out what the hell we're going to do, Will; I can't get my head around it that the bastard is one of our own. It's just not right. I mean how the hell did he get into the job in the first place?'

'Well, to be fair, boss, I don't think they ask if you have ever killed or wanted to kill someone on the application form.'

'Well, maybe it's about time they did. It's me and you until Task Force arrive from Kendal. I've asked for them because they won't have any connections with him – I hope. I've told them to rendezvous here. I hope that's all right?'

'Fine, I suppose it will have to be. We can't risk going into the station in case word gets around.'

'I've asked for two of them in plain clothes and we'll let them use your car to keep observations on the guy until we can make a move. It's a bit crap but it's the best I can come up with. I don't watch enough television to know how to deal with this.'

Will couldn't help laughing. He was right – it was turning into an episode of some brash American cop show. 'I guess we'll sit tight until they arrive then.' He led the way into the kitchen, where a relieved Grace was standing holding a heavy cast-iron frying pan.

'Phew, I don't think I could have lifted this high enough to smack anyone with, it's so damn heavy.'

They waited impatiently for the arrival of Task Force. Will couldn't stop pacing up and down and Dave was tapping his feet so hard the floor was vibrating. When the loud knock on the door came thirty minutes later, Will did exactly the same and was relieved to see the armed officers lined up outside his door. They all piled into Will's not big enough kitchen. It was a pretty scary sight to have so many armed men all dressed in black crammed around his kitchen table, but it made Will feel a whole lot better that they were here.

When he'd finished telling them what the situation was there had been some loud gasps of surprise and shock that it was one of their own they were going after. There was some debating about the best way to approach the situation between the Task Force sergeant and the DI and when they finally agreed on what they were going to do they all left in separate cars. Will, Dave and Grace left in Dave's car, the two plain-clothes officers left in Will's BMW and the rest of them piled into the back of the armed response vehicle to make their way to the agreed rendez-vous point, which was a car park at the back of a school that had been empty and boarded up for the last twelve months and was due to be demolished sometime soon.

They had to find Sean Black first. His personnel records showed he had moved here from Manchester four years ago, he was an orphan and pretty much matched everything that the priest had told them. They were relying on him being at home; if he wasn't then it could prove very tricky. They knew he had a black truck and the registration had been passed to every officer in their little group so they could keep watch for it. Sean lived in a cul-de-sac so they couldn't park in there; it would be far too obvious, so the officers in Will's car parked in a residents' only parking bay on the street that led to Sean's. Will parked at the opposite end of the street, way out of view. The response vehicle stayed on the school car park. One of the plain-clothes officers got out of the car and strolled into Sean's street, where he took a quick look around and then walked back out again. His truck wasn't there, so now it was a matter of waiting to see how long it was before he turned up.

*

Sean's feeling of being on top of the world soon passed when he noticed a black BMW that he recognised parked in the street near to his house. He had seen Will getting in and out of it enough times to know whose car it was. Instead of turning into the street, he drove straight past, across the junction and away from his house. His insides felt as if they had been filled with pure nitrogen oxide they were so cold. *They know; the bastards know. How had they figured it out? Surely they were too thick to work it out. Maybe it was a coincidence and they were doing another job and he was panicking, and then again maybe they were that good.*

Luckily for him, he had his bag with his murder kit on the floor of the passenger seat. What should he do? He had three hours before he had to pick Sophie up. Should he cut his losses and run or should he finish what he had started? If they knew about him then they would probably have worked out the connection between him and the priest. So many problems and he couldn't think straight for the sick feeling inside of him. He needed to go somewhere quiet and think things through. If they were waiting for him to go home they would be waiting around for a very long time because he wasn't going back.

He drove into the town centre and hoped they hadn't given his registration out to every copper in Barrow. This thought made his hands become slick with sweat and he found it difficult to grip the steering wheel. He drove onto one of the roads that led out of Barrow and onto the coastal road where he would find one of the small villages to park up in and sit and think everything through. The sea was on its way in and there were lots of people on the sands, enjoying a normal life and having fun. Since the day Sophie died he'd never led a normal life; it had shaped his entire future and now look where he was. He wondered how different his life would be if they hadn't died and left him all alone. Would he be married now with children of his own or would he still be the same – a cold-hearted killer?

He knew a few people that he worked with that lived along the coast road so he carried on driving past Roosebeck until he reached the road for Gleaston and turned off. There was an old water mill that had been turned into a café; he doubted that anyone he worked with would be in there right at this very moment, and if they were then they were on their days off like him so they wouldn't know what was going on. The car park for the café only had one other car in it which was an old silver VW Golf. He parked in the opposite corner to it underneath a huge oak tree and got out of his truck. He crossed the road and went into the café, which was deserted; the only person inside was the woman behind the counter. She smiled at him and he grinned back. 'Afternoon.'

He took a table in the far corner where he could see who came in and out. Picking up a menu, he pretended to read it; he felt too ill to eat anything.

The woman came over with her notebook. 'What can I get you?'

'Just a cappuccino, please. I'm waiting for my friend so we'll order food when she gets here.'

'Fine by me, darling, you're the first customer this afternoon; it's been dead. I won't be long.'

She walked away and he picked up a paper napkin, lifting it to his head to wipe the sweat that had formed on his brow. There were a stack of magazines on a coffee table near to him, so he picked one up and opened it to look as if he was busy but he couldn't concentrate because the words and pictures were one big blur. What was he going to do? He should cut his losses and leave town. He had money in a bank account under a false name so he would be OK until he could find another job, but part of him wanted to finish what he'd started. Could he live with himself if the priest didn't die? He didn't know if he could.

The waitress interrupted his thinking and placed a large mug of frothy coffee on the table in front of him. 'I'm just out the back baking for tomorrow; if you want to order anything else just give me a shout.'

He gave her his nicest smile and she smiled back. It was funny how women found him so trustworthy. They had no idea that, given the right circumstances, he would kill them and think nothing of it. He emptied four sachets of sugar into the steaming mug and stirred. *Now what am I going to do?*

*

Jake stepped into the church, closely followed by Annie. The light wasn't very good and the stench was even stronger inside. They couldn't see John but a groan came from somewhere near to the front of the building and Annie took off, running in that direction. This time Jake followed her. Annie could just make out John, who was lying on the floor near to the font. He was clutching a crucifix but what did it for Jake was the dense black shadow of a huge man who appeared to be sitting on the priest's chest. Its outline was human but Jake could see all the way through to the other side and he felt his legs turn to jelly. His feet froze to the ground and he was unable to move any further.

Annie rushed forward and saw Sophie standing near the altar with a look of terror on her face. 'Sophie, tell me what I need to do.' The girl didn't lift her gaze from the priest on the floor so Annie stepped in front of her, blocking him from view. 'Please, Sophie, he's killing him and then he's going to kill me. What can I do?'

Sophie pointed to the font. 'I don't know, Annie. Try throwing some of that holy water on him and saying a prayer. John was saying a prayer to St Michael when he got really mad. Do you know it?'

Annie racked her brain; she had heard John recite it less than an hour ago. Running to the font, she pushed the heavy piece of wood that covered it to one side with such force that it clattered onto the stone floor, then she looked around for something to scoop the water into. On the altar was a gold communion cup. Running across to grab hold of it, she plunged it into the cold water and filled it up to the brim and then ran back towards John and the scary thing sitting on top of him. John's face was grey and his eyes had rolled to the back of his head. Annie prayed to God then, begging for His help, and at that moment she believed in Him more strongly than she'd ever thought possible. She aimed the cup and emptied the contents all over the shadow man and John. She felt a tiny cold hand grasp her left hand and the words flowed from her mouth and Sophie's at the same time:

'*Saint Michael the Archangel,*
Defend us in battle.
Be our protection against the wickedness and snares of the devil.'

There was a cry from the shadow in front of her and it shifted from John's chest, pulling itself upright, and turned to face her. Annie felt her hands tremble but Sophie squeezed tighter. The shadow moved until it was standing directly in front of her, its face millimetres from her own, and the stench was overpowering. Its red eyes stared straight through her own and down into the very depths of her soul. It opened its mouth to reveal a set of razor-sharp pointed teeth and Annie had never felt so terrified. Another hand grasped her right hand; this was one much bigger, the same size as hers, and it squeezed tightly. She looked over to see a woman who was an older beautiful version of Sophie smiling at her. The woman nodded once at Annie for her to continue and Annie began to recite the rest of the prayer:

'May God rebuke him, we humbly pray;
and do Thou, O Prince of the Heavenly Host,
By the Divine Power of God,
Cast into hell Satan and all the evil spirits
Who roam throughout the world seeking the ruin of souls.

'Now, get away from here! I banish you for all of eternity from ever coming into the light. You mother fucker, go back to hell or wherever it is you come from and let Sophie go!'

The shadow man's mouth snapped shut with a look of surprise that this woman could do what the priest had failed to do. His piercing red eyes, which minutes ago had been searching for Annie's soul, faded to a very pale pink and he began to disintegrate, like pieces of ash from a fire blowing into the wind. And then he was gone.

John opened his eyes and tried to sit up. He looked across at Annie and sobbed to see her standing with Sophie and Beth on either side of her. Finally good had united against evil. Annie looked at Beth as she whispered, '*Thank you,*' and then she stepped to the side and watched with delight as Sophie stepped into her mum's arms. A warm golden light encased them both and they glowed so brightly that Annie had to shield her eyes to keep on looking; hot tears began to roll down her cheeks.

John managed to drag himself up and put his arm around

her. 'Thank you, Annie; you have done a truly wonderful thing.'

Sophie and Beth smiled at John, and again Beth spoke. 'We'll be waiting for you, John, when your time comes, I promise.' And then they too were gone.

Tears fell from John's eyes. Annie hugged him, then turned to face Jake, who hadn't moved one inch. His face was paler than Sophie's. He tried to speak but all that came out was a mumble. John bent down to pick up the communion cup, which had fallen from Annie's hands, and placed it back on the altar. 'If only Sean could have such a happy ending. Come on. Hadn't we better get back to the house; there is still a killer on the loose.'

Annie grabbed hold of Jake's elbow, pushing him forward to get his feet moving. She led him through the church to the door. It no longer smelled bad; the stench had been replaced with the sweet smell of the fresh flowers that adorned the end of each pew and they smelled of summer and hope. Annie had never felt so good. They had managed to send the shadow man back to wherever it was he'd come from and reunited Sophie with her mum. That was a truly wonderful gift and, as scary as it was, she felt as if she'd accomplished so much more in the last six months than she had in thirty-three years. John lagged behind and she waited for him and then linked her arm through his.

The presbytery was still locked up. Annie took the key from her pocket and opened the door just as a bleary-eyed woman was walking down the stairs.

Chapter 34

After almost two hours Will was beginning to get edgy. What if Sean had gone past and seen something was up? He might have no intention of coming home tonight. What they needed was to get inside his house and get real proof that Sean Black was the killer. The DI agreed with him and began phoning the people who could get him a warrant, then he told the Task Force officers to come round, ready to secure entry to the house once they had the go-ahead. They couldn't sit around much longer. There were officers stationed on each street corner watching out for Sean's truck, should he return in the middle of them searching his house.

Thirty minutes later Stu knocked on the window of the car, waving a folded piece of paper at them. 'Be nice to know what's going on like? You sod off and leave us all wondering what's happening and now this.'

'Sorry, but I couldn't risk it getting out before I'd come up with something. You haven't told anyone, have you?'

'Not a dicky bird, Will, not even Kav, who has been looking for you for the last hour and getting in a shittier mood by the minute. He's not going to be too impressed when he finds out what you've been sneaking around doing.'

'Get in the car, Stu, and shut up; it's on a strictly need-to-know basis.'

'Yeah, well, I don't know anything other than you just asked me to sneak around getting a warrant signed so you can go in and search Sean Black's house, who, by the way, is off work today – rest days. I passed his truck two hours ago driving down Roose Road.'

'Bollocks! Are you winding me up, Stu? Because it's not funny if you are.'

'No, I swear it was him.'

'Was he on his own? Where do you think he was going? Are there any Catholic churches down that way?'

'I have no idea, Will, but if you had told me what you were doing I would have known to follow him and tell you exactly where he went. Are you seriously thinking he's the killer? I mean, do you know what you're saying? He's one of us.'

Will wished everyone would stop reminding him that Sean was one of them; he felt bad enough about this and, as much as he wanted to catch the bastard, he was also hoping this was going to turn out to be some wild goose chase because it was morally wrong to even suspect one of their own of being a murderer.

'I think so, from what Grace has said, and looking at the evidence it all ties in, but your guess is as good as mine. I'd rather it turned out to be Mrs Plum in the library with a candlestick.'

Will passed the warrant to his boss, who was now outside the car smoking the cigarette he'd blagged off the sergeant in Task Force, who himself must have smoked at least twenty in the last two hours.

'Five years since I had a cigarette, five bloody years, and this is the only thing I can think of to calm my nerves.' He skimmed over the warrant, nodded at Will, then gave the all-clear to the entry team. Within three minutes the door had been put through and the house secured. Will and Dave, who were now suited and booted, went inside. The house was clean, too clean for a single man, and very sparsely furnished. It looked like a show home, nothing out of place and all very modern. They went into the lounge, where there was a sofa and a chair positioned to look out of the bay window. Next to the chair was a small table with two notebooks on it. Will walked across, picked one up and began to thumb through it. After several moments he realised it was a list of dates and times when the other residents in the street came in and out of their houses. The other book was full of pictures of churches that had been cut from newspapers. He recognised St Mary's and shouted over to Dave, who was bent on his hands and knees by the sofa. He looked at Will and Will waved the notebooks at him.

'You can call CSI out, Will; there are a couple of what look like strands of blonde hair down the side of this cushion.'

Will radioed the control room with his request and then he left the living room and went into the kitchen, pulling out drawers. They didn't contain much but the last one he pulled out had some heavy-duty clear plastic bags and tie wraps inside. He left it sticking out so they could be photographed and wondered if this was what he had used. Matt had said the girls had died by suffocation, so it was a possibility. He opened the fridge, which was stocked full of chicken, fish, veg and other assorted healthy food. Sean was planning on coming back. He wouldn't have stocked up if he was going to run. He moved a box of eggs and saw a prescription bottle of tablets – Rohypnol. Sean's backup if things went wrong or did he use it so they didn't go wrong? He wondered if they should have waited until Sean came home before searching his house.

Dave's voice shouted from upstairs and he went up them to see him standing in the doorway to one of the bedrooms, his face sombre.

'Bloody good shout, Will – he's our man.'

He stepped to one side and Will walked into the small office, his eyes fixing on the corkboards. One each for Tracy Hale and Laura Collins. Each one was named after an angel. There was a third board with a name on and a couple of pictures of a

247

blonde-haired woman who didn't look a day past twenty-three. Annie had been right; what if they were too late?

'Fuck me; this is wrong on so many levels.'

Will turned to see Dave standing in front of an open wardrobe. He walked over to see what was wrong and saw the suit Laura had been wearing in the pub hanging up all neat next to another set of clothes which he assumed belonged to Tracy Hale.

'Will, he is one sick bastard.' The DI took out his phone and began a heated conversation with someone about making Sean Black top wanted and that he was not to be approached by uniformed officers. He finished his call. 'Well, Kav's not too happy to put Sean Black as top wanted. As you may have heard, he didn't really agree with that last bit of advice and said he was going looking for him. He's a wee bit pissed off we didn't involve him in our enquiries.'

'Kav will come round; he'll be as shocked as we are. But it won't take Sean long to realise we're looking for him. He'll either go to ground or flip and I wouldn't want to bet on which one.'

*

Sean finished his coffee and wondered if he should kill the waitress. No one else had come in but he needed another car and could take hers. None of this was in his plan but he'd come to realise now that he was going to have to take some risks if he wanted to carry on. His hand had been forced and if there were any more deaths it wasn't his fault; it was Will and whoever had helped him to figure out that Sean was the killer.

The waitress came out, balancing a huge Victoria sandwich cake on a glass stand. 'Your friend's late; did she stand you up?'

'She's just texted to say she can't get her car started. I'm going to go and give her a hand.' He stood up and walked towards the woman, who was busy sorting out the fridge to make room for her magnificent creation.

248

Ten minutes later he was holding her car keys in his hand. He turned the sign on the door to Closed and turned off the lights. Then, after locking the door behind him, he strolled over to her car. This was a beautiful place, so peaceful. The sound of running water was very soothing and he thought that if he pulled the next two murders off he would leave and go as far away from Barrow as possible. Look for a small cottage in the country, one with a stream running through the garden. He could imagine stringing a hammock in a tree and lying there reading on a summer day just like this. He would get all his groceries delivered, grow his hair and a beard and no one would have a clue who he was; a fresh start.

He drove back into town, completely avoiding the area that surrounded his house, taking the long way round and the busy road that cut through the industrial estate. He passed a couple of police cars but he had a baseball cap pulled low down on his head and sunglasses; none of them gave him a second glance. He knew they would be on high alert, looking for his truck. He had purposely picked the most popular model so the police would be busy looking for every similar black truck in a five-mile radius.

He had another hour before it was time to meet Sophie, so he parked at the back of Marks and Spencer's along the side street, which was permanently busy. It was a one-hour parking bay but the cars came and went so often it was hard to keep a track of them. He got out of his car and strolled around to the small shop on the main street near to the hairdressers. He got a bottle of water and a paper then went back to his car to wait. He looked like most of the other drivers who were waiting for their wives or girlfriends to finish shopping.

It was finally time for her to finish work and he drove around to pick her up. He could see her all alone inside the shop and wondered if he should just go in there and kill her but then he realised that was a stupid idea; how was he supposed to get her body out to the car without being seen? Subway was just a few doors down and it was always full of teenagers. He wasn't thinking clearly and needed to get a grip before he did something totally stupid. She looked out of the shop window and he waved frantically at her from across the street; she grinned and waved back. Within a minute she was out of the shop, the door locked and crossing the street to get into his car. 'Hiya, thanks for picking me up; it's been a long day.'

'No problem. I bet it has. Your poor feet must get so tired standing in the same spot all day. I was wondering if you fancied a change from round here and going up the Lakes? It's such a beautiful night. This car isn't mine. It belongs to a friend – he's a priest but don't let that put you off! I thought we could stop off for a bite to eat and then while we're up there I can return his heap of junk and collect mine, which has been parked up outside the church in Windermere whilst his was getting repaired.'

He tried not to look at her whilst she made up her mind. It was a lot to ask and he didn't want her freaking out but she nodded. 'It sounds great to me. I love Windermere. It's one of my favourite places. I love the pubs up there and I haven't got anything to do tonight because my friends are either away at uni or skint.'

Sean smiled. 'Great, thank you so much. I can't stand driving around in this car much longer. I can't wait to get my own back.'

A part of him wanted to stop this and let her out of the car, tell her he felt ill and could they do it another time, but he'd already calculated that his colleagues were busy looking for a single white male driving a black truck so they wouldn't look twice at a couple in a silver VW Golf. The ANPR cameras wouldn't ping this number unless they had already discovered the woman in the café but he didn't think so. She hadn't been wearing a wedding ring so hopefully no one was looking for her yet. His hands were tied.

He continued driving and they began to chat about anything and everything. The conversation flowed easily as they drove out of Barrow and onto the bypass, which would take them through Lindal and Ulverston. Once they were through the camera on the way out of Ulverston he could relax a little and try to concentrate on exactly what he was going to do when they got to Windermere. It was unsettling for him not to have an exact plan to work to, but it was also liberating. He just hoped there wouldn't be a welcoming committee waiting for him at the priest's house, but if there was then he would be ready to do what he must.

The more he talked to Sophie the more he liked her and he would definitely regret killing her. He might even let her live if he killed the priest first. He could use her as a bargaining chip; the priest wouldn't be able to resist – he wouldn't let another pretty young thing die to save himself.

Chapter 35

The DI told everyone to meet back at the school car park, except for the four armed officers he'd left guarding the front and back of Sean's house. Will was thinking about what Stu had said. He'd seen Sean's truck heading down Roose Road so they needed to send officers to search that area. Will had an unsettling feeling that Sean had left town. He could have taken the coast road to Ulverston and from there anywhere. He'd already asked the control room to get someone to check the cameras to see if the truck had gone through them but that didn't mean much because he could have gone past Askam and headed out west towards Whitehaven. He ran his fingers through his hair. Jesus, this was a real mess.

Although Barrow was the biggest cul-de-sac in England it was also probably the easiest to escape from, with all the quiet country roads that led to the place and the lack of cameras. They did have community messaging, which was a bit like Neighbourhood Watch. He'd asked a PCSO to send out a message, which would go out to hundreds of members of the public to ask them to look out for Sean's black Mitsubishi and the registration; that had been half an hour ago.

They were just arriving back at the school when the control

room notified them that the truck had been spotted in a car park near to Gleaston Water Mill. A huge cheer erupted from the car and all the vehicles in the convoy turned around and began heading that way. There were two ways to approach the car park. Orders were given over the radio for vehicles to come in by different routes and block the road both ways; there would be no exit for Sean or his truck. As they approached the quiet road there wasn't a sound from anyone. The friendly banter had been replaced by a blanket of silence as they awaited orders from the Task Force commander who would run this from now on. Police vans parked up, forming the blockades, and the armed officers jumped out of their van and took their positions, waiting for the go-ahead to rush towards the truck. There was no indication that Sean was armed or had access to any firearms but they couldn't afford to take anything for granted. Will and Dave stood behind his BMW, which was parked behind the armed response car.

'Is it just me or do you feel sick as well, Will? I can't believe we are doing this.'

'Boss, I keep thinking it's all a dream; let's just hope he's already topped himself in the car and then it will all be over with no more lives lost.'

They watched as the officers made their way towards the truck and Will felt his heart pumping with adrenalin. After what seemed like the longest walk, all of a sudden the truck was surrounded by armed officers and they gave the all-clear; it was empty. The disappointment weighed heavy on Will. Why was life so bloody complicated? He looked across at the café, which was in darkness and closed up. They needed to go inside and check it out. Sean could be hiding in there. Four armed officers jogged over to check the perimeter of the building as the Task Force sergeant made his way over to where they were standing.

'Right then, what do we do now?'

'If he left his truck here then he knows we're onto him, so he is on foot somewhere or he's hiding out. I don't want to throw a damper on things but this is a huge area, with so many farms and outbuildings – where the fuck do we start?' Will said.

Dave shook his head. 'There is option C; he could have a car stashed or have taken someone else's. If we can locate the owner of the café they might be able to help.'

There was a lot of shouting from the back of the building and the other officers stormed around to see what was happening, closely followed by Will and Dave.

'There's a woman on the floor inside. She isn't moving and is bound and gagged.'

Two officers ran over with a battering ram to put the door through and within minutes the door was open and they were rushing in to check the building and the woman. Will watched everything from the window and felt a huge sigh of relief when the armed officer bent down to touch the woman and she flinched, trying to move away from him.

'Jesus, thank Christ for that.'

Dave peered through the window at the older, dark-haired woman on the floor. 'You know why she's still alive, don't you?'

Will looked at him. 'Not really.'

'Look at her; she doesn't fit his profile. Too old and dark brown hair.'

Will looked at the woman, who was being helped to her feet. She was crying. He was right; she wasn't young, blonde or extremely pretty. The officer who had rescued her led her from the building and passed her to Stu, who was hovering around, to wait for an ambulance to check her out; then he went back in to help secure the building.

Will walked across the road towards the woman, who was shaking. 'It's OK; you're safe now.'

She looked at him for a minute and nodded.

'What's your name?'

'Susan Letts.'

'Susan, can you tell me what happened? We need to find him.'

'He was so nice, even when he told me he was going to tie me up and take my car he was very polite and apologetic about it.'

'What kind of car do you own and what's the registration number?'

As she told him Stu was writing it down on the palm of his hand, then he stepped away to speak on his radio to the control room to get them to check the cameras for this car.

'Did he say where he was going – anything at all that could lead us in the right direction?'

'He said he had to go and pick his friend up because her car wouldn't start.'

Dave looked as if he was about to keel over from a heart attack. 'He has his next victim.'

'We don't know that for definite.'

'Will, if he has the sense to leave his car here and take Susan's it's for a reason; I don't think he's gone shopping for new shoes.'

Will didn't want to think about it. They had to save this one. He turned to Stu. 'Get back to the office and get me that list of Catholic churches and flag any that are covered by Father John; it has to be one of them.'

Stu ran back towards the car.

Chapter 36

Inside the presbytery, all four of them gathered in the kitchen. Jake had checked all the doors and windows again, making sure they were secure. It had been a while since they'd had any updates from Will and if they'd captured Sean he would have let Annie know straight away. She took out her phone to see if she had any missed calls; the screen was blank.

'What do we do now, Annie?'

'We sit tight and wait for news from Will. There's nothing else we can do.'

John looked at his sister. 'You still look worn out. Why don't you go back to bed? I think I'm going to have an early night; I'm exhausted. We can leave our very capable guards down here to keep an eye on everything, plus I'm sure they are fed up of making polite conversation with us oldies.' He winked at Annie and then walked around to where his sister was sitting and helped her up from the chair. 'You never know, we may just wake up in the morning and find out this has all been a terrible dream.'

She didn't argue with him and let him lead her from the kitchen and up the stairs. He turned around and nodded at Jake and Annie, who smiled back and then he disappeared into one of the bedrooms. Annie shut the door to their unofficial command centre so they could talk without being disturbed.

'I don't like it. Why hasn't anyone been in touch? They could at least keep us up-to-date. Is there anything happening on your radio?'

'Nothing, but they won't be running this on the normal channel; it will be on a special ops one.'

She held out her hand for Jake's radio and he passed it over to her. She pushed Will's collar number into the keypad and waited for it to ring. She heard Will's voice and felt her breath catch in the back of her throat and wondered if this would happen every single time. 'Will, it's Annie. Have you caught him?'

There was the briefest pause as Annie's voice was relayed through the handset to him. 'No, we haven't and he knows that we know. He has stolen a car and you're right; we think he has his next victim.'

Jake looked at her. Horror was etched on both of their faces.

'Where is he? Have you checked the churches?' Annie asked.

'We're on that now and Task Force are off to search them but it's a long list and we have no idea what lengths he'll go to.'

'Keep us posted, Will; it's lonely up here.'

She ended the conversation and Jake nudged her. 'He's on his way here.'

'I don't think he'd be that daft; surely he knows that someone is going to be guarding John.'

'Yes, but I don't think that matters. If he is killing women because of what happened to his family and he blames John, what do you think he'll do if he knows time is short? He'll either run and wait for another chance or finish what he's started, no matter what. He has nothing to lose now, Annie.'

She nodded as the full weight of the consequences settled on her shoulders. 'He won't know that it's just you and me, though. We should tell Will to send Task Force up here. I don't want to fight another killer. I might not win this time.'

Father John tucked his sister into her bed and knelt and prayed by her side, then he went back to his own bedroom. He didn't turn on the light; he had no reason to be afraid of the dark now. As he walked across to draw the curtains he looked out of the window and felt his heart miss a beat. There was a light on inside the church. He knew he had turned them off when he'd left but he couldn't be sure he had locked the door; his hands had been shaking so much. There was no way he would let the lovely Annie go and investigate. He had caused enough pain and suffering and she'd saved his life once already tonight. He would do the right thing; he needed to slip out. Of course he might have left the lights on but he was sure that he hadn't and he didn't want another woman's blood on his hands.

He left his room and listened from the top of the stairs to the muffled voices coming from the kitchen; the door was shut, which was good. He needed to get down the stairs and into the lounge, where he could escape for the second time tonight through those patio doors. He got to the bottom of the stairs and slowly opened the lounge door just enough so that he could squeeze through and shut it behind him. He wasn't sure what he was going to achieve if Sean was inside the church; maybe he could talk him down. Explain that he hadn't hurt Sophie and that she had died from a seizure, not as a result of what he'd tried to do. Maybe if he told him how he'd felt about his mum, Sean would realise that all he'd ever tried to do was help, not to ruin his life.

*

They finished their drinks. It was a glorious night and sitting by the lake outside one of the nicest hotels in the area, it was difficult to imagine what he was going to do in the next twenty minutes. They went back to the car and Sean opened the door for her;

she giggled and stepped inside. The light was fading now, which was better for him. Up to now they hadn't passed any police cars going in either direction so he wasn't doing too badly. He had a feeling things would go to plan. Will might be the detective of the year but he wasn't psychic and he could only guess Sean's next moves. He wouldn't have the resources for a full-on countywide manhunt – well, not for a couple more hours. One thing Sean had learned while being a police officer was that they didn't move fast, especially when they had no idea what they were dealing with. Every decision had to be agreed by several senior officers; it could be tomorrow before they got their act together. He drove on to Windermere without incident and when he pulled up outside the church and parked the car Sophie looked at him.

'Your car isn't here. What are you going to do?'

'Bloody hell, he's my friend but he can be a total pain. He's either nipped out in it or parked it somewhere else. Come on, we might as well go and wait inside the church; hopefully it will still be open, and I'll ring him.'

Sophie got out of the car and began walking towards the church. Sean opened the bag he'd thrown in the back seat and took a couple of plastic bags, some duct tape and a knife out of it. Stuffing them into his pocket, he jogged to catch up with her. There was no one around and the presbytery looked as if it was all in darkness. He didn't see the police car as Jake had parked it around the back out of sight.

If the church was locked he would have to kill her in the church grounds and then go and find Father John. Sophie was one step ahead of him and already twisting the handle on the old oak door, which opened, and Sean smiled. She didn't step inside on her own, though, and waited for him to catch up.

'I hope we find a light switch; I don't fancy sitting in here in the dark. That would be a bit spooky.'

Sean agreed with her. He didn't want to draw attention but he couldn't kill her in the pitch-black; he needed to see what he was doing or it could get messy. They stepped inside. It was so quiet and peaceful, there was nothing to give away the battle that had gone on earlier.

Sophie shivered. 'It's a bit chilly in here. I hope we don't have to wait too long.'

Sean took a small torch from his pocket and shone it around until he found a light switch. He walked over and pressed it, bathing the church with light. 'That's better; I'm not too keen on the dark.'

He felt in his pocket for the thick plastic bag and pulled it out. She was too busy looking around to take any notice of what he was doing.

'I've always loved churches since I was a kid; I mean I'm not into religion or anything, but I just find them so peaceful.'

Sean was close by her now, his hands behind his back clutching the plastic bag. He needed her to turn away from him so he could put it over her from behind. She stepped towards a plaque on the wall, turning to read its inscription. Sean stepped forward and pulled the bag over her head, holding it tight.

*

Father John stepped inside the church to hear some muffled yelling and shuffling, then he saw the man who had been committing these heinous acts and he didn't know what to do. The woman with him was fighting for her breath inside a plastic bag, which Sean was holding over her head. John did the only thing he could do and ran towards the couple, hitting Sean from the side and knocking him off balance. He stumbled and released his grip on the girl, who managed to claw at his hands enough to make his grip on the bag release. She pulled the bag from her head, throwing it away from her and taking huge gulps of air. She began coughing and crying but didn't stay still and began to run towards the door.

John looked at her. 'Go to the house; there are some police officers inside.' John turned to face Sean, who was rubbing his slightly bleeding hand onto the leg of his jeans, trying to wipe the blood away. 'It's you and me now, son. Let the girl go.'

Sean looked at the priest and nodded. 'I've waited a long time for this, Father John. You killed my sister and because of you my own mother didn't even want to be with me. She killed herself and then you let them take me away. I was bundled into a car like a criminal and driven to a place where I didn't know anyone.'

John shook his head. 'I was trying to help, don't you see? I didn't want your sister to die; I only wanted to help her. She died of a seizure. It was so sudden there wasn't anything we could have done. As for your mother, she was the only woman I ever loved and I was devastated that she took her own life. I was too afraid to tell her how I felt, maybe if I had things would have been a lot different. I'm not denying you were left broken-hearted and hurting, but there wasn't anything I could do. I'm a priest and we're not allowed to have children or I would have kept you, but it wasn't fair to make you stay in the house where both your sister and mother died within days of each other. I was scared for you, Sean, in case the shadow man came back for you and I thought that by letting them take you away I was keeping you safe.'

*

Annie was passing a mug of coffee to Jake and almost threw it at him when someone began hammering on the door. Jake rose from his chair, his baton drawn, and ran towards the front door with Annie close behind. He looked through the hole and saw a dishevelled young woman screaming at him to open the door. He threw it open and she fell inside.

'He tried to kill me; you have to stop him.'

Annie dragged her inside and slammed the door shut. 'Who tried to kill you?'

The girl struggled to speak, but she forced herself to. 'Sean. He's in the church with a priest.'

Annie looked at Jake. 'You're OK now; you're safe. Stay in here and shut the door and don't open it unless you see one of us on the other side.'

Jake was frantically talking into his radio, which he'd clipped back onto his body armour. They both began to run towards the church, barging through the door, which was still ajar. They were greeted by Sean, who had Father John in his arms with a plastic bag over his head. Jake ran one way and Annie the other.

'Sean, stop – you have to stop this – let him go!' Annie screamed.

He looked at Annie and shook his head. 'He has to pay; it was all his fault.'

Annie stepped closer. 'Come on, Sean, this is wrong, let him go. It was no one's fault; it was one big tragedy.' She pulled the broken toy that Sophie had given her out of her pocket. She held it out towards him and his grip released on the bag a little. 'Sophie wants you to stop. She's at peace now. The only person to blame for this whole mess is the shadow man and he's gone. I helped Father John to banish him for good.'

Jake took a step closer; he looked across at Annie, who nodded. She knew what he was thinking; they would both rush Sean and make him let go. Closing the distance between them, Jake threw himself at Sean and Annie lunged for his hands to make him loosen his grip on the bag. She could hear sirens; they were getting closer, and she dug her nails into his hands as hard as she could, dragging them along until they drew blood and soon the small cut that was already there was bleeding heavily. Sean let go of John and Annie dragged him away from the two men, who were now fighting. She pulled the bag from his head, but he was unconscious. There was an almighty clatter behind her as Jake landed on the altar and knocked everything off the top onto the floor.

Sean was like a man who was raging on steroids. His eyes were bulging and the muscles in his neck were straining. Annie ran over to help; taking her CS gas from her belt, she aimed for Sean's eyes and let out a jet of the liquid. He yelped but still didn't release his grip on Jake. She looked around for a weapon and picked up the heavy gold crucifix that had landed on the floor and swung it towards his head. As it connected with his forehead the skin split open and a stream of blood began pouring from the wound, down his face. In the end it was the blood that stopped him. He lifted his hand to wipe it from his eyes and when he brought his hand back down and saw that his fingers were covered in fresh, coppery-smelling blood, his legs gave way and he collapsed to the floor.

Annie didn't pause for a second; she pulled her cuffs from her belt and snapped them onto his hands before he realised what was happening. Jake sat on his legs and wrapped his black Velcro leg restraints around his calves and ankles, but all the fight had left him.

Outside, the police cars screeched to a halt and half a dozen car doors slammed at the same time. The sound of footsteps as many pairs of boots ran along the gravel path and into the church was the most comforting one Annie had ever heard. She looked up to see armed officers running towards them, closely followed by Will and the DI.

Jake pulled himself up off Sean's legs, stepping to one side, then he grabbed Annie and hugged her. 'Bloody hell, that was a bit close. I thought he was going to overpower me then.'

Will looked at the pair of them, relieved they were relatively unharmed, and grinned. 'Thank Christ you two are OK. I almost had a heart attack on the drive up here.' He looked at Annie's pale face with specks of blood on her forehead. 'Good effort, Officer Graham; did you know our Sean has a fear of blood? It's just a shame you didn't plant the cross so far into his head it bloody killed him and made everyone's life a whole lot easier.' Will kicked

Sean's foot. 'You prick.'

Annie turned and knelt down next to John, who had opened his eyes. 'Is it over? Did you stop him?'

She nodded and helped him to sit up then moved to the side so he could see Sean, who was surrounded by armed police.

'I don't know what to say, Annie; that's twice in one night you've saved my life. I owe you big time. Whenever you decide to get married it's on the house.' He winked at her and she laughed.

'What a team we are, and I mean this in the nicest possible way, but I hope I don't ever have to set foot in this church again.'

John laughed. 'So do I Annie, so do I.'

The paramedics arrived and one came over to check Father John, who shooed him away, telling him the only thing he needed was a stiff drink, which made both Annie and Jake smile. Jake was next; he had a cut above his eyebrow and his right eye was swollen. He let them fuss over him until they had stripped the cut back together again. As they walked away he whispered to Annie, 'See, I'm a proper hero now. I have the injuries to prove it.'

She poked him in the ribs. 'Yes, Jake, you are. But then you've always been my hero.'

He wrapped an arm around her and squeezed her tightly. Will, who was standing in between the Task Force sergeant and the DI, looked at his boss. 'Well, then, I suppose once he's been checked out by the paramedics we'd best get him back to custody. Are we taking him to ours or letting someone else deal – Kendal?'

Dave looked at Will. 'That bastard has caused me more heart-ache and stress this last week than twenty years of marriage. He will be coming back to ours and we will be dealing and if anyone has anything to say, send them to me. I'll tell them where to get off. I want to know exactly how much of a fucked-up copper Sean Black is and how the hell he got in the job in the first place. I'm not having someone from Kendal come in and take over when it's almost killed me.'

Will nodded. 'It's going to be a long night then.'

Annie suddenly remembered the girl they had left back in the house and, grabbing Will, she made him walk her back to the presbytery. 'Come on; I want you to meet someone.'

'Who?'

'Your star witness: his last victim that he didn't manage to kill. She got away from him because of Father John.'

'Really, Annie, you're a bloody star.'

He turned and kissed her on the lips and she felt a jolt of static electricity shoot straight into her heart. She pushed him away. 'I missed you, Will.'

His hand reached out for hers and he squeezed her fingers. 'Not as much as I've missed you.'

They reached the front door and Annie knocked on it gently. 'It's OK, it's only me, the policewoman from before. You're safe, we caught him and he's in handcuffs and being guarded by men with very big guns.'

The bolt slid back and the door opened. The girl let out a sob and Annie stepped forward to hug her. 'You're OK, I promise. I'd like you to meet Detective Sergeant Will Ashworth. He will need to talk to you soon, but first let's get you checked out by the paramedics and make sure you're OK.'

'I don't need checking; I'm fine. Well, apart from a broken nail and he's messed my hair up.'

Annie laughed. 'We are going to get along just fine.'

All three of them went into the kitchen.

'How's the priest? He saved my life.'

'He's a bit shaken up and bruised but he's fine.'

'Phew, that's good. I've had some weird dates but tonight beats them all. I'm never going for a drink with a stranger ever again.'

Chapter 37

Annie had butterflies. She had spent ages looking around town this afternoon, trying to find the perfect outfit to wear; she wanted something that was sexy yet very understated in an Audrey Hepburn kind of way. She had been into every clothes shop and hadn't found anything suitable. Her last resort was the expensive one-off designer shop in the little side street off Dalton Road. She knew everything in there would be far more than she could afford but she wanted to make a good impression on Will. After being apart for three months she knew what she wanted more than anything in this world was to get back together with him and not just for the time being; she wanted to spend the rest of her life with him. He was a changed man since she'd met him. The misunderstanding that Laura had caused had been cleared up and Annie didn't like to think ill of the dead.

The shop was empty apart from the assistant, who was having an intense conversation with someone on the phone at the back of the shop, so Annie was left to her own devices. On the rack directly in front of her was a black lace dress; it had a low-cut neck and it was gorgeous. The black silk slip underneath it gave it a touch of class and she knew that this was the one; it was the only one. She picked it up and looked at the size on the label and felt her heart sink; it was a twelve. It wouldn't fit over her hips, never mind fasten up. She must have looked devastated because the woman on the phone smiled at her. 'Megan, I have to go. I have a customer.' She put the phone under the counter and walked towards her. 'Can I help you?'

Annie felt her cheeks turn crimson. 'I don't suppose you have this in a bigger size?'

The woman smiled at her. 'I'll go and check; we may have one out the back.'

She wobbled off in her high heels and pencil skirt. Annie could never look like that in a million years. She looked at the price tag and nearly choked. *Bloody hell! I hope she doesn't have one; I won't be able to afford to eat for a month.*

The woman came back, shaking her head. She was looking at Annie as if she knew her but Annie couldn't place her. 'Do you mind me saying I know you from somewhere but I can't remember where?'

Annie laughed. 'I work for the police; you might have seen me walking around town in my uniform.'

The woman smiled. 'I'm really sorry. It must have been sold but I'll tell you what we do have. On the sale rail there is an antique cream version of this dress; it would really suit you with your colouring and it's your size.'

Annie felt her stomach drop; she had never worn anything cream in her life. The woman plucked the dress from the rail and, before she could say no thank you, she found herself being ushered into the changing room and handed the dress.

'I'll just get you a pair of shoes that will make your legs look as if they go on forever.' The assistant tottered off to the front of the shop and the display stand.

Annie wanted the floor to open and swallow her whole so she could escape the cream dress and the high heels that had just been thrust into her fingers. Instead she muttered, 'Thank you.' Whipping the curtain across, she hoped the assistant wouldn't want to see her when she had squeezed herself into it. What if she burst the zip? She undressed and took the dress from the hanger. Jake would find this all extremely hilarious. She pulled the dress on and was surprised that she didn't have to play tug-of-war to get it over her hips; in fact it slid down, even over her boobs. She struggled to reach the zip but it wasn't because it was too tight; it was the fact that the arm she had broken last year couldn't bend at that angle. She slipped on the shoes, which were a lot comfier than she'd imagined, then turned to look in the mirror and gasped. Was that her in its reflection? It didn't look like her; she looked like a proper woman.

The assistant pulled the curtain to one side and grinned. 'See, I told you that would look great on you.' She stepped in and pulled the zip up, then disappeared and came back with an elegant pearl and crystal necklace and matching bracelet. She slipped them on and nodded with approval. 'You look gorgeous.'

Annie, always the first to put herself down, actually agreed and stepped nearer to the mirror and gave herself a twirl. 'I don't think I've ever looked so ladylike and I can't believe it fits. Is it as expensive as the black one?'

'No, it isn't, it's half price. I think I know where I recognise you from. Are you the policewoman who stopped that killer last year, and helped to capture that mad policeman?'

Annie nodded. 'I am indeed – why?'

'Well, you did an amazing job and I'd like to show my appreciation for the work you do. I can let you have my staff discount, which means you can buy the whole outfit for less than a hundred quid.'

Annie felt a lump form in her throat and her eyes fill with tears. 'Thank you, but I couldn't.'

'Miss, you look amazing and whoever you want to impress will not be able to resist you. It's sophisticated but also demure and sexy at the same time. It really suits you.'

Annie looked in the mirror again. She did feel good; in fact she felt amazing. 'If that's OK with you then I'd like to take the lot, and thank you.'

She waited for the assistant to ring it all up then handed over her credit card and felt momentarily guilty, but the guilt was soon replaced with excitement to see Will's face when he opened the door. The woman handed her the two bags with her purchases in and she felt like Julia Roberts in *Pretty Woman*. Thanking her again, she left the shop and walked back to her car with a huge grin on her face.

*

Now, as she stood outside Will's front door, she hoped he would appreciate the effort she had gone to. Once she would have let herself in with a key but things hadn't been the same for a while. She hadn't been inside since the morning she'd found him with Laura. She lifted her hand and knocked softly on the door, not her usual loud copper's *bang, bang*. She couldn't wait to see him. The door opened and she watched as he took a couple of seconds to register that it was actually her; his eyes opened wide and the boyish grin she found so sexy spread across his lips. 'Wow, Annie. You look gorgeous, I mean you always do but – wow.' He opened the door wide so she could step into his hallway. Vanilla-scented candles were burning on the small table next to the photo of them both. 'Let me take your coat.'

He helped her to slip out of her coat and as his fingers brushed against her neck she felt a tremor run down the back of her spine, making her shiver. She turned to Will; he was wearing a white shirt with the top button undone and a pair of stonewashed jeans, he smelled of Chanel aftershave and he hadn't shaved for a couple of days and looked as sexy as hell. She was tempted to tell him to forget the food and just take her to bed but for once she was determined to act like a lady, so she followed him into the kitchen, where the pine table was set with candles, flowers

269

and the most exquisite place settings. She was seriously impressed; he had either bought this all especially or had it hidden away. 'It looks lovely, Will, really lovely.' She watched his cheeks turn red and realised that he was as nervous as she was.

'Thanks, Annie, it all belonged to my mum. She gave it to me when I left home but it was too good to use for the endless takeaways and cans of lager. I've kept it in the attic until I had an occasion special enough to use it for.' He turned away to take a bottle of champagne out of the ice bucket. He popped the cork and handed her a glass, which she downed and handed back.

'Phew, that's better, calm my nerves a bit. I can't believe I was so nervous coming here tonight; it's turned me into a dithering idiot.'

'I know; it must be hard for you and I'm sorry. I hope it hasn't upset you too much.'

She laughed. 'I meant I was dithering about seeing you again. I've missed you so much and you look so, so gorgeous.'

Will laughed. It was his turn to down his drink. 'Why, thanks, Miss Graham. Now we're even.' He filled the glasses again and pulled out a chair for her. 'This time I'm going to treat you like a lady and I don't care what you think or say; it's because I want to and you deserve it. You would never let me do anything for you or pay for anything and I know it's really early days but the last three months have been hell for me and they have made me realise that I can't live without you. I don't want to live without you and I hope that one day you will feel the same.'

She stopped herself from blurting out that there hadn't been a minute of every day that she hadn't been thinking about him but she knew he wanted to grovel. It would make him feel better, so she would let him do it for just a little while and then she would tell him to shut up because she loved him just as much and felt exactly the same.

They ate a meal of pan-fried fillet steak with a blue cheese sauce, homemade chips and a huge salad, followed by a white chocolate and raspberry cheesecake with freshly whipped cream.

Annie took her last bite then groaned, 'Oh, God, I'm so stuffed. That was gorgeous, thank you, Will.'

He picked up the empty champagne bottle and took a bottle of the wine that Annie loved so much from the fridge and put it in the ice bucket.

She laughed. 'I am impressed, Will; you thought of everything.' There was music playing in the background and she recognised a few of the songs but had no idea who was singing them. 'Who is this singing?'

Will picked up her hand. 'Sorry, do you hate it?'

'No, I really like it. I just don't know who it is that's singing.'

Will laughed. 'That's what happens when you date older men. It's Frank Sinatra; he was my mum's favourite singer and I guess I thought a bit of old Frank's crooning couldn't hurt.' He stood up and pulled her to her feet and started singing along to 'The Way You Look Tonight'. He took hold of her hands and began waltzing with her in time to the music.

Annie felt clumsy. She had never been much of a dancer and Will was so light on his feet but she loved it, the way that he held her, the closeness of their bodies. She was tipsy but not drunk and she knew that she would never forget tonight as long as she lived; it was what she had dreamt about since she was a teenager, her perfect romantic evening. Mike had never done anything like this for her. As she danced with Will, with good old Frank telling her she looked lovely, she didn't think she could be any happier.

The song ended and Will held her close, his lips brushed against hers and she held him tight and kissed him back. He leant close and whispered in her ear, 'Marry me, Annie Graham; I don't want to be apart from you ever again.'

She pulled him close and whispered, 'Yes.'

Author's note and acknowledgements

First of all, I would like to thank my readers, friends and supporters. Everyone who took a chance and bought *The Ghost House* then went on to tell their family and friends. I want to thank them for the messages of support and for taking the time out of their busy lives to tell me how much they enjoyed Annie Graham's first adventure. I'm forever grateful to you all.

I want to thank my family for their continued support; it means a lot and I couldn't do it without you. My colleagues at Barrow Police for their support; you have been fabulous and you really have no idea how much smoother you've made this journey.

Finally, I would like to thank my amazing team at Carina – my editor Lucy Gilmour for her encouragement, Helen Williams for her patience, the design team for the fab covers and everyone else. I'm so lucky you all helped to make my dreams come true.

Helen xx

Ready for the next thrilling instalment
in the Annie Graham series?

THE FORGOTTEN COTTAGE

Things finally seem to be looking up for police officer Annie
Graham. After a tumultuous couple of years, she is settling
into a normal, happy life. Her wedding is fast approaching,
and her fiancé Will has found a forgotten but beautiful little
cottage for them to make their own.

But as Annie begins to have increasingly vivid nightmares, she
realises their new home may not be as unoccupied as it first
seemed. Her arrival has stirred up the ghosts of a tragic past,
and she needs to put them to rest once and for all.

But while Annie's distracted, another threat is emerging from
the shadows. And if she doesn't act fast, her days may be
numbered . . .

Out in paperback and audiobook February 2025.

Out now in ebook.

Dear Reader,

We hope you enjoyed reading this book. If you did, we'd be so appreciative if you left a review. It really helps us and the author to bring more books like this to you.

Here at HQ Digital we are dedicated to publishing fiction that will keep you turning the pages into the early hours. Don't want to miss a thing? To find out more about our books, promotions, discover exclusive content and enter competitions you can keep in touch in the following ways:

JOIN OUR COMMUNITY:

Sign up to our new email newsletter: http://smarturl.it/SignUpHQ

Read our new blog www.hqstories.co.uk

🐦 https://twitter.com/HQStories

f www.facebook.com/HQStories

BUDDING WRITER?

We're also looking for authors to join the HQ Digital family!

Find out more here:

https://www.hqstories.co.uk/want-to-write-for-us/

Thanks for reading, from the HQ Digital team